Window
of
Exposure

Roccie Hill

Window of Exposure
By Roccie Hill

© 2015 Roccie Hill

ISBN-13: 978-1505344097
(Also available in Kindle format)

Library of Congress Control Number: 2014921708

Cover design: Ron Wheatley, www.ronwheatley.ca
Page design & layout: Lighthouse24

For Nicky,
who continues to be
my inspiration of integrity,
humor, generosity, and love.

Chapter 1

THEY WERE FLYING INTO THE SETTING SUN, full throttle at twenty-six thousand feet, with the light spilling blood red across the cloud floor. Kate steadied the plane, and stared at the glowing horizon. A deep purple ravine appeared before them, and she banked evenly to the left. At two hundred seventy knots, the controls were solid yet still maneuverable, as only a new Swiss plane could be, and she drove it fast through the immaculate sky.

"Oh my God," she whispered, sailing into a new tunnel of fissures where violet and orange light shot up around the aircraft. Her co-pilot nodded, both of them watching with the same calm hunger for the far curve of the earth. She had not flown through skies like this for many years, and for a moment she ignored everything else and flew the plane straight at the visceral colors.

"Jacobits has kept you on the ground too long, Kate."

She glanced at her co-pilot. "That was my decision, Tim, not his." She moved her head from side to side to release the tension in the sinews of her neck, and as she did, her brown hair swung across her shoulders. She grinned at him. "The last time I flew for work was back at Hill, and I was wearing fire retardant green pajamas."

"Best uniform ever invented," he said and laughed.

They had taken the plane that morning from the factory in Lucerne, out of a dust of snow across Mount Pilatus toward the hot desert coast of Africa. They had loaded four passengers off an unpaved landing strip near the Moroccan border port of Tarfaya. She glanced now through the open door at these men in the back cabin. Three of them sat in loose formation around steel grillwork that contained the fourth. Two were uniformed Phoenix Ravens in charge of the security of the plane, and the third, a Defense Intelligence agent for prisoner transport, was dressed so casually in jeans and a Yankee baseball cap, he might have been headed for a Saturday barbecue with his family.

The man in the cell was dark and short, with long arms and a thin body like tough black wire. One of the Swiss agents on the ground in Morocco had called him '*affe*', German for monkey. He sat now with his chest hunched over his knees, perspiring heavily and reeking from two days in a holding cell.

Kate had seen hundreds of captured criminals in her career, and they all had one thing in common: the angry look in their eyes, as unpredictable as a hidden mine. As she watched him, he began to cough, hacking down hard through a clot of thick phlegm blocking his airway.

"His lungs are about to give out," Tim said. "Even up here I can smell the cigarette stink on his clothes."

"He had a pack of Marlboros when I searched him," Kate replied. "Kind of ironic. American cigarettes killing him." She did not smile when she said it; she had handled prisoners before from the al Qaida networks, and although she had searched this man herself, she knew that she wouldn't feel entirely comfortable until she was able to transfer jurisdiction to the CIA.

She pulled the plane straight out over the water toward a necklace of islands they could not yet see, relaxing back into the newly-sewn soft leather seats and watching the burning blur of light and movement above the horizon line. She had not piloted for a living since Hill Air Force Base in Utah where she was stationed when she flew F-16's, and being in control of even this little turbo reminded her why flying would always be her first love.

A few moments later, a voice spoke to them through the radio headset on the covert frequency.

"Gabriel five two, this is Gabriel one."

"Go ahead Gabriel one," Kate said.

"We have Lieutenant Colonel Jacobits for you."

"How're you guys liking that little airframe?" the Colonel asked.

Kate smiled immediately when she heard the warm, Chicago growl.

"Amazing, Sir," she replied.

He chuckled and added, "I thought so. Okay, Captain Cardenas, give me a sit rep."

"The asset is secure, Colonel," she replied. "We're about an hour out of Lajes."

"Perfect. Now, listen up. We got a report from the analysts at Bolling and they still got no friggin' clue why he was trying to get onto the continent yesterday." He paused, and then laughed abruptly. "By the way, our colleagues at the CIA have never even heard of him. Gotta love those guys. Anyway, the only thing our own people know is that he spent some time at our favorite little summer camp in Waziristan. But we're just the taxi here. Sign him over at destination and go home. Let the CIA figure out what he was up to."

"Yes, Sir," Kate said. "Although the way he's hacking, he may not make it to the island." Even as she spoke, she could hear the prisoner retching up his lungs in the back cabin.

"Captain, we're not really worried about his health. Just be cautious when you put your wheels down. The Pentagon thinks our air base at Lajes is secure, but who the hell knows anymore."

"Gotcha, Sir," said Tim.

"*Gotcha?* What kind of friggin' response is that? Captain Cardenas, can't you keep your co-pilot under control?"

Although Jacobits could not see it, he knew he had made her smile.

Once they had passed the coastal atmosphere, they flew for an hour straight out over the Atlantic, until a heavily accented voice spoke to them in English from the airfield a hundred miles away. Kate responded and brought the power to idle. She lowered the nose of the plane to start their descent, and they slid down through the clouds leaving the western sun behind.

A storm was dying across the ocean, and once underneath the cover, the horizon was grey and murky. Before them, the slopes of the Cume hills draped deep emerald across the blue volcanic cliffs, and the lush pasture-land was criss-crossed with stone walls built from foraged lava rocks.

The wings of the plane began to tremble, and Kate leaned forward in her seat, staring at the computer-generated maps on the transparent glass screen before her.

"Sometimes the winds at Lajes are out of limits in the spring," said her co-pilot. "They might try to reroute us from Terceira to Santa Maria."

"I doubt if they would do that with this cargo. It won't be smooth, but we're okay. When did you spend time here?"

"First Lady's jet aborted mid-Atlantic. Jacobits called me in Heidelberg to go get her. We may have a base at Lajes, but they didn't think it was safe enough for her. Took her to Ramstein, waited around a couple days, brought her back. She thought I was a white knight. But the Azores are mostly cold as heck. And whatever you do, never eat their food. Portuguese islanders cook up some strange-ass things. Pots of weird smelling stew that you really only want to bury."

"You get all the easy assignments, Tim," she laughed.

"Ya think?"

"What's our call sign again?"

He grinned. "Want me to take it?"

"Not on your life. I haven't flown an airframe this new for years. I feel like I'm dancing."

"You are, baby. Gliding on butter."

She manipulated the yoke to change their altitude again by lowering the nose slightly as they approached the tiny elliptical island.

In the center of the deep green landscape she saw a black crater, dark like hell, and reminiscent of the Bikini atoll she had over-flown years before in the Pacific.

"Why did you stop flying, anyway?" Tim asked. "I heard you were a patch. And after weapons school they even sent you to test pilot school."

She glanced over at him and hesitated. Things had happened in her career that she still could not talk about, and being a woman in the fighter community was one of them. She said quickly, "They did. But when I got back from Edwards I realized I just didn't want to live in Utah." Her voice was suddenly brittle, and she smiled at her friend sharply.

"I'm just askin', Kate. Not cross-examining."

He lowered the landing gear while she pulled the turboprop around for final approach.

Kate said quietly, "I'm sorry. I just never got straight with the way things were, Tim, and I didn't want to spend my career back at Hill being that girl in the squadron who went around causing problems."

"Okay, I get it," he said, but Kate could hear in his voice that he did not.

"It was a long time ago, buddy," she said.

He nodded. "The NATO strip feeds at forty degrees into our runway over on the left, and private jets come into a terminal on the other side of that."

Kate looked down to the flatlands beside the churning gray sea. The U.S. air base spread out adjacent to the Portuguese facility, but she lined the Pilatus up with the civilian area.

She leaned back gently on the throttle until she heard the pitch of the engines shift, like a tuning fork beginning to throb. Just before they touched the ground, Kate flared the nose of the plane about ten degrees so that they would land on the main wheels. She brought it to a stop far out on the wet flight line near a solitary baggage truck. Beside the vehicle stood the CIA destination agent with his driver.

She unstrapped and stretched her arms. "Civilian runway, huh? Interesting."

Tim looked up from the landing forms. "Well, what did you expect? The Air Force never takes responsibility for the arrival of a ghost."

"Listen, I just want to get home tonight. Sleep in my own bed." She pulled her long, dark hair into a ponytail and wrapped it into a tight bun at the nape of her neck.

"Jacobits said wheels down, wheels up. You'll be back in Salon by midnight, Kate. The quicker we get the fuel truck out here, the quicker we can take off."

"You go down and sign off on this guy; I'll deal with refueling while you do pre-flight."

"Oh, sure," he replied and smiled. "Send the minion into the rain."

"You're a good guy, Tim. And while you're out there, can you hitch a ride to the terminal to get us some coffee for the trip back to the mainland?"

He adjusted the Glock pistol in his shoulder holster, and followed the passengers down the stairs to the runway. The storm had begun again with the rain hammering fast across the nose of the plane. She watched him wait in the cold while the agent loaded the prisoner into the baggage vehicle. Tim swung up onto the wet seat next to the driver, and the truck disappeared across the airfield, with the rain falling hard, boiling and splashing silver up from the tires.

She called for the Avgas truck and put a wad of Euros on the left seat of the plane. She could see her own reflection in the windshield, sharp angles of olive skin and wide-set brown eyes that reminded her of the photographs of her father as a young man. Kate had been in the Air Force her entire life, the only child of a widowed Master Sergeant, and she was used to being alone. In college at the Air Force Academy it was the only way for a woman to survive, by herself and under the radar. But when she flew F-16's, the men had expected her to be the joke of their team, to laugh with them when they pulled out the squadron porn drawer, and to join in when they forced each other into drinking binges of Jeremiah Weed. Some of them called her a whore, and some of them called her a lesbian, but none of them left her alone. Although she never had the courage to tell her father she had given up, eventually she left the fighter pilot community altogether.

She was still waiting for the refueling truck when an eerie cradle of stillness fell over the runway. She looked out of the cockpit windshield and saw the baggage van swerve. Suddenly, fierce yellow light shot out from the vehicle, followed by deafening thunder that shook the ground and every plane on the flight line. Huge plates of shrapnel blasted out, and molten metal scattered over the tarmac. The truck flipped to one side, its tires spinning in the rain, as smoke billowed higher and higher above the flames. Portuguese and American security police ran toward the crater, and the medic van and fire trucks circled the smokescreen within seconds with their sirens shrieking.

Kate raced down the steps of the plane past the Ravens, through the clouds of debris, toward the terminal. As she neared, she saw her co-pilot lying face down on the burning flight line where he had been thrown from the exploded vehicle.

She could see his bleeding fingers scraping at the asphalt as he tried to drag himself from the blast area. She shouted for a medic, and when none came, she knelt beside him.

"Hang on, Tim. You're okay. Hang on." She held his hand, and saw that his wedding ring had melted into his finger from the heat of the blast. Under his torn shirt the flesh had been seared away revealing his blackened ribcage.

She put her face alongside his, her mouth against his ear, and forced her shaking voice to calm.

"The medic will be here in a second. You'll be okay," she whispered, but they both knew this was a lie.

She had run from the plane without even a jacket, and now had nothing to cover him from the rain. When at last his breathing ceased, she crossed herself without thinking, and continued to kneel alongside him until the Portuguese ambulance finally arrived. She watched as they took his body and drove it through the falling darkness toward the rippling glow of the terminal lanterns.

When she lost sight of the vehicle, Kate grabbed her cell phone from her belt holster and touched the screen. She pressed a single button, and was connected instantly to the same rough voice that she always trusted.

"Whaddya got?" Jacobits asked.

"The ghost is dead." She added slowly, "And everyone else." She put her hand over her mouth and took a deep breath. The back of her throat was filling with saliva, and she continued to breathe slowly to keep herself from vomiting.

"Where's Tim?" he asked.

"He was in the blast. He's gone, too."

Jacobits paused, like through a kind of bleeding, then said gently, "Give me a sit rep, Kate."

"The airframe is unharmed and secure with the Ravens. The asset was no longer in our jurisdiction. He was being transported by the CIA agent. An explosion took down the truck, the passengers, everything."

"Any theories?"

"No, Sir. No idea. I searched him myself before we loaded him. It may have been an IED on the CIA truck."

"IED on a CIA vehicle? Hell, even the CIA can find something like that."

She waited in the pelting rain for a long time, her shirt soaked to her skin, until Jacobits spoke again.

"Okay, Kate, I'll get onto the analysts at Bolling and find out what the fucking hell is going on. Make sure the base commander knows that I want Lieutenant McEwing's remains brought home. Deniable or not, we're not leaving our own behind."

"Roger."

"And be safe, Kate. Remember, you already signed the ghost over to the CIA. This is their investigation now, not ours. You were just the taxi."

•

Late in the night she finally pulled her little Peugot onto the muddy back-road to her home near the town of Salon-de-Provence in southern France. Inside, she lit the furnace and poured a single finger of brandy into an old tumbler. She sat at the kitchen table beside a lamp throwing soft shadows, and sipped in the dim light until the exhaustion began to soak through her muscles.

She remained there while she typed her mission report, sending it finally into the hub server of the Defense Clandestine Service at DIA headquarters, but long after she had powered down, she continued staring at the inert screen of her computer.

Upstairs, she removed the rubber band holding a tight bun at her neck, and shook her hair loose. She undressed and stood at the window for a moment, staring out at the glistening, moonlit field beside her cottage. The shimmering light from the sky fell across her naked body, and she paused to examine two narrow dark scars across her stomach, memories left to her from past missions.

When she lay in bed, she closed her eyes almost immediately, and was instantly surrounded by the airfield again, so clear that she began to shiver. She opened her eyes quickly to remind herself that she lay in her own bedroom, with the familiar bolt of dark red Kevlar parachute cloth spreading over her bed, and the smell of the lavender field next door seeping through the raised window. She closed her eyes again and saw her co-pilot on the dark, wet tarmac, his face draining of life and his hands shuddering to quiet. This wasn't the first time she had lost a friend, and she knew that once the investigation was finished, she would be the one to tell his wife. She turned on her side and put her hands across her face, blinking furiously and wiping the tears off her skin.

Chapter 2

OF ALL THE ATTACKS Jacobits had lived through, this was the worst kind. As a young man, he had worked over a decade in Special Operations, waging deniable battles in obscure places that he remembered only as a violent blur of sun and frost. He was in the Persian Gulf during Desert Storm, before the Seabees built the road through Al Kabrit, pressing forward through a hundred miles of stark desert and sunrises burning black from chemicals. He was first into the town of Babil, where he dodged orphans who had been trained by the Iraqi government to pick off American soldiers. By the time he fought his way to Hillah, where the ancient hanging gardens of Babylon had once grown, the going rate for murdering an American Special Operations airman was a thousand U.S. dollars. A decade later in Enduring Freedom, Jacobits had led the team that fronted the fall of the Taliban, narrowly escaping enemy fire by following silent, infrared lines into the thunderous explosions of downtown Kabul.

But by far, this was the hardest, sitting in the wet evening light of the underground rabbit warren on Avenue Gabriel, watching his computer and high definition screens, connecting to his team through the best technology the United States military had to offer, and still letting one of them die.

He had told his agents to get in and get out, to be the taxi taking the prisoner to Lajes. But in his career, Jacobits had never been just a delivery boy, and now he was determined to dig until he understood exactly how the explosion was executed using a man who had been searched on three occasions within eighteen hours, and who had been deposited on an island in the middle of the Atlantic Ocean, as far from al Qaida operatives and detonators as anyone might be.

Jacobits worked straight through till dawn at his office in the Embassy, scrubbing hourly intelligence reports from the analysts at the DIA center in Huntsville. No wires or switches were found on the Lajes air base; no wireless triggers nor radio detritus. The man had been searched three times by DIA specialists and still his arrival at Lajes coincided with the bomb; the area was secured by American, NATO and Portuguese forces, and yet somewhere in the vicinity, somehow, someone had pressed a button that detonated the biggest attack in the Azores in over a hundred years.

Jacobits phoned his wife to tell her he wouldn't be home that night, and then launched himself with prehensile focus into the electronic documents, comparing facts from three different countries and five different intelligence services. At around four in the morning he clicked on Kate's report again, reading through her real-time, ground intel. She described the small man they called '*affe*', perspiring, coughing, and frightened, a Crusader caught by crazed pagans. Jacobits could picture him so clearly, and in his mind he searched the man furtively for the button that had blasted him to hazy shreds of pollution in the heavy Azorean air.

Around seven in the morning Jacobits heard people stirring along the corridor, and he locked down his computer station. He went to his private bathroom, brushed his teeth, threw cold water on his face, and changed into a fresh uniform. He stepped into the hallway and followed the blue linoleum line to the cafeteria, heading for the smell of coffee and eggs, where he would wait until it was time for his meeting with the Ambassador.

He took his tray to an empty table and sat in silence by himself. He stared at the thick ceramic plate, stained from decades of use by American compound staff, and set his elbows on the table beside it. He ran the pieces of information through his mind like football plays, waiting for them to slide into place, his body immobilized by thoughts so intense that he left only his own replica in the room.

Now approaching fifty, Jacobits was built short and square like a boxer, built tough like his father who had been a warrant officer in the Navy. He had small, dark eyes and short, grey hair, and above his left jaw was a rose-shaped scar leftover from a bomb in the Gulf, white petals of melted skin that had hardened over the years. When he and his wife made love she always touched that scar, even kissed it, although he had told her many times that he could feel nothing there.

During his years as a defense attaché at the embassy in Paris, Jacobits had made few friends. He had no skill at unnecessary conversations, and considered them dangerous opportunities to release classified information. He protected his wife and his team, and he loved his job because he loved the hunt and the truth. His preferred methods were old-fashioned, based on instinct rather than violence or electronics. Jacobits would study a situation until it spoke to him, would sit in a room with the door closed, watching a dead body until it breathed again. During Desert Storm, an analyst buddy of his had said to the wing commander that no one, not even a good guy, wanted Jake on his tail.

In Afghanistan, Jacobits had been the leader of the now-legendary team that carved a large rock with the phrase '*9-11 NYPD NYFD USA*' and added it to the protecting wall of a local Taliban battle-berm. Shortly after the fall of Kabul, he had pinned on lieutenant colonel, and was swallowed up by the Pentagon into an administrative nightmare that he had always fought hard to evade.

Jacobits grabbed a handful of sugar packets from a stainless steel cup on the table. He laid six of them side by side in front of him, and taking them two at a time, tore them open, and dumped the sugar into his coffee cup. He stirred it once, gulped it down, and his teeth tingled from the sweet shock.

•

Ambassador Henderson entered the briefing room alone, and stared at him.

"Jake, you look like shit."

"Yes, Mr. Ambassador. I know."

"If I met you on a bus, I'd be afraid," he said, and roared with laughter. A thin, ginger-haired man with pale, freckled skin, Henderson often laughed at his own jokes.

Jacobits chuckled politely, and thought to himself that the ambassador had probably not ridden a public bus for several decades.

As the senior agent in Europe for the Defense Intelligence Agency, Jacobits worked closely with Henderson, and balanced the perilous position of reporting to him, to the Pentagon, and to the DIA simultaneously. Walking this minefield had brought him close to his career coffin on several occasions.

"Who did you lose?" Henderson asked.

"McEwing. Out of Heidelberg."

"Army interrogation?"

"He was Army, yes, but not at the interrogation center. I embedded him at the university teaching math."

The conference room was over-heated, windowless, and lined on one wall with a façade of carved French limestone. Already that morning a fireplace blazed in the corner. Henderson walked to the only furniture, a gleaming table surrounded by old-fashioned leather chairs, wine-red and smelling of beaten hide. He threw three American newspapers on the table and stared at Jacobits.

"They all ran it on the front page, Jake. Who the hell issued the instructions for the airlift from Morocco?"

"The Pentagon, Mr. Ambassador. He was not a High Value Target, but they wanted to talk to him. Last week's report on internet turbulence has everyone running scared."

Henderson drew his index finger across the polished wood, tracing the hairline rings.

"This is a goddammed mess, Jake. You should have told me about this."

"Yes, Sir."

"I know your people in D.C. want me outside the loop." He paused and picked up the *International New York Times*, scrutinizing the front-page photograph. "I know that. But my guy in D.C., who just happens to be your Commander-in-Chief, actually wants me in the

loop. Goddamn it, Jake, we all look like total idiots. Not just the
Embassy in Lisbon, but all of us in Europe. Don't get me wrong, I hate
losing our people and I'm sorry about McEwing. But there is more at
stake here than a single agent. We have a major reception for Cullen,
the new Secretary of Commerce, here in a couple of weeks."

"Yes, Mr. Ambassador."

"Your people have to clean this up before then. Show some de-
pendability. I won't have that event canceled because the President
thinks we can't protect American leaders in a goddammed Allied na-
tion like goddammed France! It makes this administration look
singularly incompetent."

"We will button this up before the reception, Mr. Ambassador."

"How the hell did the explosion happen?" Henderson said
abruptly. "According to the papers, you had the man in custody the
entire day, and the night before."

Jacobits shook his head. A bitter taste slid down his throat as he responded.

"We don't really have our hands around that yet, Sir. We haven't
found the detonator, and no report has posited a theory about how the
button was pushed." He paused briefly, scarcely blinking his eyes. "Mr.
Ambassador, I'm beginning to think there wasn't a button at all."

Henderson stared at him, slightly nodding his head for Jacobits to
continue.

"Personally, I believe the explosion came from a body IED."

"A what?" asked Henderson.

"The explosives were inside of him. Last year, the Italian NATO
forces were transporting an asset and the man had swallowed an IED
that blew the whole plane up. I think this guy did the same thing,
before we even took him."

"But how did he set it off?"

"I don't know. Maybe he swallowed a timed detonator. Maybe it
was implanted. This is just a guess, Sir. We don't have the technology
yet to find internal body bombs when we do a search. But we'll never
solve this one now, because that man and everything around him is
now just another layer of Atlantic cloud cover."

"Christ almighty," Henderson whispered, staring at him.

"The CIA and the Pentagon are working on this. Portuguese security forces, too. And Interpol. But at the moment, we haven't cracked it."

"If they can do what they did at Lajes airfield, Jake, they can do anything." Henderson shook his head slowly and said, "We may just be cooked. If you are correct, we will never be able to stop that kind of thing."

Jacobits had long ago learned to cauterize himself from superstitions held by his superiors. He stared at Henderson's oval face, washed clean of courage and dull like old driftwood.

"New technology requires a period of study, Mr. Ambassador," he said calmly, "but these people aren't invincible. Every intelligence agency in the world knows how important this is."

"Listen to me, Colonel. Our ability to secure Paris against this kind of crap is critical, even in spite of the damn Parisians. James Cullen is about to be sworn in as the next Secretary of Commerce, for God's sake. There are to be no incidents while he is in France. And before he gets here, you need to convince me that you are still the man who can achieve this." Henderson rose and put his hands in his suit pockets. "I have an eight-thirty meeting, Jake. I want an update hourly. And this is 'need to know'. Nothing else is to get out about this explosion until you can confirm to me how the hell it happened."

Jacobits stared at the diplomat's silk shirt, deep purple of a shade so true it might have been a target.

"Yes, Sir."

"And stop calling me 'sir'," he replied stiffly. "You know how much that irritates me."

Chapter 3

KATE STOOD IN THE TALL GRASS, the line of forest trees behind her swelling with the passing spring rain. She wore tight indigo jeans and a dark blue sweatshirt stamped with the words 'École de l'Air'. Tall and slender, with light olive skin and huge chestnut eyes, she wore her dark hair pulled back in a ponytail, accentuating the tiredness across her face.

Before her lay a wood fire, and atop this, a dented metal vat that held ten gallons of steaming, squid-blue liquid. The acrid smell of the smoke filled her mouth and throat.

"Jacques, please let me do that," she said.

Beside her stood an elderly Frenchman wearing a heavy green waxed jacket. Jacques Morel, her nearest neighbor and teaching colleague, was a national scholar who had been engaged by the French military to teach ancient history at the nearby French air force training academy, the *École de l'Air*.

He held a three-foot long wooden pole in his large hands, and he stirred it slowly around the boiling liquid.

"Thank you, no," he replied. "The exertion will not make me collapse," he added, laughing to himself. "Oh, no."

He pulled the club from the slop and laid it in the damp grass. "I am very pleased that I finally got you out of the house, Kate. You are looking too tired and worried lately." He stepped toward her and put his tanned fingers to her face. "These dark circles near your eyes tell me a story."

"I'm fine, Jacques," she said. "Really. I just need to sleep more. But that's not going to happen until the semester finishes and our American cadets go back to America."

A few yards away stood a rickety, ochre-colored potting shed, and a graveled path leading through the grass and wildflowers. In the center of the clearing, astride a shaft of spring sunlight, slept Kate's dog, the huge Saint Bernard she called Glock.

Jacques glanced over at him, and with his eyes twinkling said, "If we painted dear Glockie with some of the blue, we could tell your American students that it is a special French breed of dog, known for its azure color. They might believe that."

"Don't be mean, Jacques," she smiled, and the indolent dog raised his head at the sound of her voice and her laughter.

Jacques leaned over the vat and began lifting cloth from the warm, dark liquid. Kate pulled on thick, yellow rubber gloves and took the dripping fabric from him, laying it across the makeshift wooden skeleton he had constructed.

"What are these markings?" she asked, and ran her fingers over the primitive figures scratched into the cloth.

He raised a sodden sheet high over his head, so the light shone through the deep blue. "*Ambiance*, my dear. This is blackout for a lecture I am giving at the university next week. I'm going to teach by firelight as though we were cruel Neanderthals in the night, about to hunt the humans."

She nodded, looking straight up through the camouflage. "I thought it was the other way around. Didn't the Neanderthals go extinct because of the humans?"

"Very good, Kate!" he exclaimed. "If only we knew for sure." He lay the material over the wooden slats, moving knee-deep into the weeds to the far side of the old vat. The fire had burned itself out, and the rich smell of charred wood rose around them. He put his hands on the beaten lip of the metal and leaned hard into it, throwing his tall frame forward until the dye emptied out across the wildflowers and weeds of the forest floor. "But I agree with you. I believe we humans ate them roasted, every last one of them." He paused, grinning. "Are you hungry for lunch? Don't worry; I have made *bouillabaisse*, my dear. Nothing but fish and vegetables."

They walked back to his old stone country cottage. The heat of the day had overpowered the rain, and as they approached, the cicadas began screaming around them.

"It would make me crazy to live with this noise so close, Jacques," she said. "If you cleared these weeds you'd have some peace. And it would also be safer in case of fire."

"Residents of Provence love *les cigales*. To us, they are a national bird, like your eagles."

At the base of the stone porch were washed-out hollows of spring mud, and Jacques strode through them with the dog following close behind, both tracking black earth as they crossed the threshold.

The first room they entered was a library, and Kate wandered slowly among the shelves on her own while Jacques went through to the kitchen. She loved this room, not for the books, but for the collection of telephones that crowded the small corner tables, dozens of telephones from all generations and every country. Most were smudged or dusty, and none of them were catalogued; instead, Jacques had placed them like raw art pieces cluttering his furniture, from his prized 1879 Viaduct top box to the pale blue Princess phone from the 1960's that had belonged to his wife.

When Kate reached the kitchen she called out, "Do you need any help, Jacques?" but he did not answer. She swung the door open, but the room was still except for the manic boil of soup on the stove.

Fresh bread lay on the table with bakery tissue still wrapped around the middle. Thick steam rose from the tureen of *bouillabaisse*, flooding the air with the smell of fish and garlic.

In the far corner of the room, Jacques sat quietly on an old wooden stool, facing his computer. His shoulders were sunken forward and his face had fallen into a sad, quizzical look.

"What's wrong?" she asked, but he did not answer. She stood behind him then, and looked at the computer screen, flashing bright red, with the words "Fuck the USA" written in thick, black letters.

"What is this?" she asked, moving closer.

"I don't know. It must be a virus. I had next week's lectures still open. I hope I have not lost them."

Quickly, she leaned across him and pressed the escape key.

"I set you up with software to protect you from viruses."

"I tried that button already. Now everything is frozen."

"Get out of the way, Jacques. And go outside. Please, quickly!"

She moved in front of him, and as though she were defusing a bomb, gently pulled the cord from the side of the computer. She tilted the plastic body up to slip the battery pack out, and then held it up to look, her fingers shuddering around it and tears of sweat sliding down her face.

Jacques stood behind her, and in this tiny chromosome of silence, put his hand firmly on her shoulder.

"My dear, I'm certain it is only a virus. There are new ones all the time. This is not a bomb, Kate. Look at me."

"You don't know that," she whispered. She stood back from his grasp.

"You are hungry and tired and you need to take better care of yourself. I will get our lunch and then you must go home and sleep."

"All right," she sighed, her face pulled back, tight and dry like a sculptor's mask. "I'm going to wash my hands."

She walked quickly to the bathroom at the far end of the house. The room was filled with sunlight, and the walls were golden, the color of ripened wheat. She sat on the edge of the old claw-footed tub, and told herself it was this brightness that took her breath away, but in the same instant she unsnapped her phone from its leather holster and placed a call to Jacobits.

"I understand your concern, Captain," he said evenly after listening to her story, "but you are still recovering from your last op. Viruses like this happen every day to millions of people."

"I have a feeling about this, Sir. I think we should check it out with Bolling and Huntsville."

"Kate, *détentes;* relax. Not everything is a plot. When you told me you were going on a picnic, I thought you were going to relax, not look for bad guys behind the trees. It's been a week now, and you need to start letting go of Lajes. If you need some PTSD counseling, just say the word."

"I'm fine, Sir," she said hoarsely.

She stood from the tub and held herself stiffly, the golden light shooting across her as though she herself had become a torch.

"Thank you, Sir."

When she reached the kitchen she stopped short at the sound of her elderly friend's voice.

"My dear," said Jacques. "You look like the dark virgin of the Mediterranean! Whatever is wrong with you?" He bent over her and set a bowl of soup at her place. "Sometimes," he said gently, "we sabotage ourselves through our memories."

"I'm like an old lady, aren't I?"

"Nothing is wrong with being old, my friend. Although, it may be time for you to fall in love! Like the dark Madonna of Provence, who fell in love with the savior of the known world. Did you know that the Madonna was also the goddess Isis? I suppose there are only so many goddesses to go around, so we humans just have to keep renaming them...."

Chapter 4

DEEP IN THE MEUDON FOREST outside of Paris, Hank Cullen sat reading the *Financial Times*. He was by himself in the lounge of one of his private clubs, surrounded by English-speaking members and waiters. His father, James, had always belonged here for just that reason, and Hank, too, loved the irony of being able to conduct business conversations in English in the middle of a country he considered to be anti-American.

His face was slick with sweat from drinking scotch all afternoon, and he took a soft, eggshell-blue handkerchief from his jacket pocket, quickly touching it to his forehead.

The waitress walked past him slowly, brushing the table and causing the empty glasses to chink together. He watched her without speaking, then leaned forward, reaching his hand out to grab the deep garnet cotton sleeve of her uniform.

"Honey, c'mere a sec," he said.

She turned and pulled her arm away from him.

"May I help you?" She was lovely and dark, Corsican he thought; small, but with confident movements.

Hank smiled and stretched against the leather armchair. He tapped an empty glass in front of him.

"Two. My brother will be here in a minute. And clean this off," he said, pointing to the ashtray. But she merely nodded, walking away without clearing the table.

For a moment, Hank stared after her. She had a tight, little body and soft black curls, but he was unused to being disobeyed. A crumpled cigarette packet lay before him alongside a soiled napkin, and she had clearly ignored his instruction. He thought about reporting her to the club manager, but instead, he stared at her as she circled around the far side of the bar. She smiled at him a little slyly, and he believed then that she was trying to seduce him.

That day he had started drinking with the other members as soon as he arrived from the airport. Most of them had now moved into the dining room with their wives, leaving Hank alone, waiting for his next scotch and watching the door for his brother. He glanced from the oak-paneled entry to the waitress behind the bar, and back to the entry again. Above the doorway hung a carved granite slab that read, *"Dieu et mon droit"*. He had noticed this on every European business trip for the past decade, but still had no idea what the words meant. In the hallway beyond, he could see his bodyguard waiting for him. Hank nodded at him now, and the man approached.

"You might as well get some dinner, Bill. I don't know how long this is going to take."

"Yes, sir. I'll have a quick bite then."

As the CEO of Cullen Industries, Hank was unaccustomed to people arriving late for meetings, and was irritated that his younger half-brother had kept him waiting so long. He began tapping his feet on the old carpet, and the waitress smiled at him as she passed again. He opened his eyes wide, grinning at her in silent invitation and she nodded. Her hair fell forward throwing a shadow across her forehead and he rose gently off the chair in anticipation.

He wore a powder blue polo shirt that he believed matched his eyes to give him a guileless, boyish air. In truth, his eyes were the color of pearl-grey cartilage, narrow and tense, but no one had ever dared to tell him this.

He was tall and slender like a swimmer, and although he had a betting interest in team sports, he did not like to play them. His preferred exercise was rock climbing. He had recently installed a climbing wall in his home near San Diego, because he loved the adrenaline rush from clinging to a sheer cliff, depending on no one but himself.

•

The other Cullen brother, Ben, paused now in the doorway, scanning the warm room. Tall and muscular, with the dark eyes and dark hair of his Italian mother, he had always been more at ease, and less complicated than his older brother. He fingered a painful blister on his lower lip, the only scar he had acquired over the past month in the desert. He took off his Giants baseball cap and slipped the brim into his back pocket. He had been traveling with uniformed airmen for the last day, and although he never felt entirely safe with civilians, he was slightly relieved to be here among people who would not judge him as a loner merely because he was out of uniform and wearing his favorite cap. Ben spotted his brother, Hank, in the corner, and walked across the room to him. As he did, the few women remaining in the bar turned from their husbands to watch.

The half-brothers shook hands when they greeted. They had been raised together as full siblings, but there were ten years between them, between the first and second wives of their father, James Cullen, and the two boys seldom trusted each other. Hank had always insisted on competing with his younger brother, culminating in the day ten years back when he tried to seduce Ben's girlfriend over Thanksgiving weekend. The incident caused them to stop speaking altogether for years, and now the most public affection they could muster for each other was this begrudging handshake.

Ben sat in a large armchair and took off his jacket. He had never really understood style or color, and had been embarrassed more than once in public as a teenager. That evening he wore a black t-shirt and black slacks, his easy default decision, and it was the same kind of black t-shirt he wore under his *dishdasha* and *keffiyeh* for meetings at work in the desert camps.

"You've got a great tan there, little brother," said Hank loudly. "How was Mortaritaville? Calming down any these days?"

Ben looked at him for a moment without speaking, wondering just how awkward the weekend ahead was going to be with his brother and father, the three of them together again after so much time.

At last he said quietly, "I haven't been to Balad for a long time. But things were okay where I was."

"I guess I don't have to tell you that Dad wants you to get out. You could have resigned your commission years ago. After all, you don't have to stay in as long as the pilots do."

Ben nodded sharply and put his hands deliberately on the arms of the chair. His career goal out of the Air Force Academy had been to fly fighters, and Hank enjoyed reminding him that he had not been able to achieve that. Once Ben's eyesight had slipped below 20/40, even James Cullen's political and military contacts had not been able to hold onto his pilot qualification for him.

"That's true," Ben said evenly, "but I like what I do."

During his last year at the Air Force Academy, he had applied for and been granted a place in Special Operations.

"You know," Hank added, "this is not really the ideal time to be a soldier."

"Some guys would say that the middle of a war is exactly the right time."

"You know what I mean. What do you want me to tell Dad?"

"Tell him I'm hoping to be home at Christmas. Anyway, I talk to him a lot. And to my mother. You don't need to carry the water for me."

Hank shrugged. "How is it out there? Do you guys get everything you need from us?"

"You mean do the tanks have enough replacement parts to keep them rolling? I'm not really on that side of things. I'm in the Air Force, remember? We don't buy from Cullen. But thanks for checking."

"Any intel I should know about for our production?"

Ben looked at his brother for a long time, his lips set together and no expression in his eyes.

The waitress brought the two glasses of scotch to their table and Ben thanked her.

"You still drink it on the rocks?" asked Hank.

Ben nodded.

"She's a good-looking girl, don't you think? Cute little butt and cute little accent," Hank said. "Maybe you should make a move."

Ben shook his head. "I won't be in Paris long enough. I have leave for Dad's reception with the Ambassador, but then I catch a lift back to the desert."

"How long do you need?" asked Hank suddenly, grinning. "I'm not suggesting you marry her."

Ben stared at him, seeing the still-brazen young man who had come home for Thanksgiving from his first Cullen job in Washington, so many years ago.

"You don't get it, do you?" Hank asked, a little too loudly. "You're wasting your life fighting this damned war just like any common soldier."

"This war has made you a rich man, Hank." Ben knew that his brother was drunk now, and that he needed to extricate himself from their meeting before it escalated into familiar arguments.

"Never mind," Hank said, "I'll open her up and get in that box."

"When is Dad getting into town?"

"He's already here. He's staying in Paris at the Ambassador's Residence. We're all supposed to go to lunch tomorrow at the Club Interallié. But I guess you know that, seeing as how you talk to him so much, right?"

Ben ignored the tone, and slowly put his own glass on the table. "You know, I'm kinda tired. And it's a long drive back to Paris from here. What did you want to talk about?"

"I want to find out when you plan to get out of the Air Force. You need to set a date. Dad is anxious for you to be safe, and he'd like you to come work at Cullen." His face tensed as he said it, and he paused to take a quick breath. "That is, we both want you to work at Cullen."

"That's not going to happen."

"Everybody has a price, Ben. Yours just may not be money."

"Even if I did leave, I would never work at Cullen. I'm not a desk job guy. But thanks for the offer," Ben added. "I know it's not easy for you."

Hank leaned his head back against the wall.

"In a few weeks Dad will be the new Secretary of Commerce, and he'll be out of Cullen altogether."

"He's been wanting a serious Washington role for a long time."

"That's about as serious as you can get for a businessman, for a genuine job maker." Hank put both hands on the arms of the chair, and did not look Ben in the eyes. "And then the company will really be mine. Finally. Of course, whether you're working for us or not, we will always take care of you, little brother."

Ben stood up.

"Thanks for the offer, Hank. I gotta go. I have a few calls to make before I hit the hay." He grabbed his jacket. "Can I drop you somewhere? I have a rental."

"No thanks. My guy is outside."

"Bill?"

"Correct."

"Tell him I said hi, will you? I haven't seen him for years."

"You tell him yourself," Hank replied sharply. "I'm not your message boy."

Ben paused, weighing whether or not to respond. Finally, he merely said, "Gotta go. I'll see you tomorrow."

•

Hank stretched back, and as he did, his head cracked against one of the sporting photographs on the wall. He jerked away suddenly.

The waitress had been watching them, and now that he was alone she came quickly over.

"Are you all right, sir?"

"Yes, of course," he said. "I'll have the check. My driver is outside. Tell him that I'm ready."

She nodded, but did not move away.

"I'm getting off work now, if you'd like me to help you find your way."

Hank had trouble focusing his eyes on her, but he had a feeling that if he was careful, he could have her in bed that night.

"My dear, that would be excellent."

•

Once outside, the driver stepped forward to take Hank's weight from the barmaid, and as he did, Hank tripped heavily over a small, dark mound on the gravel walk. He fell from their arms to the ground, and when they helped him upright, they could see that a dead hedgehog lay between his feet.

Hank laughed suddenly, and stared at it.

"Poor little shit," he mumbled, and allowed them to pull him forward.

The driver helped him into the car, and the barmaid got in beside him, putting Hank's head on her shoulder.

"I think I had a little too much," Hank said, barely opening his mouth. "But I'll be okay when we get back to town. Don't worry, baby. You'll have a good time."

"I'm not worried, Mr. Cullen. Not a bit."

He liked the way she called him Mr. Cullen, and he closed his eyes to sleep a moment.

The driver turned out of the club property, onto the two-lane road that led to the *route nationale,* and back to Paris. The first stretch was lined with tall birches, their slender branches shivering in the breeze. The light on the pavement shone from the spring moon's reflection, and out of the birches the road fell to darkness as it wound through a secluded residential area into the surrounding deep oak forest. The night lay soft and calm around them, and Hank put his hand on the woman's inner thigh, lifting her short skirt so he could feel the warmth between her legs.

He said to her, "Baby, come closer," and he put his mouth on her neck.

Before he could speak again, the driver slammed his foot on the brake and the car skidded across the pavement. Hank lurched forward against the front seat.

"What the...!" he began to shout, but then sharp light burst toward the sky in front of them, exploding into the night.

Heavy vibration rocked the car, and the driver lost control of the steering wheel. The huge Mercedes slid sideways over the damp road, and Hank's body snapped back.

When he looked ahead he saw a white light, and he knew in an instant they would skid into the center of it.

"Bill, look out!" Hank shouted, but the car continued to careen forward, while incandescent sparks showered across the road.

The fire became a violent white sinkhole of heat, taller and brighter with every second. The remains of a small car lay in the center of the street, a frame of metal and fire in their path, the flames rising over the trees.

Hank touched the shoulder of his driver, but the man's head flopped back against his hand, and he saw in a split second that a small bullet hole had pierced his temple.

The barmaid threw herself forward over the seat and swung the steering wheel firmly to the left. The car skidded a few more yards, and then slammed to a stop against a pole at the side of the road. The noise of the fire rushing to the sky beat against the night around them, and Hank lay unconscious across the seat.

The barmaid opened the door and began to pull him from the wreck. She worked quickly and with unusual strength, and as she dragged him free of the vehicle, two men ran to join her. They both carried AK-47's and their faces were covered with balaclava masks.

She shouted at them to hurry.

"Let's go, Magdy!" she shrieked. "Let's go! And take the driver, as well. Ali, come on!" She spoke now in Arabic, as the three pulled the bodies into a Renault van waiting by the trees. They drove off quickly, the two fiery crashed cars behind them, flames still flaring into the tall oaks of the quiet Parisian suburb.

Once on the highway, the barmaid pulled Cullen's body across a fiberboard platform in the back cabin. She straightened his arms and legs at the side of his torso, and unbuckled his belt.

"Is he alive?" shouted the driver to her in Arabic. "Leila! Please confirm to me!"

Her small, dark hands, with tapered fingers, held his pulse. "Ssh!" she hissed.

"Leila, he is not dead, correct?"

Without answering, she pulled a medical bag to her side and snapped it open. She lifted cotton and a plastic syringe from it. Finding his vein quickly, she slipped the needle smoothly through his skin.

"Of course he is alive. And now he must stay alive." She leaned back, exhausted, against the windowless wall of the van, but kept her fingers all the while on Hank Cullen's carotid artery.

One of the men crawled back and squatted beside her.

"Magdy," she said, "you are responsible for getting both bodies safely onto the plane when we get to Toussus." She nodded at Cullen's driver. "We will destroy the dead one when we reach my father's ship."

Magdy began to pull the driver by his limp limbs toward the back hatch where he could transfer it quickly when they stopped at the airport.

"Tckk!" she clicked her tongue and held her free arm out to stop him. "What are you thinking? There is no rush for dead bodies. First we will get Hank Cullen out of this vehicle. The other we will incinerate when we get to the *Mihrab*. I have only a few hours to do my job on Cullen once we get to the ship, only the time it takes for dawn to arrive. Then we will dump him and sail free."

She had fierce black eyes, and curly dark hair that lay across her shoulders, and as she paused she began to smile in the silence.

"It's okay, Magdy," she whispered. "I am not angry at you. You are a good boy, and I will talk to people about you when we have finished our assignment."

Chapter 5

BEN CULLEN SAT AT THE BAR of the military hotel near the center of Paris. The soft reggae song piping through the room had soothed his mood, and he closed his eyes for a moment and rocked to the backbeat beneath the lyrics. He held a cell phone to his ear, and he was smiling. He was listening to his mother in San Diego, as she told him about her tennis game that day.

In front of him sat his last scotch of the night. Around him were young enlisteds from all the American services. Most of them were Army, based in Germany and in town for some rest and relaxation. A couple of Marines had come to perform with the jazz band for his father's reception at the Ambassador's Residence. The C-21 pilot who had flown him from Riyadh sat back in the corner with his crew and a couple of girls they had met in a bar that night. It was an easy crowd: no drunks and no trouble.

Ben finished the call and said, "Okay, Mom. Gotta go now." When he put the phone in his pocket, he noticed that two young guys beside him were staring at him, grinning.

"Talking to your mom?" one of them asked.

Ben shrugged. "That's right."

"You're in Paris. You need a girl."

Ben smiled and stood up. "Have a good night, fellas."

To them, he had no rank and no name, and that was his preference. Although being the son of James Cullen had worked in his favor at the

Academy, once he was trained and operational, that identity had made him vulnerable. In the field, the son of a wealthy manufacturer became a target, and so did every soldier near him as well. The officers at Hurlburt Field in Florida had tried to reject him from Special Operations because of his family link. On the day he reported for duty, the Wing Commander even told him point blank that he considered him a liability.

Ben focused on riding under the radar, and after a few years in Air Force Special Ops, he applied to move into Joint Special Operations Command, where the jobs were more dangerous because the bad guys often had better intelligence data than he did.

Only once had he let his guard down about his family, and that had resulted in a car bombing in Pakistan that killed three of the six in his field team. The attack was carried out by a suicide bomber who had laced the IED with rat poison to make sure that blood coagulation in Ben's buddies was hampered so that they bled to death. In the years since then, he had never allowed his identity to surface, and he felt most at ease in moments like this, out of uniform among military people who did not know him.

He checked his watch and put his ear to the door of his hotel room, pausing for a few seconds to reassure himself. Inside, the room was sparse as in most military hotels: old, barely functional furniture, with only the basic supplies. Ben was not accustomed to better, and in fact he had spent six hours that day on a crude airlift from northern Iraq to Qatar, then an hour flying to Riyadh, followed by ten hours into Paris. The last bathroom he remembered apart from the planes was a hole in some nameless corner of the upland desert southwest of Mosul.

Ben took off his t-shirt and slacks, and sat on the foot of the bed in his boxers, watching French television. He had learned French from the Rosetta Stone CD's the Air Force gave him when he was a 2nd Lieutenant, but he had also studied Arabic and German in college. Years ago, the Air Force had sent him to the Defense Language Institute in Monterey to teach him Russian. At moments like this, when he was raw-tired and a little drunk, he could hear all the languages together, jostling for prominence in his mind.

He stared at the television screen. Rhinestone-clad women with heavy makeup were dancing to cabaret music on some French sound-stage, and Ben watched, thinking about the people who had been telling him that night to find a woman. He wondered if it showed somehow on his face how isolated he had become. The last girl he had been close to was at the Academy, a beautiful Latin girl who went on to become a pilot. He still remembered every detail about her, and if he closed his eyes long enough he could feel her breasts in his hands again, and he could see her luminous smile. But their ending had been rough, not long after the Thanksgiving incident with Hank. It made no sense to him now, but he had taken her up to the woods above the dorms, all the way up to Cathedral Rock in the darkness. Both of them were shivering from the scattered snow around them, and there, with no reason except his own callowness, he had broken off their relation-ship. All the years since, he always gave his friends the joking excuse that women just did not spend time in the Central American jungles or the Middle Eastern deserts where he worked.

When his cell rang, he had already been sound asleep for half an hour.

"Where the hell have you been, Ben?" It was the C-21 pilot he had seen in the bar earlier.

"Asleep. What's up, JJ?"

"They've been calling you for twenty minutes. We need to get you over to Gabriel A-SAP."

Gabriel was the name the military gave to the American Embassy in Paris. Ben sat up quickly.

"What's going on?"

"Your brother's been taken. Get your clothes on. The guys coming to escort you are just about at your door now."

Ben jumped out of bed and grabbed the slacks he had worn that day. Shortly after, the knock came and the Embassy guards announced themselves. He grabbed his Baby Glock and opened the door slowly. Two young Marines stood on the other side in fatigues, with M16 rifles at their sides.

"Major Cullen? We have orders to take you with us."

"Come in, guys. What's going on?"

"They'll explain it to you when we get to the embassy."

He grabbed a cotton shirt from the closet and sat on the bed to put his shoes on. "Let's go."

"You won't get in the embassy with that, Sir," said one of the Marines, pointing at his gun.

"I'm licensed."

"We know that, Sir. But no one but us gets in with weapons."

The Marines transported their cargo in a black Mercedes Benz SUV with bulletproof windows, and brought him not to Avenue Gabriel, but to the adjoining Ambassador's Residence, the Pontalba building on the rue St Honoré. They walked through a band of special French security forces outside the fortress, past the Marine guards on the inside of the iron gates, to the cobbled courtyard. Instead of crossing through the darkness to the glass entry doors of the residence, they led Ben swiftly to a sunken wooden door at the far side of the courtyard. The façade was carved with Roman Catholic gargoyles, and three ancient steps led down to the small platform before the door.

One of the Marines opened a small, steel cover to a keypad and punched in a security code that allowed him to push the door open.

Before them lay a metal staircase, lit only by dim floor lights. They ran quickly down the stairs, and entered another code at the keypad on the bottom door. Inside this heavy steel door stood more Marines, and before them lay a maze of starkly lit corridors beneath the block of buildings that belonged to the United States. The guards took Ben between them, walking more easily now into the deep cavern of activity below the quiet Parisian streets.

Dozens of people, uniformed and not, worked below the Embassy and the Residence, through the day and the night. Shifts of diplomatic workers, cultural, security and economic, as well as service members from all branches, made this steel-encrusted underground refuge a matter-of-fact American city, twenty-four hours a day.

Without speaking, they led Ben past offices, briefing rooms, an American grocery store, a couple of fast-food restaurants, and a small athletic facility, to another steel door, unmarked, and flagged by more military guards. One of the Marines stepped onto a platform that determined his weight, and then faced a mirrored panel that scanned his eyes for identity. The light turned amber when he was approved, and he entered a code on the security pad. The door clicked, and the guards checked his identification, before allowing him to enter.

•

James Cullen stood up immediately when Ben arrived. He was tall and slender, much like his elder son, Hank. His thin, short hair was entirely white, and his face and hands were tanned from the sun of southern California. His eyes were pale, crystal blue, and were sunk into the thin, crepe-wrinkled skin around his eye sockets.

He threw his arms around Ben's shoulders.

"They almost got you, too," he said.

Ben smiled. "That's not so easy to do, Dad," he said. "Don't worry about me." He turned to the Ambassador, who extended his hand.

"We're doing everything we can, Ben," he whispered. He put his other arm around Ben's shoulders and leaned close. The Ambassador's pale, freckled skin was mottled as well with liver spots, and though Ben had known the man since childhood, he had never been able to tolerate the heavy smell of German cologne that always surrounded him. "We hope to have a briefing in a few minutes."

Ben nodded. "Thank you, sir."

The Ambassador's aide stood behind the couch and without instruction, left the room.

"Has it hit the news, yet?" Ben asked. "We should let Hank's mom know what's going on before she sees it on TV."

James Cullen said immediately, "Until we know for sure, I don't want to phone her. As soon as we get the report, I'll phone Utah, and your mother as well."

"Let me get you something to drink," said the Ambassador's wife suddenly. "Some coffee? A little stronger?"

"Coffee would be great, ma'am." Ben sat on the couch, and leaned back, exhausted. He had seen many safe rooms in his career, but this was one of the best to provide the illusion of safety. Designed to be an oasis of familiarity for the Ambassador during moments of threat and hysteria, it looked exactly like his upstairs study. It contained a deep cherry desk, a couch and two austere 18th Century Colonial American chairs, as well as photographs of former Presidents and their wives. This false little oasis was situated far underground at the center of the fortress of American activity, behind several steel shells of protection and the most sophisticated electronic surveillance equipment, run by the most sophisticated teams in the world. Just alongside the fortress under the streets, ran the rats of the Paris sewers.

Ben closed his eyes for a moment, trying to rest in the bright light. Ironically, he had felt safer in the desert outside of Mosul than he did in this room next to the heavily guarded American Ambassador. Ben's normal team was small: usually not more than six people working in some village street, guys who had been together for years and whom he trusted. Here in the Embassy, his family's safety was dependent on a bureaucracy of men and women who were small components in a large security system. As a lead in JSOC, Ben was many years past believing in the efficiency and capability of the entire military force. For a long time now his life had depended on small moments within his team, little flutters of knowledge and violence unfolding in silence between them.

He heard the brittle crackle of a china cup as the Ambassador's wife placed his coffee on the small table in front of him, and he opened his eyes.

"Thank you, ma'am."

She placed her hand on his shoulder and said gently, "Ben, I've known you since you were born, honey. You don't need to call me ma'am."

"I'm sorry, Anita. It's just a habit."

Anita and Paul Henderson had known the Cullen family since Jim's law school days at the University of Utah, as well as through both of his wives and families. In the beginning, the two men did little more than drink together, late at night across the Utah state line in Wyoming. Jim Cullen would pay for their weekend binges because Paul Henderson, who came from a working-class Ogden family, never had an extra dollar for Saturday night. When the men practiced law in Salt Lake, their families became close and the Henderson children and the Cullen boys attended the same boarding schools.

Ben watched these men now across the room, his father holding a landline receiver to his ear. He saw him so seldom, he had a hard time understanding that Jim Cullen had become an old man. His face was wrinkled from too many hours on southern California golf courses, and his sharp cheekbones were permanently rouged from the decades of business cocktails that had become his life.

Ben leaned forward and took the coffee cup between his hands.

"Are you cold?" asked Anita Henderson.

"I guess so," he said and smiled.

"Let me get you a blanket. We've been down here twice before," she said calmly, "and they never seem to be able to get the climate control right."

The Ambassador came and sat beside him on the couch.

"We've got a situation report now, Ben." He sat forward, leaning heavily with his hands on his knees. He was focused but tired, and his voice sounded to Ben like his mouth was stuffed with cotton. "The French police found Hank's car in the forest, on fire. There were no human remains inside, so we believe he was kidnapped, and we are hoping he's alive. No one has claimed responsibility, but we have some local reports that may help. The French police are working on this around the clock. And we are, as well. The CIA is bringing in a Dutchman, an older man connected with Arab kids at a public high school in the suburbs at Drancy. He seems to have some information on activity in the area."

Ben nodded slowly. "I would like to talk to him, if I could, Mr. Ambassador. On my own."

"You know I can't let that happen, Ben. We're not at war with France, and our military has no authority here. It's the CIA's jurisdiction during peacetime – not Spec Ops." Henderson put his hand lightly upon his shoulder. "You know that," he said softly. "The French are bringing in this witness so that our special agency representatives here can interview him."

"Do we know whether the kidnap was executed by terrorists or private criminals?"

Henderson shrugged. "I'm not sure I know the difference between the two anymore," he said. "But no demands have been made and we have no confirmed information about who took Hank. However, there are many reasons why someone would want to." The Ambassador added, "You and your father have permission to hear the taped recording of the interrogation, if you want. They'll let us know when it is ready. Ben, any idea if Hank had friends in Paris? A girlfriend, maybe?"

"Not that I know of."

"Because reports are that he left the bar with a woman."

Ben's face was as still as a sheet of glass, and he could see the woman's eyes as she leaned across the bar table earlier that evening. He knew instantly what had happened. After so many years of seeing dead soldiers and politicians, Ben understood that their vulnerability was almost never defined by professional errors, but by a slim window of personal exposure usually opened by their own vanity.

He nodded and said quietly, "I think I may be able to identify her. It may be the woman who served us at the club in Meudon."

Henderson glanced over at his aide. "Get that French detective back here right away."

Chapter 6

BY THE NEXT MORNING, Ben and the others had been released from the underground compound, and they sat in the breakfast room of the 19th Century residence complex. The spring sun drenched across the lead-paned doors and the interior courtyard, covering Ben's exhausted face. On the wall opposite him was an American oil painting of scarlet poppies thrown across a mythical field, and as he stared at it, he felt with overwhelming nausea that he was sitting in a junkyard.

He had not slept that night. He was unused to being off the street in moments of crisis, and was agitated by having to listen to his father and Ambassador Henderson speculate about the political strategy behind his brother's kidnapping. Ben had learned early in his career that micro view intel, or ground truth, was always more valuable than intel handed down from his superiors, yet now that he was incarcerated in the elegant, highly-guarded American fortress, he had lost access to any movement out in the city. Moving, scanning, thinking, deducing, and calculating: a working soldier could do many things simultaneously in a smooth, beautiful way, but the key to it was direct access to the fighting.

"Ever since the rise of the gangster state," he heard his father say, as though practicing for a speech, "war has revolved around only one question: what stops a suicide bomber? There is no answer to that. This is an entirely new way of playing."

"There have always been gangster states, Jim," said Paul Henderson. "As long as there have been human beings."

"Perhaps. But until now our principal threats have come from the standing armies of our enemies. Today we have small groups of soldiers who are unaligned to any particular government and who wage war from the shadows."

Both men paused to chew, and in that quiet pocket, Ben began to see much he had known about Henderson and his father distilled before him. He understood now that although they might feign sincerity in the most difficult political meetings, they were really just *fobbits*, the kind of soldier who remains uncommitted and within the safe wire of the Forward Operating Base.

"This is no more than well-organized armed robbery by terrorists. Politically-motivated violence aimed at non-combatants," said Jim Cullen. "We need to respond, quickly and hard. They are trying to bring down Cullen Industries, and our whole American economy."

"Jim, I really have a hard time believing that the fall of one company, however big, could bring down our whole economy," said Henderson. "But I agree that we need to respond hard."

Ben leaned forward abruptly. "Just get my brother free before you start another all-out war." His voice was unforgiving. "We don't even know if terrorists lifted him."

Both Cullen and Henderson turned to look at him, and his father's face was sour. Once, Ben had watched his father whelp out a litter of show dog puppies, one at a time they came out of the mother, each covered in a glaze of serum, and when one of them emerged not breathing, he remembered that his father had thrown it matter-of-factly into the garbage pail.

"Calm down, Ben," Henderson said. "Your father and I are not the enemy. I think we are pretty certain this is a terrorist action. There are many rich people in this country who could be kidnapped more easily if all they want is money. This is more than just a private crime. And please realize, son, there is nothing we can do at the moment. Hank is not military and he is not diplomatic. He is a private American citizen. This is a French police matter unless they decide to bring our people in, or unless our President gets involved."

The dining room filled with voices as the Ambassador's visiting grandchildren came for food. They immediately ran to Ben and the youngest jumped on his lap. An aide followed them and whispered to the Ambassador.

"They're ready for us at Gabriel," he said. "We've had accreditation and a demand."

They followed the aide through a series of underground passageways to the main buildings of the U.S. Embassy, to a small briefing room where gathered the highest-ranking men from international intelligence services in Paris. Although they rarely collaborated, they sat at the table this morning because the American Ambassador had phoned each of them personally.

In the room were the senior CIA analyst from the Office of Russian and European Analysis; the CIA Special Assistant to the Ambassador; Lieutenant Colonel Jacobits, the U.S. Embassy military Defense Attaché from the DIA; a representative from *"Cristina"*, the terrorism department of the *Direction Centrale du Renseignement Intérieur*; and an agent, a French national, from the international collaborative against al Qaeda terrorism, *Alliance Base*.

Ben could hear a phone droning off the hook somewhere behind a wall. He sat in a narrow, grey chair next to his father, in the windowless theater. On the screen before them was a map of France, with red circles over the likely holding points for his brother. Ben tried to focus on the report of the CIA analyst, squinting at the rivers and the roads before them, all descending across the map like delicate fissures, but he had not yet fully accepted that his own brother had become the asset to be rescued.

The CIA analyst finished his report and sat down.

Colonel Jacobits leaned stiffly forward and said tightly, "I'm sorry, did I miss the agency's conclusion? I didn't hear your recommendation."

"Our data isn't sufficient yet, Jake. You know we haven't made a recommendation," said the Special CIA Assistant to the Ambassador.

"Well, what have you been doing all this time? You spent hours analyzing the data without letting us see it. We have deadlines now, until Monday to respond, Wednesday to deliver cash. Every piece of extra data you want to collect before you feel able to offer a solution is time deducted from Hank Cullen's life."

Ben glanced up, grateful for someone else's frustration.

"Jake," said Henderson sharply. "Keep this moving, please. We only have a coordinating role in this data gathering, remember."

"I'm sorry, Mr. Ambassador." He nodded to the *Alliance Base* agent, who began typing quickly on a keyboard embedded in the desktop before him. Suddenly, a map of the Paris region appeared, and the tobacco-crackled voice of the Dutchman, interviewed earlier, dropped through the room. Ben thought he made Paris sound like a fairy tale land of good and evil, and when he began describing the poverty and violence of Muslim boys in one of the northeastern suburbs, he did so with the greatest sympathy. The Dutchman had taught them in Drancy schools, and he spoke of a covert network of communication across the French countryside, a network he believed would one day lead to the downfall of the French government.

Ben listened, his back hunched over the desk so that he did not have to look at the eyes of the men sitting near him. He was rarely invited to meetings at this level, with ambassadors and key security officers. He had learned over the years not to wonder too much about why they fought or what happened when they were finished with a mission.

The *Alliance Base* agent stood, and watched the screen with the rest of them. As he did, he put his large red hands over his belly. He was perspiring faintly, and his face had begun to shine. He fingered a laser pen in his right hand, and when the audio recording stopped, he began to draw a path with red light across the map. He clicked a computer mouse and a map of the Mediterranean coastline appeared.

"The demand comes to us from AQIM, al Qaida in the Maghreb. This is an Algerian fundamentalist group committed to a variety of goals, including bringing down the Algerian and the French govern-ments. And the Americans, of course," he said quickly, "but that pretty much goes without saying, doesn't it? Also, they publicly support the Islamic State."

Colonel Jacobits interrupted him quickly. "The man in the Lajes explosion last month was AQIM."

"Correct. We have been watching the Maghreb for some time. We know their funding comes from al Qaeda sources, but we have also traced income streams from local wealthy fundamentalist Algerians. With financing they have never before possessed, this group in that North African region is about to explode in capacity."

"This is intel we have had for years," muttered the CIA analyst.

"Perhaps it took a collaboration like the *Alliance Base* to make it relevant," replied the Frenchman.

"Let's circle back to Hank Cullen, gentleman," said Ambassador Henderson.

The *Alliance Base* representative continued, "They lifted him from outside of Paris in the Meudon Forest, and according to our expert, the suburbs of Paris are teeming with young Islamic fundamentalists who would aid this effort."

"I doubt that Meudon is 'teeming' with Algerians," said the CIA representative. "Don't you French usually keep your darker citizens in their own suburbs on the other side of town?"

"That is totally unnecessary. Please let me continue. International air space is now monitored, so a flight will be impossible. We believe they have moved him to the south by road in order to get him out of the country on a boat over to Algeria."

"Your 'expert'?" asked Jacobits. "The old left-wing English teacher from Holland? Are you kidding me?"

"No, Colonel, I am not making any jokes here."

"Did my ID of the girl help you any?" Ben asked quickly.

"Frankly, Major," said the representative from the French *"Cristina"* agency, "you had a good description, but we haven't had anything further on it. The woman was not a permanent employee, and no one seems to be able to find her now." He looked at the *Alliance Base* agent and continued, "All of us have known for years about the Drancy activity. Even before the *Alliance* was created, *Cristina* was reporting on it."

The CIA analyst looked at Ambassador Henderson. "That's true. The tenements in Drancy have always been filled with teenage Muslim boys. Their parents came over after the Algerian War to work any job they could get. These kids have grown up here, in the poorest sections of the capital. They were educated by French teachers who resent them, and were beaten by Algerian parents who don't understand why their kids are so westernized. These are the thugs who burned that little Muslim girl alive a few years ago. In the name of God. Now they are political capital. No big surprise to anyone."

Paul Henderson closed the paper file in front of him. He drank from a water glass, and leaned forward with his arms folded across the table.

"Gentlemen, I'm not hearing much hard intelligence. You are assuming a lot to connect schoolchildren in Drancy to Hank Cullen's kidnap simply because some leftwing, alcoholic teacher believes it. What you are really telling me is that none of you has any idea where Hank Cullen is, or how to get him back."

"With due respect, Mr. Ambassador," said the *Alliance Base* agent, "this teacher has worked with us for years. He has always been a trustworthy source. He taught English and German to foreigners in Paris for three decades. Before the Gulf War, he was hired by EADS at their old manufacturing facility in Tarbes to teach English to the fighter pilots from Saudi, Syria, and Iraq."

"We all remember those times," muttered Jacobits. "When the French sold weapons to nations of questionable loyalty."

"And that, too, is unnecessary," said the *Alliance Base* representative. "France is not at fault for this kidnap, and my government is not at fault for the ills of the world."

The CIA agent pressed a button in the table before him and the screen went black. "Actually, we do agree with you about the connection between the Drancy gangs and the Muslims on the south coast, because many of these boys have ended up in the Waziristan training camps in north Pakistan. This teacher may be Dutch and he may be an alcoholic, but Mr. Ambassador, our best HUMINT tells us that Hank Cullen is being taken to a port in Provence to be lifted to Algeria. This could be a kidnap, or they might be after him for information; our worst case scenario is that this is political *dim mak*, and he could be dead already."

Ben moved to speak, but somehow could not. *Dim mak*, poison hand, a forbidden kung fu technique where the attacker strikes a vital point with precise, balanced force at an instant in time with the intention of killing, was one of his own combat specialties.

The *Alliance Base* agent stood and put his laptop into a soft black Hermes leather portfolio.

"My friends, I am due back to brief my Director soon. Please keep us advised as the day unfolds."

When he and the other French representative from *Cristina* had left the room, Paul Henderson said, "Well, Jake, if it is the Med coast, what is our next step?"

The Colonel shrugged. "The French police are investigating. We have consulted the French President at the Élysées. He has promised a response by this afternoon."

"My brother could be dead by this afternoon," Ben said.

"Please, Major Cullen," said Henderson. "You are an observer here." He turned to the Colonel. "Would you speculate about the options, Jake? The man's family is sitting here, and we would all like to know the possibilities."

"The French police have refused to bless us into their investigation. They will determine on their own where Cullen is being held, and then I'm sure they will take immediate action. Since the crime was committed in France, this is an investigation by the French national police. It has nothing to do with the Agency." He turned the computers off. "But I can tell you this, AQIM is not after the cash. The ransom price is too low for that. Either they want information or Cullen is dead already. There aren't thirty-seven scenarios here. And stopping him at the coast is still our best option."

The Ambassador's aide turned the theater lights on.

"Waiting for the French to take action on the kidnapping of an American businessman doesn't seem to me like the best solution," said Jim Cullen. "The torture and death of the CEO of a principal American weapons supplier will be a signal of extreme weakness for the U.S."

His eyes were the color of gunmetal, and beneath his shirt, the heft of his chest entirely dissolved now into an old man's body.

"Do we know they are doing all they should?" asked Ben.

"The French police are the best detectives in the world," said the CIA analyst.

"That wasn't really my question," Ben said.

"Then that is a political question, and no one in this room can answer it."

Colonel Jacobits looked up. "Of course, there is no reason for us to stop our own investigation, Mr. Ambassador. We have a skilled DIA agent in the south. An Air Force captain embedded at the École de l'Air in Salon. I would need your authorization for this. But I could have her here by noon for a briefing."

"Her?" asked Henderson.

"Yes, a woman, but she's excellent, Sir. She has been on my team for a few years," said Colonel Jacobits. "A former F-16 pilot ostensibly working as the coordinator of our cadet exchange program for the Academy. She's multi-skilled, fluent in French and Arabic, and an expert shot. If you give the word, Mr. Ambassador, we can pull a team together and get our own people on the ground undercover."

Paul Henderson looked over at his friend. "You know, Jim, I can authorize fact-finding. But I cannot give the go-ahead for a Title 10 or Title 50 action without consulting the President. Even a clandestine operation would need his okay."

"I understand."

"And my bet is, the President will not authorize any American military or CIA action in France.

Ben stirred slightly, seeing a lake of space between him and the others. In his world, he would have stopped discussion long ago.

"You have my okay to continue the investigation," said Henderson to Colonel Jacobits. "And I'm trusting you, Jake, to expand the possibilities of rescue for us. But gentlemen, I have a nine a.m. appointment and I will need to leave you for the planning. And you will, too, Ben. You and your father are not authorized to participate."

Ben did not want the others to know that his nerves were entirely shredded, and so he stood strongly and nodded. "We need to get you on a plane back home, Dad," he said.

"What do you mean? I have a speech to give at dinner tonight."

"We have to cancel that, Jim," agreed Henderson. "Every principal economic advisor in Paris is coming. And all the financial journalists. It's a huge risk to take after what's happened. Tonight was intended to be a media event. You will soon be the new Secretary of Commerce, and the President wants you safe. He certainly would not want this news of Hank's kidnap to get out."

"You don't see the OECD leaving town," Jim Cullen replied. "What kind of reason would you give for canceling? And what kind of message are we sending to AQIM? It's your decision, Paul, of course, but I'm here and willing to continue."

The Ambassador's aide stood at the door, silent as always, shifting from one foot to the other across the thick, blue carpet, brushing aside everything around him but a look from his superior.

Slowly, Henderson looked over at him. Finally he said, "I don't think God intended us to be cowards, do you?"

Ben watched his father reach out to Henderson, relieved. Long ago, he had stopped believing that courage or survival had anything to do with God. His operations were dependent on correct information and instant communication. He knew that the American Embassy in Paris was a dwarfed United States planet that could be broken down in twenty-four hours by skilled agents from a thousand miles away, if only they had better intel and quicker communication. The brash confidence of leaders, whether political or military, was something he had come to mistrust; even their belief in this American god, concealed in the clouds and protecting the country, even this god eluded Ben now after so many years as an operative.

"We won't cancel tonight," Henderson said. "But you and Ben will have to remain here in the compound until then. We'll make you comfortable and get you whatever you need for now."

Ben nodded automatically, his body stiffening slightly as though to attention.

"Thank you, Paul," his father said.

On his way out the door, the Ambassador stopped in front of Colonel Jacobits. He leaned close, and said gently, "The President wants Hank Cullen back alive. Whatever you need to do – do it."

Chapter 7

KATE WAS NOT YET DRESSED for the day when she received the call from Lieutenant Colonel Jacobits. She stood at her window looking out into the damp forest, holding her cell phone to her ear. She wore a white lace bra and a plain white thong that glowed against her skin. Her stomach was taut and brown, and in her pierced navel lodged a golden ring. She put her hand over it, fingering the band while she listened to the Colonel. Occasionally, she nodded to the phone. She had lived alone for so many years that she did not think it odd when she responded to the telephone as though it were a human being standing beside her.

Jacobits gave her the order with little information, merely telling her when and where the transport would arrive. The copper morning light lay over her face like a veil, and without looking down, she reached to the table for her coffee cup.

"Within the hour? This is fairly short notice, Sir," she said. "I have a dog, you know."

Jacobits laughed. "When did you get that? You never used to have a dog."

"At Christmas. He was a present to myself."

"Captain Cardenas, you need to get out more. Be at the airfield by ten hundred to meet them. I'll see you before lunch."

•

Kate pulled her service blues out of the wardrobe and put the uniform on. She grabbed her go-bag, already packed and ready for such call-ups. She took her dog downstairs and put his food and blanket in a backpack.

"Come on, Glock," she said to him. "You're going on a sleepover at Jacques' house."

Jacques lived at the end of a tiny hedgerow-lined lane. When she pulled up the drive to his house, he waved at her like an excited schoolboy, and called out, "Halloo!" in broad, accented English.

As she got out of her car, she noticed that he still had not repaired the collapsed garden shack near his house.

"You better get someone to fix those boards," she said. "This is going to be a hot summer, and then they say a very wet winter. I could help if you want."

He shrugged. "Hmmm. A potting shed in tip-top shape; not really a priority of mine, Kate, but thank you." He bent forward and kissed her cheeks three times.

He was six feet tall, much taller than most Frenchmen of his generation, and slender. He was clean-shaven with short, curly white hair and small wire-rimmed glasses. He wore American hiking clothes and Australian-made boots, and was in perfect physical condition for a man of fifty, even though he had actually celebrated his seventy-fourth birthday at the beginning of the spring.

"*Viens ici, mon pétit Glock!*" he called, and the dog ran up the steps to greet him. Jacques knelt on the old stone porch floor and it began licking his face. "This is much better than going to Paris tonight! Well, I was just looking for a good excuse to stay home when you called."

"Thank you, Jacques. I'm sorry this is so last minute."

He began shaking his head, and stood up, putting his arm around her shoulders. "Don't be sorry. I was going to Paris to hobnob with some rich American donors. I'd much rather be here with Glockie."

"I should be back on Thursday."

"Okay, Glockie and I will be waiting for you with baited breath! Professor Lowell just called to cancel my visit to the gorge over the weekend. I was going to rappel down to some Roman antiquities and examine the rock art, but now he says there are bigger VIP's than me touring my Ardèche forest and they can't have me jumping off cliffs frightening them! Imagine! Though Lowell will never allow them into the caves, no matter how much money they donate."

"Is there anything you won't do?" Kate laughed. "I still can't believe you dived the underwater caves at Cosquer last year."

"All in the name of science, my dear. The drawings at Cosquer are the earliest record of medicinal herbs in existence on those walls at Marseille. A fabulous discovery. Besides, at my age you always worry that if you sit still you will turn to stone. Why Catalina," he exclaimed, touching the shoulder of her uniform, "you are all dressed up in your outfit already. Don't you have time for tea with me? I also have fresh *pain au chocolat!*"

"No, I have to get to the airfield soon. Maybe when I get back, you could come for dinner and bring your guitar?"

"Of course," he said. "It would be my pleasure!"

Kate drove out the back road, swinging wide to avoid the deep ditch left the previous winter by the last-minute *mazout* heating oil delivery. She heard the soft engines of a nearby canal barge through the wide farming fields, and turned onto the main road to the airfield.

•

A couple of hours later, when the Gulfstream touched down at Le Bourget, she stared calmly out at the empty pavement around the plane, still with no idea why she had been brought to Paris. A light spring breeze had come up that morning, and a fine paste of pollen now lay on the surrounding planes. When Kate debarked she breathed deeply, inhaling the fuel fumes. Flying had been her love since she was a teenager, and jet fuel was still the smell of freedom for her.

At the Embassy on Avenue Gabriel, she was taken immediately to the DIA offices, a long hallway of nondescript rooms along the steel-hulled corridor underneath the tree-lined avenue. The Marines deposited her at the door of Jacobits' office, and she sat down across the wide oak desk from him. On top of the desk lay three brass paperweights, anchoring three neat stacks of files. She lifted one paperweight in her hand, and as she did, a smear of sweet gum clung to her sleeve from the object.

"Colonel, your cleaner missed something here." She took her handkerchief from her pocket and began to rub at the spot.

Jacobits watched her patiently.

"Are you finished now?" he asked. "I've always thought, Captain Cardenas, that we are so alike you could have been my daughter."

She flashed an easy grin, and he felt as though the room had come alive.

"How's your father doing? I heard they moved him to a hospital in San Diego." Carefully, he folded his hands together on the desk.

"I think he's a strong person," she said. "But I know it won't be many more months. I have leave to go back after the semester finishes at Salon. But you probably know that."

He nodded, and said quietly, "I do, Captain. It's my job to know everything that might impact the team's performance."

"Why did you bring me to Paris, Sir?"

"There's been a kidnapping, of an American. I'll be straight up with you, Captain: Ambassador Henderson wants us to find the victim and get him back without official involvement or knowledge."

"Who is it?"

"Hank Cullen, the son of his best friend. CEO of Cullen Industries. Since they're one of our biggest vendors in this war, the Secretary of Defense has also phoned me. And the Chairman of the Joint Chiefs." Jacobits chuckled and added, "All my bosses have checked in this morning."

Kate's face froze, and Jacobits saw it. "What's the matter, Kate? You've run big-time ops before." She shook her head, and Jacobits added, "Henderson's best friend, James Cullen, founded the company, and will shortly retire so he can be appointed the new Secretary of Commerce. He's also the President's best friend. In fact, James Cullen has so many good buddies that I've been instructed to get his son back at all costs. Without letting anyone know."

"Have we had any demands?"

"It's AQIM again. That bunch of Algerians trained in the north of Pakistan. We just heard they want ten million dollars or they kill him and announce it to the media. We have a deadline of next Wednesday."

She lifted a thin smile. "Only ten million? I guess American businessmen aren't worth what they used to be."

"Who knows? Maybe they just want information from him. Maybe they want to show us that they can lift an important target under our noses. Who knows what their point is. But the deadline is very quick. We need to move today."

She stared at him, her expression unflinching.

"AQIM is active along the coastal provinces, in Marseille, of course. That's why you are here. You have a better knowledge of the agents and movements in the south of France than anyone I know. We think they took him by road to an embarkation point along the coast. I figure they are going to sail him into the Med if they don't kill him. Take him over to North Africa."

"Do you think Cullen knows anything they might want to know?"

"I'm sure he does, but my gut tells me that if they wanted intel on our strategy in Iraq, Afghanistan, Iran, or anywhere else, there are a dozen guys they could have lifted more easily. Hell, all they have to do is read the damned *Canard Enchaîné* or *Wikileaks* and they can find out what our plans are. I haven't a friggin' clue why they did this. We've asked for proof of life by tomorrow."

"Title 10?" asked Kate.

"This is more than Title 10. This is not just a clandestine operation. The U.S. government will wholly deny any involvement in this action, whether or not it is successful, because they will be denying that he was lifted in the first place. We can't admit the enemy is able to kidnap our major war suppliers, now can we?" Jacobits shook his head slowly. "By next Wednesday, if James Cullen doesn't pay the ten million to get his son back, I'm guessing they will kill him. If he does pay, they will probably kill him anyway. I called you because I know you can do the job. I am not ordering you to take part; I'm asking. But if you decide to do this, whether you succeed or fail, I promise you I won't let them hang you out to dry."

"Colonel, if you need me, I'm there. Of course." She saw dust laying on the ridges of his desk, but she was afraid to wipe it and reveal how her fingers were shaking. "What about the French police? Are they involved?"

"The Agency thinks they are dragging their heels. Who even knows what instructions they had from the Élysées? I'm not sure I believe anything they said at the briefing today."

She moved her hand suddenly across the desk, swinging it wide and loose, like a drill bit breaking from its socket.

"Captain, what is wrong with you?"

"Nothing, Sir. I must have had too much coffee on the jet. Is *Cristina* involved in data gathering?"

Jacobits nodded. "We met with them this morning. And I have a buddy at the bureau in Marseille who may be able to cooperate behind the scenes."

"What about the *Alliance Base?*"

"They've been sharing intel. But we have gone as far as we can go with them. I don't trust any of the usual partners on this. The CIA can help a little, but I want our own guys on it. Those cretins in the CIA haven't gotten anything right since they saved the Dead Sea scrolls in the Forties."

She knew he wanted her to laugh, but she could not muster it.

"Colonel, there's something I have to tell you."

"I can see that. What is it?"

" I know Hank Cullen."

"Well, since you used to date his younger brother, I assumed you did. What I can't figure out from your file is just how well you know the older Cullen brother...."

"I met him once."

Jacobits sighed. "...and whether or not this is going to be a problem."

"Of course not, Sir."

He rubbed his eyes and sat back to watch her. The room was honey yellow in the artificial lamplight. "I hope Hank Cullen is worth all of this," he said hollowly. "There's only a very minor opportunity for anything good to come out of it." He leaned back in his chair. "We have a briefing with the CIA now, and then you will need to go and meet your team."

"Who do I have, Sir?"

"This is deniable. It's a small team. Chad Witt out of Spain. Jenny Abernathy. I would have used McEwing....now I gotta find someone else for you but I don't know who yet."

"Just four of us, Sir?"

"That's all you get, Captain. Not exactly poolside in San Diego, is it?"

"Six would be better, but I'm still in, Colonel. You know that."

"Thank you, Kate. They are gathering in the old Basque monastery outside of Mauléon near the Spanish border. Those monks have always been on our side before. You could go home to your Salon base and wait, but I figured you would want to meet up with the team as soon as they land. One of the monks will be your driver to get you to base to prep the op. By the time you get home, I'm hoping I can have another agent there for you."

"When do we move?"

"Tomorrow dawn. Get yourself some go pills. This is going to be a long week. And a hard one. I have a gut feeling that they won't let Cullen live very long. I hope you have overnight care for your dog. What kind did you get, anyway?"

"A Saint Bernard."

"The big kind, then."

"Of course," she replied, grinning.

Kate and Jacobits moved down the DIA corridor to the main underground crossroads of the embassy maze. The recirculated air was soaked with the metallic taste of synthetic purification, all of it shining stark and bright. When they came to the crossing, a signpost indicated the Gabriel offices to the left, the Residence to the right, and the CIA stronghold straight ahead.

Kate paused at the sign, as though wandering lost by a river, and she leaned against a corner while the flow of people moved past.

"Captain Cardenas, what are you doing?" asked Jacobits, but she did not answer. She was staring across the corridor at a non-uniformed man. He had seen her and was staring back.

In just a few seconds, Ben had crossed the corridor. He stood before her, tall and wearing rumpled black clothing.

Kate wiped her palms against the sides of her uniform, again and again as though her hands were covered in oil.

"Hello," she whispered.

Ben nodded sharply, his mouth trembling.

She nodded back, and said, "I heard about your brother. I'm sorry." She knew what she had just said was a lie, and that they both carried another pain like light on their backs.

She could feel the sweat forming small drops on the back of her neck, but she could not find vocabulary for what she wanted to tell him. Awkwardly and quietly, she moved out into the passage and found her place beside the Colonel. As they walked on, Jacobits turned back and nodded at Ben Cullen, at once aware of the sprawling complexity of this job.

Chapter 8

AT TEN MINUTES TO THREE that afternoon, Kate sat alone over-looking the *Gave Uhaitza* in the center of the town of Mauléon-Licharre in the French *pays Basque.* She was outdoors in the hot sun, alone on a cafe patio along the railing that protected customers from the sheer drop to the river below. She wore blue jeans and an American college sweatshirt, and sat quietly writing post cards and sipping an Orangina.

Like other young tourists to this town, Kate carried a backpack containing her essential belongings, but unlike most of them, hers was crammed with a secure cell, German-made Hanwag boots, CQB gloves, recon wrap head gear, dog tags, knife, night vision goggles and her Escape and Evade Kit. A camouflaged holster secured around her waist held her 45 ACP pistol.

This spring day in the foothills of the Pyrénées was slow for the little market town of Mauléon. Earlier, Kate had bought her father a souvenir crucifix from the 12th Century St. Blaise church, and now she held it, Jesus-down, idly stroking the tiny vial of holy water inlaid at the back.

The old wisteria vines on the patio were in bloom, and heavy clusters of purple flowers hung like a frame above the bright river. Indoors a group of teenagers were drinking soda and laughing loudly with each other. The lone girl in the group, a tall, black-eyed beauty, sat suddenly in the lap of one of the boys. She put her arms around his shoulders and kissed him quickly on the mouth. Just as suddenly, the girl stood and strutted to the café bar without looking behind her. The boy called out to her, and Kate tried to interpret what he was saying, but only half of the words were French. When he shouted the word '*neskuto*', Kate realized that they were speaking pidgin French mixed with Basque. She looked down at her postcards and continued writing, alert to the words she could understand.

When the girl reappeared she strolled to Kate's table and stood beside her. She was wearing a white dishtowel as an apron over skin-tight black Capri's.

"*Voulez-vous aut'chose, mademoiselle?*" she asked. Her hair was straight and black, and Kate speculated that her family had come from the Spanish side of the Basque country, the activist side.

"*Non, merci,*" replied Kate. The girl continued to look at her for a few moments, and then swiveled abruptly on her heels.

Kate and the boys were the only customers now, and they had fallen silent. She stared at the postcard on the table before her, sensing a shift in the atmosphere. Casually, she put one hand near her belt buckle, her fingers unhooking the clasp of her holster so she could unlatch the safety on her pistol. She breathed slowly, barely moving.

She heard footsteps across the cobblestones, and her fingers moved onto the safety. She looked up quickly and saw the girl's boyfriend advancing toward her.

"Hello," he said in clear, crisp English. "You are a tourist to the *pays Basque*, no?" He spoke confidently, and Kate nodded her head. "You may want a guide for your travels, then," he said.

His tone was slightly commanding.

"Maybe," Kate replied. She took a sip of Orangina from the thick red glass on the table. "It depends on your knowledge of the area."

"I am particularly familiar with the monastery up the mountain. Would you like to see it?"

Relieved, Kate leaned back in her chair and took her hand from the pistol.

"I am Teobaldo. Teo, please."

"Hello Teo. I'm Kate."

"I know that. I've heard about your work from my uncle. It's a privilege to be your driver this afternoon. Your people helped us at the monastery several times already, and I am happy to repay it. My car is down by the *gave*, and one of your team is already there. Shall we get started?"

They set off, walking toward the river, and Teo said stiffly to her, "I would offer to carry your backpack, but I suppose you would not let me."

"You're correct," she said.

When they reached the parking lot below, he stopped at a small, blue Renault Clio. Inside sat a black man, his head against the window and his eyes closed.

Kate tapped lightly on the car and he opened his eyes quickly, grinning. Teo unlocked the car door and the man leaned out, stretching his muscled arms.

"Thought you caught me, huh?" he asked Kate.

She smiled and shook her head. "Hey, Chad. How was the flight in?"

"Got an Execujet from the consulate in Santander this morning into Mont de Marsan. Flies like an Aston Martin. Can't beat working for rich people. *Los ricos* are the best," he said. He opened his eyes wildly, pulling a small, tungsten case close to his chest.

"You're a funny guy," she said. "Shove over."

Chad was the senior DIA communications expert in Europe. He had been embedded at a minor consulate in Spain by the Defense Intelligence Agency, to collect and forward data reports to the DIA headquarters at Bolling Air Force Base in DC.

The Department Chief at the Directorate for Science and Technology had been so pleased with his work during the previous year that the DIA had attempted to recall him to Washington for a promotion, but they hadn't counted on him falling in love. Before they could stop him, he had married a Cantabrian girl from the coast near Santander and he refused to return to the States. He told his supervisor, Colonel Jacobits, that he would just as soon get out of the DIA as leave Spain. Anyway, he said, his wife was pregnant and he wanted his children to grow up in Cantabria.

Jacobits had been secretly pleased about this, and he fought to keep him. He might spend years looking for key personnel, and he resented the Directorate when they tried to promote successful agents away from his team. Somewhere along the way, Jacobits had realized that the psychological profile of his team members was an unusual one, and necessitated both a scorching pride in being an American as well as a fear of being engulfed in its culture.

"Got everything you need?" Kate asked him.

"I do. We gotta get in and out tomorrow, though," he said. "I have an *Hola Bébé* class with Adriana on Wednesday at the hospital."

"Yeah, right," Kate said, and relaxed back against the seat. "Maybe you shouldn't plan on that."

Teo turned on the radio as they pulled out onto the *route nationale*. "I take you now to the monastery where my uncle will join us."

Outside of the town, they turned up a winding mountain road through the pines. As the road climbed into the trees, the warm air thickened with the humidity of the deep forest, and the tiny car began to strain at the steep grade. Teo pounded the accelerator and clutch mercilessly, driving heavily and quickly around the narrow bends. Neither Kate nor Chad showed any fear, even though the left side was an unprotected drop to a deep mountain gully and the right was lined by an ancient, ill-kept dry stone wall that had crumbled, scattering large quartzite chunks across the road.

The tarmac eventually gave way to hard-packed dirt and gravel, and after about a mile Teo slowed the car, rounding a switchback curve. He stopped suddenly in the center of the road and got out. He strolled to the cliff edge and looked over the side.

"We will wait for a moment," he said, leaning precariously forward and peering into the hot, shadowed forest below. "Another of your team is meeting us here." He lit a cigarette and continued watching the dark glade.

Kate and Chad stood side by side without conversation in the steamy sunlight of the forest road. Each of them moved slowly back into a defensible position in case the need arose to fight.

Within minutes, a small woman with white-blonde hair made her way down the mountainside to the road. She carried a backpack over one shoulder, and she wore shorts and a sleeveless, blue t-shirt with a huge sunflower painted like a bulls eye on the front. She was eating a ripe peach as she stepped out through the moist, dark dirt, and the juices were running down the sides of her mouth and her throat. When she reached the stone wall, she climbed easily onto it and jumped to the road with the heavy clatter of her hiking boots. Dry pine needles scattered everywhere, and she smiled at the group.

Chad walked over to her and put his arms around her shoulders.

"Hey, baby, I didn't know you were coming! Haven't seen you since last November in the Alps. How the hell are you?"

She grinned at him again. "Pretty good, Chad." She tossed the peach pit into the soft roadside soil, and said, "It'll grow, won't it, eco-boy?" She wiped the back of her hand across her mouth and throat.

"Were you waiting long, Jenny?" asked Kate.

She shook her head slowly. "They lifted me into the 1st Marine regiment at Bayonne in one of those new French 725 helos, and I dropped not far from here. I just sat down to relax when you pulled up." She yawned and stretched her arms high over her head. Her body was small and tight; delicately formed but for shoulders that were broad and muscular. "Good to see y'all."

Kate and Jenny were both '02 grads from the Academy. In those days only about 400 of the 4000 cadets were women, which translated to fewer than 100 girls in each of the graduating years. Every girl knew every other girl in her class, and though Kate and Jenny had not been in the same squadron, they had instantly recognized each other when they met years ago in Jacobits' office. Jenny had been a cheerleader at the Academy, and Kate had remembered her huge all-American grin from four years of watching her scream to the crowd at football games.

Now she coordinated intel for Jacobits' team, and worked the plum of all embedded DIA jobs, in Venice at the quiet little UNESCO office as a document restorer. Although all of Jacobits' DIA team members were multi-lingual, Jenny's key attribute was her ability to speak Italian, French, Spanish, German, Russian, and several Arabic dialects, all as though they were her mother tongue. Her ability to assimilate into a local community and retrieve information was unparalleled in the American forces in Europe, and Kate was relieved that she would be doing reconnaissance on this mission.

"Okay," said Kate, rising from the stone wall. "Let's get moving. We need to be at the airfield in Tarbes by five."

"When do we brief?" Jenny asked.

"When we get to the base in Provence. We're meeting our PJ there."

"Did you get Tim McEwing?" Chad asked.

"No," she said, and her skin began a cold burn. "Tim died in an explosion at the beginning of the month."

Chad did not move. He held the shaft of his pistol perfectly still against the hot stone wall, and silently a huge mantis touched down upon him, scratching at his skin with its thin legs.

"Was that the op in the Azores?"

"Yes," she replied.

"I never got the news," Chad said quietly. "Have they stopped telling us when we lose a buddy? Or aren't we expected to care anymore?"

"Bolling didn't publish it because they haven't done the final report yet."

"Why not?" asked Jenny.

"That's a question for Jacobits," Kate said. "He's still obsessed with it. Can't figure out how the ordnance slipped by us all."

"Ya know, Katie, I know Tim from way back. From years ago in Germany. My wife and Tim's wife are friends. Not being told is total crap. Does his wife even know yet?" Chad had lifted his pistol and slipped it into the holster. "This is friggin' bullshit."

"I'm sorry, Chad. But we need to get going. We have to catch a flight from Tarbes at five. I don't know who our PJ will be and that's all I can tell you. This assignment is Secret Squirrel, and if we don't move fast, we may not have an asset to rescue."

"Who else have we got? Who's our medic?" asked Jenny.

Kate shrugged. "Me. There's only four of us. Jacobits wants it done under the radar – even our radar. As few of us as possible are to be involved. I told him we needed six, so he may clear one other to work with us. But for now, there is no one else."

"Katie, Katie," said Chad, "what are we walking into?"

Kate felt something warm on her fingers, and looked down. Her index finger was smeared with a warm, sticky substance. Quietly, she glanced around, and along the top stone of the wall lay a small trail of blood red wax, viscous and warmed by the sun. It looked a little like napalm, and she tensed for a moment, unconsciously, to scan the forest. She knew the smell of napalm, the raging odor of raw petrol burning through clean air, but the red wax was odorless. She looked again at her fingers, smiling to herself as she coated them in the plain candle wax that had melted from the heat.

"Anyone wanting out now is welcome to leave."

"We must go," called Teo from the car, and they all began to move.

•

After the steep ascent to the top of the mountain overlooking the Soule Valley, they could see the high point of the Pic d'Orhy and the silvery pines of the Spanish frontier beyond. Below them, in a small cul-de-sac over a narrow bridge, lay the old grey stone buildings of the monastery. They drove through the high arch of the entry gate, built five hundred years before by soldiers and peasants under the rule of the King of Navarre. Above the arch, the letters "*EGIAZ*" had been carved deep into the stone. This word, 'TRUTH' in the language of the Basques, was in turn riddled with more than a hundred bullet holes.

"This is our home," said Teo, and a monk in the inner courtyard closed the heavy wooden gates behind them. "And you are welcome here."

Kate climbed out of the back seat of the car and slung her backpack over her shoulder. She had opened her holster again, and as she looked around the quiet courtyard, her hand hovered gently on the metal.

The monk was dressed in the traditional long, rough brown robe and white rope belt. He was six feet tall, with blond hair and a flat, crooked nose that had once been broken. He held his hand out to Kate, and smiled when he saw her gun holster.

"*Semper paratus*, Captain Cardenas? Just like a Boy Scout."

"Please call me Kate."

"And I am Marko. From time to time I work with Colonel Jacobits. He has asked me to help you on this run." His accent was neither French nor Spanish, and he spoke flawless English.

"We're grateful for your help getting us over to Tarbes for our flight," said Jenny.

"Not just the driving," Marko replied. "He has assigned me to the operation. I'm performing your pararescue."

The mountain air was crisp with the sweet scent of cool pines. The courtyard was still, and each of them turned to stare at the monk. Kate's eyes narrowed, but she did not move.

"I'm sorry," Marko said, and untied the white cord around his waist. He lifted the heavy robe from his body, and slung it over his shoulder. He wore blue jeans and a thin cotton shirt underneath, and the damp cloth was shadowed from his sweat. "I'm sorry to have surprised you with the news."

Kate had pulled her phone from the backpack, and was texting Jacobits for confirmation. She nodded slowly when it came through, and said to the others, "This is Captain Marko Eskibel of the French Spec Ops out of Pau. Combat pararescue and recon. He is our PJ. Let's get going."

Jenny slid on her back underneath the blue van, while Chad pulled a long-handled square mirror from his kit and began examining the inner tread of the tires. Every single time they got into a vehicle, they checked for explosives.

Teo took the driver's seat while the others crouched on the metal floor in the back of the windowless cab.

Marko held a FAMAS assault rifle in his lap.

"I thought you guys had moved across to the German equipment," Kate said.

He smiled gently, staring at her with stark blue eyes, and said in French, "This piece has been with me a long time, Captain."

She nodded quickly at him. "We can land on the airfield at Salon. By the time we get there all the students will be out of the air. They are the most dangerous part of flying into *l'École*."

"You are piloting us down?"

"I am."

"We may have a tricky bit in Tarbes. Did the Colonel tell you? Some of the manufacturing houses are in production again. When we reach the main trunk road to the airport, there will be security guarding. It will be better to take the old road at the back. Longer, but safer. There's a cut-off there that takes us directly into the private airfield. We need to access the jet with our equipment without being noticed. We need to be in the air by dix-sept heures. What do you think?"

She nodded, and asked, "Chad, do you have a take on activity at the N21?"

He squatted on the floor of the van in front of the Toughbook laptop contained in the tungsten case. A radio pod was lodged in his ear, and he was speaking to the ground informant in Aerospace Valley outside of Tarbes. As he spoke, his fingers tapped across the keyboard, relaying movement to the DIA analysts in Alabama and Bolling.

"My guy is confirming activity."

Marko looked up at her. "Our jet is at Turbotag. This is a small facility owned by a couple of Saudi brothers who used to manufacture executive jets. They stopped production in the late Nineties when the government began investigating their arms connections. They still own the property, though, and my people have used them for discreet flights. But now that EADS has new contracts, the production in Aerospace Valley is increasing. This will probably be the last time we can fly out of Tarbes unnoticed."

Kate stirred in the cool dark, and moved to the front of the van. The sounds of the rough local road vibrated through the metal of the car hull, and she put her hand on Teo's shoulder to alert him.

"Take the next lay-by road to the left, then five clicks from the target on your scanner, sheer up to the trees, and we'll move on foot from there to the old north runway where our transport is waiting."

Teo nodded. Within a few moments, he had pulled the van off the road into the damp woods beyond. He ground down on the accelerator and the van bore forward through the sycamore maple trees. The noise of the wind and the slapping branches magnified around them, until they swerved suddenly to a halt. The van was half-hidden under a rain-slicked cradle of leaves, and as the team jumped out of the side door, they landed in soft, wet forest soil. They took a few seconds adjusting to the silence, listening for animals and scanning for movement.

Chad pressed the stealth communications pod in his ear, and signaled them one-by-one to sound-check with his station.

"Good to go," he whispered. Jenny waved goodbye to Teo, and shoved the side panel door closed.

"Wait until the jet is gone," said Kate into the mic, "then go straight back to the monastery."

They moved fast through the tall, wet grass, keeping low so as not to silhouette themselves against the sky. They fanned out to opposite sides of the woods, and on either side were shadows of disused aircraft, rusting steel carcasses littering the grassy knolls beside the runway. As they approached they could see the blinking lights, and the amber glow of the test hangar lit from within.

Kate followed the flight line, between three executive jets that were parked about fifty yards from the closed hangar door of the Turbotag facility. When she reached it, she slid it open and stood in the dim light against the steel wall. She moved silently along her own shadow until she had circled the building interior. She smelled chocolate and tobacco, but she could not find it, nor release the sense of it. She searched for a moment in the dim light for men who would have brought the scent with them; finding no one, she declared the area clear.

"Good to go," she whispered, "ours is on the left, the little Learjet."

Her colleagues arrived from all sides of the runway, their arms filled with sacks of explosives, communications and clothing. Chad and Marko began to load the cargo, while Kate climbed into the cockpit to grab the pre-flight checklist. She scrambled down the hatch stairs, and began running her hands carefully along the flaps and rudder as though they were sharpened blades. She touched everything herself, and began a recheck when at last, Chad spoke to her furiously.

"Kate, we're clear. It's okay. Get us in the air now."

Jenny pulled herself into the left seat, calling out numbers from the instrument screen before them.

"When is the last time you flew?" Marko squatted behind Kate and put his hand on her shoulder.

"Last month. Don't worry. I flew Lear jets as a kid. The 45XR is just a new version of an old toy."

"Okay," he said. "Taxi off the flight line to the left onto the old runway. We don't need much distance to take off in this, and it is more secluded there. We have about ten minutes now before the gentlemen come to look why one of the engines is rolling."

"You mean we are stealing this?"

"Not exactly," Marko grinned, "but among my contacts, nothing is entirely clear-cut."

Chapter 9

A COLD SPRING RAIN covered the rue St. Honoré that evening, coating the old cobblestone drive in front of the Ambassador's Residence. Ben waited alone in the darkened inner courtyard, leaning against the far wall, and listening distractedly to the Marine Jazz Combo that had flown in from Germany for this occasion. The trumpet player was meandering through the *Basin Street Blues*, standing straight in his dress blues with the blood-red stripe down his legs, as he blew his way around the corners of the Louisiana music.

Ben recognized him from the military hotel the night before. He had been just another guy with a high-and-tight haircut, sitting in an old t-shirt with a beer and no prospects, laughing with his buddies. Now he was lost in these notes, not noticing any of the guests move through to the reception rooms, but Ben knew instinctively that this was a mask. Even this trumpet player, intoxicated as he was with the music, could snap to defense in seconds if need be.

When the Marine finished the song, he looked over at Ben and nodded without smiling.

The moon seemed to hang directly above them, the color of sand through the rainy, black sky. Ben's face was smeared with the thick mist that clung to him. He had been standing under the old grey stone eave for about thirty minutes, having unofficially assigned himself the task of observing the visitors before they were able to get close to his father. His training had taught him to power-down his breathing and

movement in the face of unfamiliar situations requiring tactical analysis, but this evening he knew he was failing. He could feel his own
short breaths as he silently challenged the guests walking past him. He
was used to quick surges of adrenaline and cortisol, and he had been
taught that the sudden rise and fall of these levels in his bloodstream
were what differentiated his kind of operative. He had been tested
many times for the remarkable speed with which his adrenaline returned to normal, but tonight, with his family at stake, he was
witnessing the lasting, painful palpitation of his own fear.

The Ambassador's wife came into the courtyard toward the band,
but stopped when she saw Ben in the shadow against the wall.

"Ben, love, come inside out of the rain. What are you doing here?"
She put her arm around his broad shoulders, and led him like a child
to the musicians. "All of you, it's cold and wet out here. Come inside
and have some food. Enjoy yourselves now." She was smiling inno-
cently, talking to hungry men about food, and Ben recognized this
smile from his childhood. He knew that she was acutely aware of the
instability around them tonight, and now he understood that all the
years he had known her, this same smile had been her camouflage.

"Thank you, ma'am," said the trumpet player, and the band turned
smoothly on their heels and walked into the Residence.

"Stop worrying, Ben. We are like Fort Knox here. In a couple of
hours this will be over and you can take your father safely home."

Every Spec Ops soldier had a weak spot, and waiting was Ben's. In
training, he had been told that kicking in doors was an idiot's job, that
the battlefield had nothing to do with geography or weapons, but that
it was a careful fight for the minds of the enemy. Particularly in the
elite JSOC forces where information was more important than attack,
sitting around a fire with the local people and listening to them was
always the critical component of an operation. It had taken a long time
for Ben to identify his own liability, and he had learned the hard way
that the rush he got from capturing the bad guys was only the smallest
part of his job.

Once, years ago, he had waited for two straight days at the media
center in Bagram, a small windowless room filled with journalists

moving in and out of Afghanistan. He had missed his helicopter out, and had been told he could catch a ride in the next media chopper. After forty-eight hours of waiting for a window of safety in the fighting, Ben had begun to go stir-crazy. He sat for hours under a sign that read, *"No drinking while armed"*, playing Texas Hold 'Em with the reporters. Eventually, he renamed the media ops center the Hotel California, because he came to understand that hell was not the battle; hell was the waiting.

He had counted about fifty people wander into his father's private reception, most of them dressed in serious, dark-colored business suits, intent on shaking hands with James Cullen. He had watched them walk through the labyrinthine arches of the Residence, through doors paned with clear glass or with mirrors, and in his mind he had marked some of their reflections with an invisible handprint of suspicion. He knew that the identity of each guest had been verified long before they arrived at the immense iron doors, and that each of them had passed through the metal detectors. He knew that every known risk had been mitigated by the embassy security. After that there could be no control: it was God's will or the luck of the draw, whatever theory you subscribed to.

He followed the Ambassador's wife into the parlors of the Residence public areas. He approached a group of two men and a woman standing around a low, ornate table, upon which sat a huge Limoges bowl, lavishly-painted with horned devils and unicorns, and filled with packets of American cigarettes of different brands. The men were sifting through them like thieves shuffling contraband. In Mosul, where success depended on perception and where damn near every container held a threat, he would have swerved around this group to watch from afar. Now, as he approached them, he felt his pulse quickening.

Behind them on the wall hung a large oil painting of an American baptism, of a preacher-man lowering a young girl headfirst into a pool of dark water. The three at the bowl were oblivious to the picture, and snickered about the piles of American tobacco they could take.

"It's free," said the slighter of the two men. "We might as well fill our pockets." He wore a badly-fitting, mustard-colored suit, and spoke with an English accent. A waiter passed by, holding a silver tray of wine glasses. The Englishman stopped him and said, "I'd like a gin and tonic, please."

The woman smiled at the waiter and said, "He'll take anything he can get."

The taller of the two men put his arm on the woman's thick back and said, "Let's go in. I want to see if I can get an interview before he starts speaking."

"Don't be so neurotic," said the other. "Everything you need to write will be in the press packet. Our job is to drink and eat the dead things on toast they serve."

"Alastair, that's why you're here for *Estates Times* and I'm here for the *International New York Times*. You're always such a scam artist. Don't you have any pride in what you do?"

"Not particularly," he replied, and giggled through his nose with a loud, cynical snort.

Ben smiled slightly at the group. "Hello. Are you here to see James Cullen?"

"Not all of us," laughed the woman. "Some of us are just here for the alcohol."

As she spoke, a short elderly man pushed past suddenly. He wore brown tweed with a thick turtleneck sweater, and carried a worn leather portfolio under his arm.

"I'm terribly sorry. Do pardon me," he said, as he lurched away from them and scurried toward the next room.

The journalist from the *New York Times* said, "For God's sake. I hate that guy. Who does he think he is?"

"I don't know. Who is it?" asked the woman.

"We've met him before, Jane. That's Dirk Lowell, the Berkeley archeologist who's been working on the Riviera sites since the Sixties. He's always in Paris looking for movie stars and rich donors; he's a total rat bastard."

She cackled loudly and said, "Well, honey, why don't you tell us what you really think?"

"You can make fun of me if you want, but it's true. You remember the American election night party last year at the *Tour Montparnasse?*

Remember the drunk Englishman wandering around bragging about his political friends? That was him."

"I thought you said he was from Berkeley?"

"He is. He just pretends to be English."

"Typical American," snorted the other journalist.

"You know that Lowell actually grew up in Kansas? So he pretended he was from Berkeley, until he could pretend he was from England. Come now, we better go in before we miss the next round of drinks, Alastair."

Dirk Lowell had stopped at the doorway and was staring back at them. He strode quickly across the room to join them.

"Why, you are Ben Cullen, aren't you?" he asked, and the others stared at Ben. "My boy, I haven't seen you in so many years, but I could see your mother's eyes immediately in yours. How wonderful to see you!"

"Hello, sir," said Ben, shaking his hand and thinking how unnaturally soft his skin was. He did not remember meeting him, but he had been introduced to so many of his father's business acquaintances over the years that he had grown used to vaguely recognizing a large number of people in James Cullen's world.

"Well, this is a great night for the Cullens!" the old man said. "And I am, as I always have been, very grateful for the generous and truly critical support that James Cullen has given my little project over these many, many years. Protecting our prehistoric sites, in my opinion, is one of the truly urgent historical jobs of today's scientists."

"Why?" asked the Englishman called Alastair, but Lowell did not even glance in his direction.

Ben noticed that under the turtleneck, a large portion of the scientist's neck was missing, and a huge concave scar was visible as though the flesh and skin had fallen into his larynx.

"Come, come," said Lowell. "We don't want to miss your father's speech." He put his misshapen, liver-spotted hand on Ben's shoulder and leaned against him. "I think I should sit down," he whispered. "I'm feeling a little weak. Would you mind?"

Ben took his arm and led him into the next parlor, which was lined with pink silk couches.

"Not here," said Lowell, suddenly waving his hand forward. "In the next room. I want to hear what your father has to say. This is such a great occasion."

Ben walked him forward across the room and into a long hallway lined with potted palms and a mural of a Tahitian beach washed with shocking, carnal shades of blue and red. They came to a wide doorway, and inside was a large ballroom set with rows of narrow, satin-backed chairs.

"Sit here," said Ben and pointed to the back row. "I'll get you some water."

When Ben returned, his father was at the man's side.

"Dr. Lowell," he said. "It's very kind of you to travel all this way just to hear me ramble on about world trade." He held his hand out to the archeologist, and leaned closely to him. "Are you feeling all right? Would you like to step outside and get some air?"

Lowell nodded slightly.

"Let's get you comfortable, then." He turned to his son. "Ben, let's walk Dr. Lowell out to the terrace." The two of them stood on either side of the man, helping him to stand and leading him through the crowd to the far doors. An embassy bodyguard followed along behind James Cullen.

"Do you need help, sir?" he asked.

"Not at all. Dr. Lowell is one of my oldest friends. We're accompanying him to the garden for some fresh air."

They sat on wrought iron chairs on the broad patio overlooking the Residence gardens. Lowell's breathing was shallow and labored, and he stared quizzically at Ben. He chuckled then and his head dropped to his chest.

"Ben, go get Henderson's physician. Quickly."

"No, I'm fine, James. I'm absolutely, amazingly fine. Just tired. It was quite a train trip from the south today. Quite hot. But I," he held his hand up as though to halt their efforts, "can see everything apparent to Berkeley's God! I am fine." Lowell chuckled and put his hand on Cullen's arm.

"You really shouldn't have tried to make this trip, Dirk. It's much too hard a journey by train for a man of your age."

"If I had not come, I never would have seen your handsome grown son here! How proud you must be!"

"Of course," he replied, and lay his arm around Ben's shoulders.

"What do you do, my boy?" he asked, and the scientist's upper lip curled uncontrollably.

"Ben is a Major in the Air Force. Always flying off somewhere. He'll be in town with me for a couple of days, and then back on a rotator somewhere."

"Dangerous work, I imagine. So brave you are. And your other boy? Or should I say, that other handsome grown son of yours? Is he here?"

"Not tonight," Cullen said. "Our business, you know. How long are you in Paris, Dirk?"

"Oh, I return tomorrow morning. The cost of hotels are prohibitive in the capital, or I would stay for the week."

"If the project is running short of money, Dirk, I'll write you a check tonight. You didn't have to come all this way just to pay respects to me for the evening."

"My poor old skeleton. I am getting old, I think."

"Do you think we might get in this year, Dirk? For a short visit to see the art? I have a friend, a financier from Chile, who is interested in contributing substantially, but he wants to experience it first."

"My friend, I'm so sorry. These paintings are thirty thousand years old, and so technically perfect. Any external microbe could destroy them forever. Not even the President of France was allowed in when he requested. This is quite simply the greatest prehistoric site the world possesses!" Lowell sat up in his chair and looked out across the immense and serene velvet lawn, lit now with lamps. "No one gets in but me, I'm afraid. James, you really are the very best of friends, to continue funding us so blindly. You have sent us millions over the years, and you never flinch from a new request, even without seeing the fruits of our work. So trusting! You are like Emerson, believing in the goodness of man and in the rigor of science. And it's true, we do need to hire a new specialist from South Africa, and that will cost us unexpectedly. A check would help enormously."

"Of course, Dirk. I will have it delivered to you tonight before we are finished here. But one day, I really would like to see the caves again. One day."

Suddenly, they heard the crack of a door behind them, and one of the journalists stepped onto the terrace. The embassy bodyguard walked quickly to him.

"This is a private meeting, sir."

"But I'm media," he said, affronted, and pulled his press card from his jacket pocket.

Through the door after him came Ambassador Henderson, followed by his own bodyguard.

"Jim, it's almost seven o'clock. We really ought to get started. How is Dr. Lowell doing?" The Ambassador looked to the pale old man. "My doctor is here, and I can ask him to come and sit with you, sir."

"I'm sorry to trouble you," said the reporter, looking past the Ambassador to James Cullen. "I was hoping for a comment about your cabinet post, sir." He inhaled from his cigarette. "For your supporters in the UK. Just something quick about foreign investments."

Ben moved swiftly to put himself between his father and the reporter. As he began to speak, Dirk Lowell's cell phone rang from his front jacket pocket. Lowell pulled to the side to answer it, and began speaking furiously in French. Turning back to them at last, he said, "Oh gentlemen, this is frustrating news, indeed. In fact, I am afraid I must leave this happy party immediately. That was one of the young graduate students in the caves, and it seems I must return at once, even before your special lecture, James. I am so sorry. But you are so generous, so unpretentious, my friend, to offer a check with none of the proverbial strings attached. It will enable us to pull that scientist from South Africa."

"Yes, the check, of course. And I will ask the Ambassador to make arrangements for your trip back tonight. However, I do need to begin my address."

"Yes, yes," said Lowell. "Sing for your supper, by all means!"

Suddenly, a tall magnolia at the back of the garden path began to tremble in the humid night air. They turned to this rustling sound, and

Ben noticed several broken paving stones at the bottom of the velvet slope.

"Take my father and Dr. Lowell inside," he said to the bodyguard. "Get them all inside."

Once the others were safely in the building, Ben jumped to the bottom of the wide stone steps and knelt in the darkness, watching and waiting. Without a gun or a weapon of any kind, his ability to observe was his only defense.

A few seconds of silence passed, and Ben remained motionless and alone, until at last he began to inch along the perimeter of the garden toward the far slope and the Avenue Gabriel beyond. When he reached the paving stones, he paused to turn one over, and suddenly all around him lights as bright as day flashed on, illuminating every square inch of the area.

A swarm of plain clothes Americans came from nowhere, surrounding him with rifles. Three moved fast against him, and threw him to the ground, his face in the grass and dirt.

Ben did not struggle, but lay without moving underneath the leather soles of their boots. He allowed them to wrench his arms behind his back and handcuff him, and just as suddenly, the lights were snapped off, and he was dragged down into a hole in the earth, along a dark, stone passageway to a modern steel door.

****

Ben leaned back into the overstuffed leather chair in the dim light of the Avenue Gabriel library. Before him on the old oak table lay a white porcelain cup of half-drunk black coffee. The brass reading lamp on the table had been turned on for him, and except for this, the room was dark and silent. Next to the coffee cup was a washcloth that he had been given to wipe the mud from his face and clothing. He stretched his arms over his head, pulling his elbows from side to side to release the tension. Finally, he sat back in his chair and put his feet on the table. He looked up at the Marines surrounding him and grinned.

"Pretty great assignment, guys. Embassy in Paris. I bet you have some great weekends." He had rolled his sleeves up over his muscled forearms, and the crisp black cotton was still caked with grass and mud from the garden. "Does it really take four of you to keep me here?"

"They're not here to jail you, Major," said a man's voice from between the darkened library stacks.

Ben saw Colonel Jacobits emerge into the silver glow of the corner. "They're protecting you."

"Oh, I see. That must be why they cuffed me, Colonel. To protect me."

"What were you doing at the bottom of the garden, anyway?"

"Just trying to keep another member of my family from being taken out from under your nose."

"Don't be a smart ass with me, Major. We're on the same side. All you spec ops guys are the same, one huge messiah complex." Jacobits sat down across from Ben. He nodded to the Marines, and they filed out of the room. "You're here because I need your help, and I need it quietly. I have no jurisdiction over you, so I'm asking you a favor."

Ben leaned back against the leather chair. At the far edge of the table stood a heavy, white marble bust of Copernicus, and he began tapping it gently with his shoe.

"My brother was taken twenty-four hours ago. And I'd guess that my father doesn't know that the chances of him still being alive after the first four hours of a terrorist kidnap have dropped by eighty percent. I'd say you're getting pretty desperate right about now. Sir, why the hell is my brother still out there? And what has your team been doing for the last twenty-four hours?"

"Get your damn feet off the table when you talk to me, Major."

Ben did not move. He stared at the Colonel in silence. Slowly and evenly, he began to lift his feet from the table.

"I don't need any more crap from you tonight. What I need is your help. I have been given the assignment of getting your brother back under everyone's friggin' radar."

"Deniable?"

"What do you think?" Jacobits' face was stark and remote. "And so far our intel is pretty sketchy. I'm not really trusting any of our usual partners, I've got nobody available to work this op, and I need your help."

"You're asking me to join the mission?" Ben asked.

Jacobits nodded.

"Who's on the team?"

"Three of my agents, Chad Witt, Jennifer Abernathy, and Kate Cardenas. And a French spec ops agent, a Basque, who owes me a lot of favors."

"Kate Cardenas?"

"That's the one," he said.

"She was in one of the classes below me at the Academy."

"Don't be coy with me. I know you had a relationship with her. What I want to know now is whether you can work with her in spite of it."

"There's more to it than that."

"Unless I need to know it, Major, I don't need to know it. Look, AQIM made these demands. Second time in a month they've pulled off a high profile attack. I don't have time for the Desperate Housewives version of your life. Are you in or not?"

Ben closed his eyes, nodding slowly.

"You know, Major, my team doesn't fail very often. The consequences are huge if we do. Years ago, we missed a friggin' bomb in Madrid, and that was disastrous. And in '02 we were chasing *haji* across Italy. They had the daughter of the American Consul in Milan. By the time we got to Brindisi it was too late. They had murdered her. You know what they left us? A pair of dice they'd carved from her femur."

Jacobits leaned forward and cracked open one of the old lead-paned windows. The balmy damp air seeped in, and he sat on the ledge against the starless night.

"I know what they do, Colonel."

"I know you do, Ben. There's a shitload of unorganized intel floating around about AQIM. These incidents are disjointed, and it's making me very nervous. And I don't like being nervous. You know, our analysts have let us down a couple of times on the eve of something big, and I don't want another 9/11 on our hands. I gotta have a team small enough to remain stealth and big enough to do the job. That means I have to have the best for each job, and we all know that you, Major Cullen, are the best."

"Who'll be doing intel?"

"I will."

Ben smiled slowly. "Rumor is that when they promoted you out of the field a lot of disappointed agents took Palace Chase into easy jobs in the Guard, knowing they'd never be able to work with you again."

The glimmer of a grin appeared on Jacobits' face. "Is that a yes?"

"It would be a privilege, Colonel."

"You know, Ben, there's no glory in this. We're just a bunch of DIA cowboys trying to save an American. We can't call out 'sprint' if we get trapped."

Ben stared at Jacobits, but his expression did not change. 'Sprint' was the common code for spec ops teams in a jam, a last resort shout that told everyone in the vicinity, 'If we do not get help immediately, Americans are going to die.'

"I understand. What do you want me to do, Colonel?"

"Go back to the lecture now and make excuses. You're on leave anyway. We're going tonight from the helo pad here."

"Where to?"

"We're heading to our base of operations in the south. I'll brief you in the air."

Chapter 10

KATE STOOD OVER the deep white porcelain sink in the kitchen of her home, her hands submerged in soapy water. She pulled out a handful of modern silver-handled steak knives and rinsed them under the cool stream from the tap. Chad moved in behind her and took them in a white linen towel.

"You're not too bad a cook," she said.

He shrugged. "Anyone can grill a steak." He dried the knives and put them in the cutlery drawer.

Kate saw the knives lying with their handles scattered, and she quietly rearranged them, all handle curves to the left.

Her house was a permanent station of the United States Air Force, always assigned to the liaison officer in charge of the exchange student cadets from the American Academy. Situated on the old Roman Aurelian Way, the house was buried in a cluster of tall sycamores. The kitchen held a large Aga stove she fed with coal each morning to heat her water and rooms and to cook her food.

She sat at the broad table in the center of the kitchen and watched as Marko opened the iron door to tend the flame. In that bright room, with the glowing fire of the stove, the night seemed to melt away around them.

Jenny and the two men came and pulled out the heavy wooden chairs to sit at the table together.

"What's the plan now?" Marko asked quietly.

"We have two people coming tonight. With new intel. We'll mission plan as soon as they get here. Leave before dawn."

"Who is it?"

"Colonel Jacobits is coming as our fox. I don't know who the other is."

"I hope he's got the damn cavalry with him," Chad muttered.

Kate shrugged. "I'm going upstairs to get some sleep." She stood from the table. "Wake me up when he gets here, okay?"

Kate opened the window of her bedroom to let the cool night mist in. She slipped under the coverlet wearing only her bra and pants, and lay her head on her arms.

A new cut on her shin from the Azores explosion was throbbing, but she had many like it from other missions, small smears of darkened skin on her forearms and belly that were all that remained from bombs and guns of now-distant battles. The deepest scar on her body had been left by a Yemeni terrorist, the first enemy Kate had ever watched die. He had cut deep into the underside of her left bicep with an American Kershaw knife, as she held him from behind and strangled him in broad daylight near the Volvo he had packed with explosives. She ran her index finger around the circle of this rough skin, and eventually she closed her eyes.

Thirty minutes later she awoke to several sharp knocks at her door. Chad was calling out to her, and she sat up quickly, immediately alert.

"They're here, Kate. Let's get rolling."

"Okay. I'm coming."

She had already dressed in full mission gear when she joined them in the kitchen. She carried her M-4 over her shoulder, and night vision goggles in one hand.

Across the room from her stood Colonel Jacobits, also in full gear.

"Captain Cardenas," he said gently, "so glad your beauty sleep is over. We have an hour to brief before our transport arrives at the base airfield. Take a seat and let's get into this. You know Major Cullen, right?"

Ben sat directly across the table from her. His rifle lay in his lap, and he folded his hands together over it. He, too, was dressed for battle, and over the back of his chair hung his ballistic vest. He looked up slowly at Kate, breathing unevenly. Like ringing that would never disappear, neither of them had been able to shake off the memories of the years they had loved each other. Between the two of them lay an imaginary line containing an infinite number of points, as between any two objects on earth. Yet they sat quietly across the table from each other, both of them oath-bound to a document lying in a vault in the American capital, neither of them allowed to acknowledge a single point on the line between them.

Kate's breathing quickened as she moved forward and put her hand out. Ben stood and leaned across the table to shake it, and just before they clasped, both of them hesitated.

"It's good to see you again, Ben."

Awkwardly, he bent his tall body toward her and put his arms around her shoulders. The smell of fresh soap still clung to his skin, and Kate smiled at this familiar smell. She pulled away quickly and nodded, concealing her memory.

"Is this the team, then?" Marko asked.

"One more," said Jacobits. "A helo driver from the French base. Alain Rifault. He's our transport and our medic. He'll be here in a few minutes to brief. Let's get the maps out."

"How'd you manage that?" asked Kate. "I never thought the French military would approve participation."

"They didn't. He owes me a favor." He handed Chad a flash-drive. "Fire up your comp and stick this in." He turned to Kate. "Where's your weapons room, Captain?"

Kate led Jacobits down into the cool, stone basement off the kitchen. Around them lay the heavy smells of dust and damp, and Kate flipped the old plastic light switch. In the far corner of the mildewed floor, Jacobits saw a five-foot high steel door.

"In here," Kate said, and keyed a series of numbers into the pad beside it.

Once inside the vault, a purple light shone automatically across their faces.

"What have you got for us?" Jacobits asked, and Kate led him to locked steel boxes of ordnance. He knelt on the floor beside her while she put the combinations into several of the boxes. Before them lay all manner of weaponry: mortars, antitank guns, sniper rifles, RPK and PKM machine guns, pistols, and ammunition.

He put his hand on her shoulder, and she did not move. "We can do this job. We have the best now. Our orders are to get Hank Cullen back safe, but our bigger mission is getting some validated intel about AQIM and what the goddammed hell they're up to before we have another international disaster on our doorstep."

There was no light between them but the deep violet, like an expiring sun. Without speaking, Jacobits began to lift the flat, heavy cartridges from the steel case, the tenderness of his pause spanning them both.

•

Chad sat at the old pine table, and inserted the thumb-drive into his laptop. Immediately, a color photograph of a city at night filled the screen: a narrow street of 18th Century buildings, a pedestrian shopping district in a congested urban area, a blue and gold neon sign that illuminated the word '*Chaussures*' against a sparkling evening.

Jacobits stood across the kitchen, staring into the coffee mug he held between his tanned, chunky fingers. He squeezed the mug between his palms, and as he did his knuckles went white and his biceps swelled under his shirtsleeves.

"Folks, take a good look at this photograph and tell me what you see."

A mirror hung on the far wall of the kitchen, framed with rough wood and painted bright red. The group of warriors was reflected in this glass like infinity, their faces glowing under the high-watt bulb.

"City street," said Kate. "Commerce. Islam is an ancient culture of merchants. Our war is not just military, but economic. Terrorism has a corporate component that fires it, and we need to keep our eyes on that as well."

Jacobits shrugged. "True, but you're overthinking."

Jacobits looked over at Marko. Underneath his heavy brow-bone, his eyes were the palest blue.

"I am only a guest among you."

"If you consider yourself just a guest, this team does not have a chance," Jacobits said.

"Very well then, Colonel. It is my opinion that we need to believe in our success in order to have strategic factors on our side."

"Sun Tzu. *Art of War*," said Jacobits.

Marko nodded.

"What the hell?" said Chad. "Are you telling us we don't believe we can do this? What kind of crap is that?"

"We are unprepared because our leader feels trapped by the circumstances, the lack of information, the deniable nature of this mission, the unknown goals of the enemy, and the small size of the team."

Kate stood up from the table abruptly, and shoved her chair across the tile floor.

"For God's sake, Marko," she said sharply, "when they call our team in, it's always because a mission is trapped by circumstances. You're not saying anything we don't know. That's what we do for a living. Lieutenant Colonel Jacobits isn't responsible for the lack of intel in an op."

Marko shrugged and leaned back into the uneven shadows. The circle of light cast out by the computer screen throbbed softly across the team, now silent with nothing left but the bled-out hurt of the night.

Chad folded his arms on the table and stared closely at the evening shopping street in the photograph, and the illuminated shoe store sign.

"Of course, my wife would say, '*Zapatos son la vida*'," he said abruptly, and grinned. "I know I can always find her in a shoe store."

Jenny spoke in a slight voice. "I see a city street on the comp. We know our battlefield is social. We're fighting an unconventional war. Our enemies often do business with our allies."

Ben leaned back in his chair, balancing on the rear legs. "In spec ops work," he said quietly, "the key to success is the local people. You gotta let them lead you to the answers. I don't know anything about this photograph, but I know we don't have a lot of intel from the ground. One old alcoholic Dutch guy is all, in a country of French people."

"Why do you think we don't have good ground truth?" asked Jacobits.

"Because we didn't have time to infiltrate," said Jenny.

"If we don't make time for ground intel, then we shouldn't attempt the op," said Jacobits.

"The French police were dragging their heels getting us info," said Kate.

Jacobits could feel his throat go dry. He put the coffee cup on the counter behind him, because his palms were suddenly cold, as though his vital signs had slipped a bit. He wore a thin, grey turtleneck, the jersey clinging to the small mounds of flesh over his belly. His weathered jeans were slack over his thin legs, but were pressed to a crisp fold down the center of each leg. Slowly, he raised his face to the group, and each of them could see the look in his eyes, his heart blown open to them like a boiler door.

"The truth is," he said, his voice hoarse like something jagged had caught in his throat, "I didn't trust them. I didn't want them in this. When they first refused to bless us in, I was angry and believed I could do it myself. I stopped trusting the French police. How many times have we worked on our own without the local people?"

"Never," said Chad quietly.

"Correct. Never. Because to think we are the best and don't need help is just damned American cowboy arrogance. My job as your team leader is to take you down the right road, not just any road, not just to be your Custer. The Paris police have been investigating this kidnapping all along. They put an entire team of detectives on it, and I finally called them tonight to ask for help. Truth is, if I hadn't been such an arrogant asshole, we might have Hank back already.

"So I gave 'em what I know about AQIM, and the French blessed me in." He pointed at the computer screen. "Go ahead, Chad," he whispered. "Next up is a video recording."

Chad clicked the keyboard once, and the image of the shoe shop was replaced by a Western man sitting at a bare, metal table against a pale lime-colored wall covered with empty metal shelving. A flicker of a gaze passed between Ben and Kate, as they recognized the man to be Hank Cullen. He held the *Wall Street Journal* in his hands, and the date printed on it was the evening edition of that very day.

"AQIM's proof of life for Hank Cullen. Shot somewhere in Marseille, maybe even in the back room of that shoe store."

Hank Cullen spoke to them in the broad, hollow accent of his Utah childhood. He looked straight at the camera, his face unharmed, but his eyes clouded with fright.

"In the name of Allah, the Beneficent, the Merciful. All praise is due to Allah, the Lord of the Worlds." Ben brought his chair-legs back to level ground, and all in the room could hear his deep breath.

"I am here because of my own mistakes," said Hank. "I am here because of my greed." He stopped speaking, but did not move a muscle. Suddenly, a woman's voice from outside of the camera range said something scarcely audible, and Hank Cullen began again.

"The United States is a fascist aggressor against good people of the world community. I am ashamed today to be an American, and hope that my family in the USA will help me stop the cycle of violence that we have brought upon other nations. The money that has been asked of you is not for my return, but for war reparations to the people who follow the prophet Muhammad, whose lives have been torn apart by American politicians and businessmen and soldiers. When you pay what is due, Allah will send me home to continue making amends for the harm our country has done. Pay this money right away. The deadline is soon, and I will be killed if they do not receive these war reparations from you in the manner they have requested. You cannot escape them. They will attack you in your innermost sanctum. Please."

Jacobits began speaking almost immediately. "Hank Cullen was taken from the Meudon Forest straight to Marseille. He was brought into this store in the Centre Bourse by AQIM. The shoe shop is on the border between the Arab Quarter and the wealthy fashion district in Marseille, and is owned by an Algerian importer called Assim Hosni. It was Hosni's daughter, Leila, who took Cullen from Meudon."

Ben moved his rifle from across his knees and placed it upright at his side.

"This recording and Ben's first description of the barmaid at the Meudon club, gave the French police what they needed. This is what they have been working on for the past several hours. That woman's voice you hear in the recording is a Welsh-educated Algerian woman. The police were able to pull that out, and when they ID'd the group of French Algerians who were educated in Wales and who also traveled in and out of France over the last two years, they came up with half a dozen women. One of them matched Ben's description. Leila Hosni, a graduate of the medical school in Cardiff."

"Christ," said Chad.

"The best detectives in the world," Jacobits said. "Right, Marko?"

"But how is this chick affiliated with AQIM?" asked Jenny. "They don't let their women hold top positions."

"Well, Captain, I'll tell you something I learned a long time ago. I don't care who you are, when someone offers enough money, almost anyone will modify their beliefs pretty quick. *Cristina* jumped in with data that Leila here was trained in the Khyber Gateway camp that al Qaeda abandoned last year in Pakistan's Northwest Frontier Province. She was one of a handful of women who were allowed to work there, partly because she's a doctor, but mostly because her father bought that slot for her. And they trained her to fight pretty good, I'd say."

He paused and glanced over at Ben. "You see, we all thought you were the best, Major Cullen, but it turns out that Leila Hosni takes that honor. She's a doctor, and a killer."

Kate walked to the kitchen sink and took the dishrag from the deep porcelain rim. She turned her back to her friends, and began wiping the blue-tiled counter. Jacobits glanced at her quickly and continued.

"Chad, roll forward now. Okay, once AQIM sent the recording of Hank to the French police, they knew we would all close in pretty quick. So they need to cycle Cullen out fast, and if they're gonna make use of him, they need to get him somewhere we can't infiltrate. AQIM's base is in the coastal capital, Algiers. That's where we think they are heading with him. The airports in Provence are locked down, so they can't get him out of France on a plane now. Most of the major roads in this country are being monitored. *Cristina* believes the only way they can move him out is by water, and the *flics* down here believe he will be taken on a ship over the next few hours to North Africa. Here's the image series from our analysts in Alabama."

A photograph of the Marseille harbor appeared, once Greek, then Celtic, later Roman, the blocks of the quay crusted over with millennia of seafaring cultures. A small black image appeared of a man squatting on the waterside near the yacht slips, a shadow braced against the satellite grain. The screen changed and there appeared the Canebiére Way, an ancient road lining the Mediterranean sea and named after fields of cannabis that had once been farmed for sailors' hemp.

"We are looking for a boat, or a ship, or some damned bathtub that could take him across undetected," said Jacobits. "And, here it is," he grunted, "the yacht belonging to Leila Hosni's father. That's their target. A hundred feet on three levels, swimming pool and sea doo, all of it just waiting for your brother, Major Cullen. Our job is to lift him before they get him there." A photograph appeared of the yacht silhouetted by dusk, its stateroom windows glowing yellow in the falling night. "They are transporting him to this, to the *Mihrab*."

"It's been a long afternoon," said Jacobits. "Let's take a break. We'll brief the mission as soon as the helo driver arrives."

Chad shut the computer and stood up. "Come on, Jenny," he said. "Let's go watch '*Apostrophe*' on TV."

Ben lifted his rifle and walked outside into the clear night.

Marko remained silent at the table, while Jacobits sat near the warm, iron stove.

"Colonel," said Marko finally, "may I ask you a question?"

Jacobits nodded.

"AQIM obviously must have suspected we might discover the woman's identity. Why then would they bring Hank Cullen to her father's ship?"

"Maybe they think we're stupid, or maybe they had no place else to take him. But I'm thinking that it's not really a yacht; it's probably

Allah's little battleship. Who knows what's inside? I think they've been planning this for a long time."

"This kidnapping?"

Jacobits shook his head. "You and I both know there's something more here. Too much is random; too much doesn't add up. Friggin' token ransom amount, random Azores kill; AQIM is doing something the hard way now, and they got us running after them."

"Yes," Marko said. "I wondered if you realized. And taking the elder Cullen son, when they might just have easily had the father."

"Of course I friggin' see it. No successful op I've ever been in was fought by running *after* the bad guys. That's why God invented the phrase, 'cut 'em off at the pass' for God's sake."

"And yet we are here, chasing after them."

"You got any better ideas, Capitaine Eskibel?" Marko did not answer, and Jacobits continued to stare at him. "You gotta get with the program, my friend. I can't have you on this op if you are questioning my decisions."

"Do not worry about me. You have done much for my people, and you will never have to worry about my loyalty."

Jacobits nodded, and opened the stove door, turning the coals with the poker.

Kate remained at the sink, and above her on the wall hung an old photograph from her pilot training days in Oklahoma. Two rows of pilots were lined up and smiling at a distant photographer, while Kate looked in another direction, grinning broadly and waving to a different observer. She stared at this photo for a moment and turned back to Colonel Jacobits.

"I don't know what happened between you and Major Cullen, Kate," he said, "but in case you didn't realize, this is the time to make your peace with him."

Chapter 11

A NEIGHBORING FARMER'S FIELD stretched dark and silent beyond the sycamores behind Kate's house. Ben leaned over the rail fence that separated the properties, his body a shadow against the soft, indigo night. Kate stood alongside him, and for a moment they watched a bird in the far corner of the field, a slender white crane lit like a candle from the moonlight.

Kate flicked a light switch on the outdoor wall, and amber lamps glowed along the back porch.

"Come sit with me, Ben," she said. "I'll turn the propane heater on."

"I'm not cold, Katie," he said, and walked over to the old, heavy white wicker chairs where she stood.

She smiled when he called her 'Katie', and they sat for a moment without speaking. The lights threw copper reflections along the path against the house and adjoining garage. Gauze curtains hung behind them, and the smell of lavender surrounded them from the farmer's thriving field.

Ben looked out at the garage wall, and saw that it was smeared with old graffiti.

"'*I will kill you, American*'," he read. "Who did that?"

"I don't know. It happened just after I arrived a few years ago."

"Nice welcome."

"Goes with the territory," she said quietly.

"You should get that repainted."

She shrugged. "I left it there to remind myself to be careful."

"Katie, I'm sorry you were called into this op. I'm sorry for what this has gotta be doing to you, Hank and all."

"That Thanksgiving was a long time ago. I've forgotten about it." She smiled at him. "I've been attacked by a lot of people since then, with grenade launchers and knives and you name it. One horny guy in San Diego is nothing anymore. If you hadn't stopped him, things would have been a lot different. But I was lucky."

"He never changed. He's my brother, but you and I both know he's not really worth all this effort."

"You don't rescue people because they're worth it. You go after them because they shouldn't be kidnapped."

He held his breath, and took her hand, unfolding her fingers from the fist she had made. She noticed that he had the same serious line to his mouth that he had as a young college boy. He was staring hard at the palm of her hand, and said, "I never forgot about you."

"I couldn't, either." Under the lamp, Kate could see a large, oval bruise, yellow and green at the corners, sunk deep under his skin and covering most of his forearm. She wondered how he had come by this, but their kind of operative never bothered to ask.

"Are you happy?" Ben asked suddenly. "This is really the back of beyond out here."

She pulled her turtleneck up over her chin to warm away the chill that had begun closing through the night.

"Did you know that Nostradamus lived out his life in this town?" she asked. "Creepy, isn't it? That this was the center of the future of history. You don't believe in anything like that, do you?"

Ben shrugged, and smiled, and looked away from her. "Not really."

"I like this empty Nostradamus sky. The only things you see are stars and Jupiter. And the air always smells like lavender. It's a very simple place."

"Do you remember that Labor Day we spent with your family on the beach?"

"Sure," she said cautiously.

"Playing volleyball with your cousins. That was fun. How's everyone these days?"

"My dad is pretty sick, but the rest of them are okay. My family lives in different states now. We don't see each other much. I don't get home very often." She looked away from him in embarrassment, to the fields where leftover fence wire hung in loose coils from the posts. She did not speak again, and crossed her arms over her chest.

"Katie, did you ever think that you would be the one to run out of adrenaline like this?"

She turned to look at Ben, and was still staring at him when they heard the engine of a car revving up her driveway. The back glow of its headlights extinguished and the door opened. Instantly and unconsciously, Ben reached for his rifle.

"That'll be Alain, our helo pilot."

Ben nodded. He leaned close to her, still holding the rifle against his chest, and kissed her cheek.

"Maybe we could try again. After this is all over."

Kate stood up and stepped down into the moist dirt path to meet the new team member.

"*Salut*," said the man.

" '*Soir*, Alain," Kate replied, and the two of them leaned together mechanically to kiss each other's cheeks. "This is Ben Cullen, of Joint Spec Ops Comm. Jacobits is inside. We should get a move on."

Chapter 12

KATE FLEW RIGHT SEAT on the EC725 helicopter, as it lifted smoothly above the military airport in blackout against the moon. As co-pilot, she ran the checklist aloud in flawless French. Her voice was calm and full, unfaltering through the unfamiliar tasks of this vehicle. She read and confirmed each item, through the avionics, the hydraulic system, and the engines, all as though she might have been reciting a liturgy.

Once above the dark seam of the night horizon, she relaxed back as the French pilot flew the short distance down to the private Euro Copter manufacturing terminal adjacent to the Marseille airport.

"How did you score this helo for our mission?" she asked. "Even the pedals are clean. Has it ever been operational?"

"No," he replied. "Technically, we're delivering it now. We're just making a few stops along the way."

She could see his grin beneath the helmet mike.

"On Monday," he said, "this helicopter has to be in Corsica. Intact."

Within minutes they were circling above the Marignane airport to the north of Marseille. On the left side of the darkened cabin she could make out the darkness of the coastal lake that bordered the landing strip. As they drew down through the moonlit sky, she saw the suburbs of Marseille and the disused fairgrounds to the north, where the metal skeleton of an old Ferris wheel stood frozen with rust like a gatekeeper to the ancient city.

Kate lowered the landing gear lever with a smooth, strong heave of her arm, and both she and the pilot focused on the liquid crystal display of a digital chart drawn across the transparent cockpit glass. This 725 was a combat search and rescue model of the newest, most lethal helicopter produced by the arms industry. It contained the latest weapons systems and technology available, including armor plating, integrated machine guns, side-mounted rocket launchers, and search radar, and although Kate knew that a piece of hardware rarely made the determining difference in a covert operation, she was grateful nonetheless that Alain had managed to bring the 725. The helicopter was huge, with capacity for 29 soldiers, but this night there were only seven: Kate, Alain, and their five team members.

The hissing rhythm of the blades shifted as the helicopter banked left and began its descent, a dismal, howling siren of cool air pulling hard at the aircraft through the night. Alain put the machine delicately on the ground, twenty yards from the blacked-out hangar. The running lights were off, and the helicopter blades churned a cloud of dust up into the air across his face.

"Would you grade that landing an 'Excellent'?" he asked Kate.

She began to run the landing check, and smiled at him. In the back the others pulled their weapons and packs together.

Suddenly, the side door sprung open and Jacobits leapt out into the night. He pulled his night vision goggles down over his eyes and saw a crisp picture bathed in ghostly green light, and a thin red laser beam spitting out from the front of the helicopter.

"Okay, folks," he said, "tonight they are moving the asset from the old docks to the yacht. We need to take him before they get him on board, and Alain will meet us in the helo at the landing zone at Pastré Parc in the middle of Le Point Rouge, with many thanks to la Comtesse de Pastré for the use of her meadow. Our transport down to the water is an armored truck in the hangar over there. We drive to the yacht. Serge, my buddy from *Cristina* out of Marseille is tailing *haji* at the moment along the quay to the port of Le Pointe Rouge where the yacht is moored."

Kate stepped forward across the damp tarmac. She pushed her sleeve above her wrist and looked at the face of her watch. Immediately, the others did the same. "Time hack. Twenty-three fifteen in ten seconds, nine, eight, seven, six, five, four, three, two, one, hack." She looked up. "We're thirty-five minutes from the yacht at La Pointe Rouge. We leave here in fifteen, at twenty-three thirty. We get as close as we can in the vehicle, and then the rest on foot. Ben, you and Chad are advance. Get out to the yachts and ID the *Mihrab*. Then backtrack and build your berm where you think their most vulnerable transport point will be. The rest of us will follow. Any questions?"

She reached into her pack and pulled out a thick roll of fluorescent orange tape. "Marko, you mark the top of our vehicle so Alain can identify us from above in the dark."

She looked over at Chad who took a sandwich from his top pocket and began eating it. She stared at him, and the others followed her gaze and began to laugh.

"I'm still hungry. I can do the transmitter check and eat at the same time," he said.

"Oh, I believe that," said Jenny. She pulled her goggles down over her face, and they all began to move without speaking, without reflection, their breathing sharp with anticipation.

Kate slipped into the back and checked her equipment. She pulled a black sheath over her thigh, and fixed the Velcro straps into place. Into this, she slotted her special Applegate-Fairburn knife that opened and locked with the touch of one finger. Finally, she loaded a second medic kit into her belt, softly snapping it into place with her thumb. She sat down hard on the metal floor, and pulled out a mirror and her camo sticks, and began covering her face with dark paint.

Ben pulled the vehicle out from the airport complex to the main road that crossed the peninsula from the marsh to the Marseille harbor. Once in sight of the sea, he turned onto the quay, which lay nearly deserted in the darkness. The Corniche road wound around the great arc of the bay of Marseille, past the ancient docks of old Massalia that had sheltered trading ships since the Iron Age.

"Look at that," Marko said to him, pointing to an island miles off-shore and the ghostly green tower rising from it. "The Château d'If. Where the Monte Cristo Count was held captive for so long."

"I always thought that was a fairy tale," Ben said.

"No," said Marko. "The man was held there for decades. We human beings have a bottomless capacity for evil, don't we?"

"That's pretty cynical, coming from a priest."

"I am not a priest any longer, Major Cullen." Marko had propped his FAMAS assault rifle beside him, and the metal shaft was warm now from his body heat. He spread his fingers around the barrel, and kept a constant scan from left to right across the road ahead. "Many years ago I realized that some things are indeed worth fighting for. Since then I have not been a priest."

"But you still live at the monastery?"

"We are not a monastery anymore. We have all become soldiers of one kind or another. Like the apostles of Jesus, who were warriors before the history of Christ was rewritten by fat popes and greedy kings. This is now my calling."

The stench of the water of the old seafaring city rose up as the truck rounded the corner beyond the old port. The acrid smell of blue oil and rotting gull carcasses in the commercial quay mingled around them, and they drove past a long line of silent container ships, shadows of grey and black in the night, but washed for these soldiers with the grainy green light of their night vision goggles.

Ben shifted the engine to come fast out of the crescent of the port onto the short drive down to the Pointe Rouge. He nodded to Marko.

"This is it," he said.

Marko spoke into his mike, "Okay, my friends, we'll be there in five minutes. We're entering La Pointe Rouge now and are almost to the entrance of the yacht harbor."

Chad punched up the Falcon View terrain maps on his laptop on the back floor of the truck.

"Keep sight of the sea," he said. "We'll be nearing the harbor peninsula and we need to swing left at the fork before we do."

"Be careful at that fork, Ben," said Kate.

The truck was silent then, except for the grinding of the gears and the breathing of the soldiers.

"Piece of cake," said Chad softly.

Almost upon his last word, the first shot hit the truck with a flash.

Ben swung the vehicle sharp right down the street bordering the bay. The road dropped down to the water, and the buildings formed a line on their left side. Ahead, Ben saw a row of sandbags laid across the street, and he knew he would have to slow down to roll over them.

"This is a fucking ambush!" he shouted. At the end of the street they heard machine gun firing.

"Go, go, go!" yelled Jacobits, rushing forward to the cabin.

Ben spun the truck around into an abrupt three-point turn and raced down the bay road back to the fork. The truck lurched and swung out over the intersection.

"What are they shooting?" he called out. "How wide is that danger zone?"

A burst of machine gun fire erupted several hundred meters behind them. They could hear another rocket propelled grenade launcher flaming toward them, but so far it had missed the mark.

"You'll be out of the range of fire in a hundred meters," said Kate, and her voice was low and solid. "Follow this street to the end. Chad, right or left? Right or left, dammit!"

"Take the left back along the bay. We're not chancing a fight in the city tonight." Quickly, he shouted, "Alain! Give me some news! What the hell do you see up there?"

The hollow echo of the French pilot overhead rang through the microphone.

"You have a small enemy jeep at the church waiting for you to turn the corner. Not likely to be the transport of Cullen. Too small and open for guards to protect the asset. If you take the next road to your right you will miss it."

"What if it is my brother?" asked Ben.

Calmly, Kate said, "The helo call is that it isn't Hank. Ben, that's the only intel we have. But if we take the turn and avoid it, they will just follow us. Alain, can you put us behind them so we can engage?"

Jacobits looked at her suddenly. "You fight with your fangs out, don't you, Captain?"

"Major Cullen, a new vehicle has just entered the road to le Point Rouge. A Land Rover, coming behind you along the bay," said the French pilot. "Chad, can you see that passage on the screen? This is the asset. I am sure of it."

"Get behind the first vehicle! Now!" shouted Kate.

"Ben, sharp right in ten yards," said Chad. "Follow that street to the next intersection, hang another right and wait. I think that will get us behind them."

Ben wheeled the truck at best speed around the corners, slamming to a halt in the shadows of a blackened corner façade. "Kate," he said, "get the Colt launcher ready. It'll be seconds."

Kate fixed the grenade launcher to her M4 and wheeled it to train on the spit of damp, dark tarmac before them. "Marko," she said, "I can't get a line from inside this truck. I'm going out. Give me cover."

The two of them leapt simultaneously from the truck. Kate hit the pavement and lay alone in the dark with her weapon fixed on where the vehicle would cross. Marko climbed to the top of the truck, his back against the adjacent concrete wall, his muscled body fiercely tight, trembling and waiting.

Within seconds, they heard the groan of the tires on the pavement, as the enemy vehicle pushed steadily into the open without headlights. One marksman rode in the back, scanning the black streets for Kate's team.

In the split second before the combatant detected their truck, Kate squeezed off the grenade launcher with a tight, accurate hit through the gunman's narrow opening. An instant later, at one hundred meters, Marko shot the back tire off. With a small white flash of that bullet, the vehicle swerved into a lamppost, flipped onto its side, and the grenade exploded.

Kate and Marko ripped their goggles from their faces, before they could be blinded by the white light. They ran to the car with their rifles raised, to the back gunner's window that had become a dark hole of bent metal. Marko put two shots into the driver, blasting his chest into hamburger. The crackling sound of electricity and shooting had swelled to the thunder of raging fire, and amid this oppressive noise, they quickly scanned the car for capacity.

"Marko, look, they've got a tracker. Grab it and let's go." He wrenched the American Blue Force Tracker box mounted on the dash.

They ran to the truck and jumped into the open back hatch.

"All here, all safe?" asked Kate, breathless. She flung the tracker on the floor beside Chad.

He picked it up, and put it beside his laptop. "Katie, you're the best, baby. Now when the bad guys see the blue dot moving again on their radar, they're gonna think their ambush team won."

Kate shrugged. "Let's get back on track," she said. "We lost ten minutes then." Kate slouched back against the hard spine of the truck wall, breathing unevenly, backing into the darkness. The team around her was speaking, but she only heard it as faraway music. She put her fingers to her dry lips to feel if she had chewed them raw during the fight. For a moment her eyes glazed over, and she saw the most beautiful colors, apple green and crimson, with tangerine streaks washing over. She grabbed a blanket from the floor and pulled it over her, and sat quietly for the next few moments of the ride, hardly breathing while a few tears slipped down her face.

Chapter 13

BEN AND CHAD SPRINTED out of Pastré Parc across the Avenue de Montredon toward the quay. They crossed into a web of narrow alleys lined by towering, derelict buildings that blocked the fog-shrouded moon.

Once they reached the wide turn at the Avenue d'Odessa, they moved across it, staying low so they would not reveal their own outlines against the sea. They smelled the putrid air of trash fires burning in the abandoned buildings, and the sweet, heady smell of tires and refuse rose around them in steam across the bay.

"How much time do we have?" Ben asked.

"Thirty minutes."

Once at the Port de la Pointe Rouge, Chad squatted against a wall and grabbed the transmitter from his utility belt. "We're here," he said with a slight clamber of excitement in his voice.

"What's happening? Give me a sitrep," said Kate.

"We're heading out to find the *Mihrab*. Not a soul on the quay." They moved onto the tarmac of the darkened causeway, where the fog pulled in close around the moorings and gave them cover in the cold, raw night.

Ben edged out onto a narrow bridge leading to the yacht slips, as he heard the black water slapping against the pylons beneath him. The nasal call of two migrating gulls screamed out through the fog, and the soft, grey birds rose above him.

Chad followed several meters behind while Ben moved through the moorings to the end of the smaller, parallel slips.

"Look," he said, nodding at the opposite quay, towards a white ship, sleek and huge, lit like a flight of gold against the indigo horizon. "There is the *Mihrab*."

"Gateway to Paradise," whispered Ben. "That's what *mihrab* means. Probably a hundred feet of torture, all the way across to North Africa." Dampness rolled down his face and arms like anesthesia. Both men squatted on the concrete plank, and Ben grabbed his spotting scope to scan the ship. "Can't see a damn thing in this fog. What do you think? How many people does it take to run that monster?"

"Could be six, or it could be a platoon."

Ben smiled slowly at him. "Hell's gonna fly, Chad. You know that, buddy."

Chad nodded at him and spoke into his mike. "We got the *Mihrab*. Shit, Kate, it's a big one, baby. Get all the back-up you can. This could be the fucking Algerian navy here."

"Gotcha," said Kate. "Can we blow it before we lift the asset?"

"If we do, Captain, we'll have all of Marseille down here. This is the yacht of one of the richest merchants in town," said Jacobits. "The French cops will not stand up for us."

"Copy," she said quietly. "Okay, guys, find the best position for cover. When the Land Rover advances, stop it anyway you can. so we can open it up and get the asset out."

Ben recognized her tone, the same doomed electricity of her voice from that Thanksgiving years ago when he had caught his drunken brother tearing at her.

Ben touched the pod in his ear and said gently, "It's the garden of Eden, Katie. And they're soft like ghost soldiers. We can do it." He turned from the ship shimmering in the fog, and said, "Come on, Chad, we gotta find a defensible position between the town and here."

They retreated silently along the ramps until they no longer stood over water, but on the first street of the ancient village harbor. A small traffic circle lay before them, the last space before the sea that would be large enough to park a vehicle. Power lines slung low beside the nearby chandlery buildings, and the ripe smell of yesterday's fish heads permeated the now-thinning yellow fog.

"It's gotta be here," said Ben into his mike so all the team could hear him. "This is where they'll unload him and take him to the ship. But we'll be caught in cross-fire if we set up at this intersection. The *Mihrab* could have twenty soldiers on it, and they're behind us. The truck arriving has four and they're in front of us. It's suicide to try to lift him here."

"Ben," said Kate, and her voice was calm and low, "you have to build your berm far enough away from the ship so the crew can't join the fight. Maybe you install above. Get off the street. Alain, give us a picture. Where are they now?"

"You have time, Kate. They have not turned off the Corniche yet."

Within seconds she asked, "Ben? Have you got a back-up plan?"

"Katie, they'll be coming down avenue de Montredon and then turn at the fork heading here to the water. There's a triangle where Odessa, Montredon and Pointe Rouge all meet. There's a two-story building in the middle of that triangle with a bar on the ground floor. That'll be our best position. They'll know that, if their driver is familiar with the city, but that's the best I can do."

"Get yourselves installed up over the bar to give us fire so that you can stop the truck. Lay some in the street. Marko, the Colonel and I will open it up and pull Hank. How long do we have before we can expect the *Mihrab*'s crew to get to the fight?"

"I'd give 'em five minutes," said Chad. "One to receive communication, two to muster, two to get here."

"So we have to be back at Pastré by then," said Kate. "Everyone?"

"That's pretty tight, Kate," said Chad.

"Alain, we will need air cover," she said.

"Can't do it, Captain. If I delay my landing to strike with you, I won't be able to install in the Park in time to exfiltrate you."

"Copy that. Do the French cops know about what is going down here tonight?"

"They do, but they also know to stay away." said Jacobits. "We are, after all, deniable."

Kate breathed deeply and said, "Let's talk about abort options, guys. If I call 'knock it off', get back to the helo without the asset. Colonel, do you agree?"

"I do, Captain. Get your butts out of there. Regardless of the consequences. I don't care who we piss off by aborting. We don't leave any of our own behind."

"Ben," asked Kate, "did you hear that?"

Ben stood in the deep shadows of the fog, in the moment before swinging a rope up the side of the café, before slicing a knife through the space between the door and the lock of the second floor office. "Yeah," he said. "I did." Even after he had agreed to her plan, the others on the hot mike remained silent.

Chad squatted beside Ben against the steel shutters of the café window. He put his hand lightly on Ben's back and looked up at the building they were about to scale. An enormous vessel-shaped bird's nest of twigs was lodged above them at the juncture of the old granite building blocks and the loose power lines. Ben looked over his shoulder and nodded silently at Chad.

"These people are asleep now, invisible," Marko whispered into the mike, "but when they wake up with our noise, every single one of them could come after us. To attack an American here gets you a hundred Euros. To kill one gets you seven thousand now. We are so close to North Africa – just across the water; don't underestimate their network."

"Get back here alive," said Kate to her team.

"The fog's gonna lift in an hour or so," said Jacobits. "Maybe sooner. We need to be out of here by then."

The mikes went silent, and within minutes Chad and Ben began laying the SLAMS, the explosive devices, across the road.

"SLAMS are in," said Ben. "We're good to go."

They hoisted themselves up the nylon lines to the second floor office windows, and slipped inside the empty room, where Chad placed an explosive SLAM on the old window-frame and silently blew a hole through it. Ben positioned himself alongside, spreading his legs wide like an anchor and leaning against the thick old wall. He pulled a

Barrett .50 rifle high on his chest like a human tripod. He looked through the 10-x scope, and trained his gaze on the intersection below.

Chad quietly arranged the rocket-propelled grenade launcher to be first fire, and set a cache of explosives on the floor beside him as follow-up. At last, he leaned his own M4 against the wall adjacent the window-frame, where he knew he could take it and run within seconds.

Marko led off from Pastré Park through the dark streets, jogging and ducking along the building lines, with Jenny and Jacobits following, and Kate bringing up the rear. Once at the triangle they stopped, and without speaking, each chose a defensible position from which they could attack the enemy with firepower, or if needed, face to face. The only rule they fought by was the last fighter alive was the winner.

The street lamps threw yellow light into pools on the damp, cobbled gutters. There were trees on the corner of Odessa and Montredon, and their branches tugged with the April breeze rising up from the sea. Jacobits was shielded by the heavy, granite arch of a church doorway, out of Kate's line of sight, but she could still imagine his familiar, emotionless expression in her mind. Kate crouched against the cold wall of a blackened restaurant down Odessa, and stared straight at the dead center of the intersection, led there by the red laser line from her rifle.

"All in?" she asked. "Colonel?"

"I'm here, Kate."

"Marko?"

"Yes, madame."

"Jen?"

She did not answer. Jenny had followed Jacobits down the darkness of the church side alley, and had spun from there to the right, where she had taken cover against the windowless wall of the annex.

"Jen, if you can hear me, let me know." Every instant she expected the Land Rover to roll across the intersection. Her heart was pounding furiously and in the lower corner of her peripheral vision, just below the edge of her goggles, she caught sight of her own assault vest. Her heartbeat was moving it.

Still no answer from Jenny, and Kate knew she could not move to investigate.

"I'll go," Marko said. "I believe she stopped about twenty meters behind me." Marko ran quickly back down the block, ducking into every blackened, filthy crevice looking for her. Once around the far corner, he heard a loud rifle crack break through the night, but detected no firing pin thump behind it. He hit the ground at once, knowing instantly that this meant a gunman was close. He bellied back against the door and scanned the street. A single man stood at the cobbled curb, looming above Jenny's small body sprawled in the gutter.

Marko leveled his rifle calmly and squeezed the trigger hard and smooth. The head of the man snapped back, and he fell to the ground alongside Jenny.

Marko ran to him. His neck had been penetrated cleanly with the first shot. Blood lay on the ground around him. Marko lifted his rifle then and avoiding the assault vest the man wore, aimed directly at his face and pulled the trigger once more. At this close range, the man's eyeballs turned to liquid as they spattered. Marko wiped the man's blood from his own face, and knelt on the ground by his colleague. He checked her carotid, but finding no pulse, pulled her body back into the alley.

"She's gone," Marko whispered, leaning at last back on his heels, his arms limp at his sides. "Jenny was taken out by a gunman back here. I have hidden her body."

"Fucking hell," Jacobits grunted. "Well, get your Basque ass back here now. We need you!"

"I'm on my way," he said.

Alain watching far above through the infrared sniper pod affixed to the helicopter, shouted, "They're approaching! Down Montredon, as predicted."

Kate pulled her goggles down over her helmet, and lifted her rifle. "Be patient," she whispered. "Wait till they're in the open."

"I hear the engine," said Marko. "No lights." The weight of the heavily armored Land Rover caused the brakes to shudder as it slowed for the intersection. Marko saw the front grill of the vehicle push out beyond the corner buildings. Suddenly the entire vehicle was in the open. "It's picking up speed!" Marko said, and the truck heaved to a higher gear as it rolled across to the Pointe Rouge.

"Wait," said Kate, as she followed the vehicle for three more seconds, her adrenaline hammering the blood through valves opened wide to fear. Then at the count of three, calmly and loudly, she said, "Chad, engage now!"

He fired the rocket-propelled grenade through the second-story window, and a dozen concealed pigeons lifted up to safety. The RPG whistled through the night, reverberating against the granite walls until it struck the front of the Land Rover, burying deep into the grill and exploding in a shriek of shell and fire.

The truck rolled on a few feet over the SLAMS explosives, and then jerked out wide toward the far sidewalk. Chad reloaded immediately and launched the next one at the windshield of the slowed vehicle. The blast shattered the glass and metal frame, catapulting shrapnel across the intersection.

"Perfect, buddy," said Ben quietly. He lifted his sniper rifle and held steady for the first escaping soldier, while Chad put the grenade launcher down and grabbed his rifle to cover the team on the street below.

Jacobits and Marko advanced quickly to the halted Land Rover. Jacobits flung open the door, and the driver fell to the damp street in blood and shock. Jacobits lifted his rifle and fired, putting a hole in the man's skull.

The front seat passenger emerged through the gap blown through the windshield, screaming and staring at his arms, his missing hands blown straight off his wrists by the explosion. He looked at the stumps for a few seconds, and then he blacked out, fell hard to the tarmac, and a moment later he was dead.

Ben and Chad fired furiously through the smoke and lifting fog, raining brass down onto the vehicle.

"Cease fire," Kate said, as, Jacobits and Marko surrounded the back of the vehicle. Jacobits swiftly lay explosive pods around the door. "Blow," said Kate sharply, and Chad detonated the blasts. The door sprung open, and the three agents leveled their rifles at the men inside.

A boy of about fifteen leapt from the dark, screaming at Jacobits, his arms flailing as he landed on him. He held a knife in one hand, and he and Jacobits struggled momentarily for it. When Jacobits took hold of the handle he turned it quickly toward the boy, sinking the blade deep into his chest, all the while staring at his face.

"*Merci, mon ami,*" said the boy, and his copper eyes lay glazed open. His skin was soft and smooth, and Jacobits reached to touch his forehead, closing his eyes.

Marko took hold of the asset, dragging him from the truck. Hank Cullen's wrists and ankles were bound together by plastic flex cuffs, and Kate grabbed cutters from her belt to free him.

"Can you walk?" she asked. Cullen nodded at her and she shouted, "Then come with me and run like hell!"

Ben and Chad scaled down the building and jumped to the street. The team moved out then, down Montredon back toward the helicopter waiting at Pastre Park.

After one block, they heard the pounding of boots following them, and the pummel of heavy machine gun rounds chopping the air behind them. Kate grabbed hold of Hank's arm and dragged him forward through the street, pulling him at last into an alley.

"I'm going for Jenny's body," Jacobits said into the mike. "The rest of you keep moving to the parc."

Marko dropped back to cover the team, shielding himself against a bank along the main street. He scanned the avenue behind, and saw eight gunmen moving toward him from several blocks away. He crouched down to cover himself and lifted his rifle. He squeezed off a burst that brought down one of the gunmen.

Kate heard the round of his rifle and looked over her shoulder. She saw that he was trapped in a narrow passage, and the seven gunmen would be upon him within minutes.

She looked at Hank Cullen beside her and shouted, "Keep going. Follow your brother to the helicopter!"

Kate ran through the gunfire, panic thumping across her heart. Just short of the corner where Marko hid, Kate understood she would not be able to make it to him. She looked up to see the tops of the old buildings and the moon, clear now against the fogless ceiling. She saw the gunmen thundering toward Marko, spraying bullets at him.

Across the sidewalk she saw a parked postal van, and she sprinted for it, ducking through the flashes of shrieking gunfire until she reached the driver's door. She jimmied the lock and slipped inside, and lay across the floorboards, fumbling for the wires, until suddenly the engine gunned to life with a deep roar.

Kate pulled the vehicle out into the street, driving hard for the space between Marko and the men.

Kate shouted at him, "Get to the helo!"

She floored the accelerator and aimed the van toward the men. As her foot pushed the pedal to the floor, an explosion encompassed her, a light made scorching by her night vision goggles, blinding her and throwing her up through a ghostly electronic tunnel, through the glass and night, across the black street.

Then she lay motionless, speaking but hearing no words coming out, her back cold against the cobbled street. She was washed up on a beach, chasing a ball in the warm, foamy surf, and she heard her family around her shouting. Her fingers moved against the old street stones as she searched for sound and color, and slowly all noise was obliterated and the surge of blood at her temples silenced her thoughts.

Chapter 14

KATE AWOKE, NOT KNOWING how long she had been unconscious. All she could see was a sky the color of crows, black and glistening, woven together above her like tufted wings. A slow shadow loosened the blackness of her peripheral vision, and she tried to lift her arm but could not. It was then she realized her hands were tied behind her back and her eyes were taped shut. Water leaked around her, soaking her back, and she heard soft dripping behind her. A dog barked loudly in the distance, and she heard voices, but she could not make out any words.

A sharp, sour odor surrounded her; she thought it might be the rotting carcass of an animal or a human. She knew she was outside, because the faraway voices vibrated like open bells, unmuffled by walls. She heard a simple engine turn over, and rushing water, and wondered if she was on the *Mihrab*.

With great caution, she began to move her legs, but her ankles and knees were bound together so tightly the plastic cuffs had cut tender ridges into her skin. She rolled slowly to one side, and a piercing pain shot across her back. She bit hard into her lip to keep from crying out. Blinded and alone, her mind pounded with fear. She lay quietly for a few moments, focusing on her breathing, forcing the terror back down her throat.

Once she sensed the adrenalin dissipating and her muscles relaxing, Kate evaluated her physical state, slowly contracting muscle groups and releasing them. After a few moments, she knew she had not lost the use of any limbs. She was still unsure about the condition of her back, and tried again to move onto her side. She felt the ground give slightly, as though she lay on soft-packed soil. She smelled a thick, musky smell, damp and heavy around her. This time when she moved, she understood the pain to be shooting from her left shoulder, and she moved quickly to shift her weight off of it. As she lurched, she felt her body butt against another object, soft and yielding. She bent her head close to it, and smelled a man's sweat.

Kate lay still, her thoughts so fast and so clear she could almost hear them. She listened carefully for the voices again, but only heard the harsh call of a large bird as it flew from a tree, and the rustle of leaves as it moved to find the sky.

"What's that?" she heard a man's voice whisper in English. "Where have you taken me?"

"Who are you?" Kate asked, but the man did not answer. "Where are we?" she whispered. "Can you see anything?"

Suddenly, someone grabbed her injured arm and pulled her to a standing position. The blindfold and tape were ripped from her eyes, and she stood facing two men and a woman. One of the men was older and short, with a thick, dark face and tough leathered skin. The younger man was tall and wiry, in his twenties, and his large black eyes were circled with ruptured veins like fireworks across his skin.

The two men dragged her from the narrow path into the adjoining oak forest where she sank ankle deep into black mud. She heard the gurgle of a sluice surge across rocks somewhere below them, but her gaze remained fixed on her captors.

The woman leaned forward, roughly grabbing the man who still lay blindfolded on the dirt path. She clipped the ties around his ankles, and tore the blindfold from his face.

"Get up!" she said, and her English was accented with British inflections.

The man stood cautiously, as though in great pain. His face was bruised and muddied, and he wore a wrinkled powder blue polo shirt.

He looked straight at his female captor. "What now?" he asked loudly. The woman lifted her rifle suddenly and jabbed his stomach hard with the butt until he doubled over again.

Kate watched silently, and when Hank was standing, she said to him, "Keep your mouth shut, for God's sake."

"Yes, Captain," the woman said. "That is a very good idea. Mr. Cullen, I would listen to her if I were you."

She spoke to one of the men in Arabic, and he pulled metal shears from his belt and cut Kate's ankles free. The woman, small and olive-skinned, pushed Hank forward into the woods. "Get going. We have a long walk ahead now."

They stood at the head of a deep canyon, and the sun shone directly overhead through the oaks. They crossed through the mud to another path, and followed that down to a fast-flowing, glistening river.

The five of them walked for several minutes. All around them were large granite boulders and limestone canyon cliffs, and everywhere was the dank smell of dense oaks growing in the dark riverside soil. Kate began to rack her memory for where they might be, what country, and what forest. The path bent to the left along the meandering river, and when they rounded this, she saw above them a natural stone arch shaped like the face of a lion, smeared with thick layers of tan and cream, and she suddenly realized their location.

One of the men stopped walking and pulled a water bottle from his backpack. He handed the bottle to the other man, and then to the woman, who refused to drink. Kate saw that all three of her captors carried the old Russian AK-47 rifles over their shoulders, and they wore military utility belts with other weapons and communications equipment.

"Let's go," said the woman, and the two men pushed their prisoners forward down the track. Once beyond the arch, they walked for another half hour along a narrow animal path, until they came to a large stainless steel door set into the limestone canyon wall.

The woman made a call on her cell phone, and in a few moments, she and the two men put their palms against a sensitized steel plate on the electronic door. Suddenly it opened.

"Here," said one of the men, and grabbed Kate by the arm. He pulled her across the entryway and spun her around to cut the flex cuffs that bound her wrists together. He pushed her toward the door, and she had to stoop inside it to enter the black hole in the cliff.

She stumbled down a small dark passage of stone, followed by the others, and was shoved onto all fours. All of them, captor and captive alike, knelt to the ground and entered a narrow crawl space.

The woman behind pushed at her with a rifle point and said, "Go!"

Eventually, they came to a precipice deep within the cavern, and a stainless steel ladder secured to the wall that projected far down into the depths of the cave. One by one, the five of them swung out over the abyss onto the ladder and climbed down the sheer drop to the bottom of the second landing.

Once they could descend no farther, the lantern light of the captors pierced the blackness to reveal a range of stalactites and stalagmites, pink and golden yellow, surrounded by sparkling white crystal.

"Sit down," said the woman, and Kate and Hank Cullen squatted to the damp earth, staring up at the immense cavern.

The other men reached into a trough of boot slipcovers, and pulled plastic sleeves over their shoes. The woman laughed and shook her head.

"Leila, the doctor told us to put these on," said one of the men.

"Don't be absurd," she said. "He is not a real doctor like me, and anyway we will blow this cave up when we finish here. Tie them up and let's go."

Kate was bound again and dragged across the painful terrain into the corner of a far cavern. Her hands were chained to thick steel rings that had been drilled into the wall, and even with the lamplight around her, she could not see the entrance to the chamber, nor where they took Cullen.

●

In the main cavern at the front, the voice of an old man called out for the Algerian woman.

"Mademoiselle Hosni!" he shrieked. "There are topics we need to discuss!"

Dirk Lowell had followed Leila into the electric light of the Brunel chamber. She stood beneath a wall painting of yellow horses, packing medical instruments into a steel box. Her eyes widened at his tone, but she did not respond immediately. Instead, she bent over, lifted a swath of surgical draping, and folded it slowly. Around her feet were bloodied bandages.

"Once again, your men are making a mess of my work," he said. "They leave your medical detritus everywhere."

"Dear, dear Dr. Lowell, I did not realize that part of our contract was to be tidy."

"We never talked about the possibility of such urgent changes in plans. We never spoke of medical work. You and I have only discussed storage. That's all we bargained for. Valuable items and some higher value people. Nothing more."

Leila Hosni closed the steel box and spun the combination lock.

"Did you forget that day three years ago when my father invited you to our home in Juan-les-Pins. We had sweet tea on the terrace. It was not too hot that day, and I remember that the sea was a miracle of glass." She smiled slowly at him. "You remember that beautiful sea, correct? Well, that was the day you destroyed this place, all by yourself. For the money, Dr. Lowell. My father requested that you help our efforts, and offered to pay for your support. You told us that the Americans would not have been so generous. And now you have far more than you ever needed, don't you?"

She pulled off her latex gloves and put her delicate fingers to tighten her bun of tangled black hair.

"You will be clearing out soon," he said. "I will be leaving as well. It is time to turn the caves back to the French and for me to go home. After all, we should leave them some salvageable history here."

She walked closer to him and folded her arms across her chest.

"Magdy! Please come here!" she shouted in Arabic.

The tall young man came down the dark passageway, carrying an oil flame into the bright light.

"Mister Lowell, you will stay here until Cullen is safely returned. We will kill the woman and destroy everything in this cave that we cannot carry away. Then you may leave if you want."

"Destroy the cave? I never agreed to that."

She turned to Magdy without speaking, and nothing, not even her hands, betrayed her intention. "Mister Lowell," she said, staring down at his feet in the dim light. Her mouth lifted to a smile as though by a far-off current. "Mister Lowell, you are standing in blood. Please do not track it through the chambers. Cullen's DNA must not be discoverable anywhere."

•

Kate put her head on the limestone behind her, and noticed two handprints at eye level, their outlines blown in red pigment against the stone. She sat staring at these, while Hank was chained to the wall alongside her.

Then, the muzzle of light disappeared with their captors down the passageway, and she could no longer see the hands, nor Hank's face, nor anything in the cavern. She closed her eyes quickly, bringing darkness upon darkness, trying to think clearly. *They will be searching for us*, she thought, *but they will get it wrong. We need to get out of here on our own.*

"How do we do that?" Hank asked, and Kate realized she had been speaking aloud.

She looked over to where he sat, though she could not make out his eyes in the deep black of the cave.

"If you can get us out of here," he whispered, his voice was rasping like a crow cawing, "I will give you anything you want. What's your name, dear?"

Kate sat silently, considering his simple question. Hank Cullen had long been her nightmare, and so many pieces of her life had become silent because of him. She had worn a lavender cotton dress the day he tried to rape her, and had never worn lavender again; all rain seemed thereafter to be poisoned, and her fear had dulled at last to squirming mistrust of living people. The consequences of answering his question crackled through her.

"My name is Kate," she said at last. "How long did they interrogate you?" she asked.

"They haven't done that yet."

He has no idea, she thought, and like a crazy woman marooned alone, she nodded several times to herself.

"If they haven't interrogated you already, then they really are only looking for the ransom."

"I think I hear a helicopter," he said suddenly. "Can you hear it?"

"No, there's no helicopter. We're a hundred feet into a cave. You can't hear anything from here." Kate leaned back against the hard, cold cavern, and knew that she had just lied to him. She could hear lots of sounds, the soft, quick flamenco guitar of her old neighbor in Salon, the sizzle of the waves crashing against the San Diego shore, even her dog whining to go outside. She could hear all of it, and she could see it, too.

"What do you think they want from you?" she asked Hank.

"I don't know. Nobody's asked me anything. My guess is you're right. They're going for the money, although these stupid Arabs could get a lot more from my company than they're asking."

"These people are from the Maghreb, not Arabs. Do you think you have any broken bones?" she asked.

"My wrist is pretty sore, but I can still move it. It may just be cracked. My stomach is killing me. And the side of my head feels like it's going to explode. I think my ear is infected."

They heard a loud vibration begin, hard hammering of a motor and the sound of large blades circulating in the distance.

"What's that?" asked Hank, his voice shaking with stress and dehydration.

"I think it's an electric fan." Slowly the smoke of burning charcoal blew toward them, and then they began to smell roasted meats.

"Do you know my brother, Ben?" he said. "Fat lot of good that did me to have a brother in spec ops."

"Say that where they can hear you and we'll all be skeletons: Ben, you, me and your damned company, too."

When finally Hank spoke again he put his hand out first, reaching in the darkness to touch Kate with his soft fingers.

"Do I know you?" he asked, but she did not reply.

After some time, the darkness began to loosen in the distance with approaching lantern light. A new soldier they had not seen before came toward them. He carried a plastic bag in his fist, and threw it on the ground between them. He unchained one of Hank's hands from the wall shackle and sat down across the cavern, pointing his rifle at them.

"Eat," he said. "You first."

Hank grabbed the bag quickly and pulled a piece of meat from it. He devoured this in two swallows.

"Do it slowly," whispered Kate. "Don't choke on the food they give you."

Hank nodded, and lifted another piece from the bag. As he did, Kate noticed bright circles on the bag, yellow, red, and blue, and then she saw the word '*wonder*' printed across the plastic in thick red letters. *American bread,* she thought, and stared at the colored plastic for several moments. *Where do they get that?*

Their captor grabbed the bag from Hank, and chained his wrist back to the wall. Hank winced with the sharp pain, and said to the soldier, "Easy, friend."

The captor lifted his boot and kicked him in the ribs. "Is this easy enough?" he asked, with a thick accent. He squatted again by the far wall, leaning on his rifle. "You lady," he said to Kate, "you can eat now."

He tossed the bag toward her, but did not unshackle her. Kate stared at him, and after a moment she realized that his intention was to see her struggle to eat without hands, like an animal.

She had not eaten in a very long time, and knew that she needed protein if she was to be able to think clearly about an escape. She leaned forward so that her lips were close to the damp soil of the cave floor. Carefully, she maneuvered herself into a position to open the bag with her teeth. She lodged it against her leg, and with her mouth pulled a piece of meat from inside the plastic. She chewed slowly at it, the taste sour and pungent, but she knew even the juices would help her strength.

Suddenly, the man grabbed the bag and the meat slid into the dirt. "There, you can finish that." He walked away with the bag and the lantern, leaving them in darkness again.

Hank leaned back against the hard, jagged wall. "Do you know where we are?" he asked.

"Yes," Kate said. "I think we're in the Ardèche."

"What?"

"Just north of Provence."

"Yes, I know where it is! Idiot. What are we doing there?"

"I have no idea," Kate replied. "They wanted to take you out on a boat across to North Africa. If that had happened, you might have been dead within the night. After we ID'd the operation, they couldn't get away on open sea, so I guess they decided to hide us here."

"How long do you think we have?"

"Until they get from me what they want. My guess is they probably intend to kill us."

The sound of the engine droning in the cave grew more urgent, and the smell of gasoline permeated the thin air around them.

"I want to get out of here," said Hank, caught suddenly in his own panic. "You need to get me out of here!"

Kate closed her eyes and took a deep, slow breath. She tried to recant the principles of withstanding torture that she had learned from the Fairchild trainers, but the only thing that came to her mind was the rule of how to cross the threshold of a Muslim home, always with the right foot, because the left foot is reserved for dirty places. She repeated this aloud to Hank.

"What?" he asked. "Are you crazy?"

"It's my job to return you alive," she whispered, "and I will do that."

Kate saw a candle flicker in the distance, and a moment later she thought she heard a jackhammer rattle through the cavern.

"What the hell was that?" asked Hank, and he jerked suddenly back against the wall.

Kate did not move, sat absolutely motionless; listening and waiting, but the cave was silent.

Kate felt a light weight across her pant leg, a rapid movement over her knee. She looked down and could see nothing in the blackness until the tiny eyes of a rat, climbing up her clothing to her chest, began to glow.

Chapter 15

BEN SAT ALONE in Kate's bedroom, watching as first light touched the surrounding lavender fields and olive grove. He heard the landline ringing in the hall, but did not move to answer it. He had taken the beginning watch, and sat on an oak bench by the corner window, scanning the paths approaching Kate's home.

He and the rest of his team had arrived back at the house early that morning. Shortly after, they were joined by Serge, a French agent out of the Marseille bureau of *Cristina,* and together they set up a briefing room in the basement, integrating intelligence from both the DIA and the *Direction Central du Renseignement Intérieur.* The agent came armed with a five by ten foot detailed map of the south of France, and they unrolled it onto the basement floor. Chad set up the Toughbook on an old drafting bench under the grimy storm window, and ran the METT-T software to start war-gaming protocol. They began running the components, drilling over and over through mission, enemy, troops, terrain, and time, refining the intel they held and gaming the possibilities.

They had shuttered all the windows but Kate's second story bedroom where Ben sat in darkness, so that even the faintest glow of the basement lights could not escape into what was left of the night. The men took turns sleeping, guarding, and constructing trial ops that might be a successful mission to rescue Hank Cullen and Kate, if indeed either was still alive.

The pod in Ben's ear was hot, and as the light began to follow the dawn across the fields, Chad's voice spoke to him.

"Time to get some sleep, buddy. I'm coming up to relieve you."

Ben stood and walked across the room through the grey shadows. He was both curious and cautious to be able to see the private things of Kate's life, her jewelry laid out on her dresser, her dusty mirror, and the photographs of her family. He stared like a thief at each of the mementos she had displayed around the old pewter frame, until suddenly he saw one secret she had never meant for him to see.

An old envelope lay on her dresser, crinkled and smudged from the number of times it had been handled. Kate's name was on the front of the envelope, and Ben recognized his own handwriting. He stood motionless for a few seconds, seeing the memory of her in his dorm room at the Academy the day he had given it to her. He remembered kissing her in the hot Colorado summer as she held a mouthful of crushed ice, the cool of his tongue as it pressed through her lips, and slowly he took the envelope from her dresser and opened it.

Inside he found a note with his jump wings pinned to it. He looked at the words, remembering exactly the moment he had written it, in that same dorm room, alone with taps blaring through the loudspeakers and young men shouting in the hallways.

"These are for you because I love you. I know that with all the crazy things I'm going to do in my life, as long as you hang onto my jump wings I'll be safe."

•

Ben heard Chad's footsteps on the stairs, and folded the old notepaper. He put the envelope back in its place on Kate's dresser, and looked up to the door, waiting for Chad to come through.

"Make any progress?" he asked too quickly, and Chad watched him cautiously, as though he might have uncovered a secret he did not understand.

Chad walked past him to the chair, and sat down with his rifle slanted through the opening of the window.

"No, only that it would be pretty hard for them to get out in the Med at this point," he said. "It's gotta be a land escape." After a moment, he added, "You know, she was my best friend. But she was never really a rough girl; not like she could have been." He was speaking gently, and he put his hand to his face to rub the tiredness away.

Ben nodded. He stood in the deep iris shadows of the rising light and said, "We'll get her back."

The first hour of Chad's watch passed in quiet. Ben slept on the basement cot, while the others worked around him mapping the possibilities of the geography and local transport to identify anywhere they might uncover the AQIM group.

Near six a.m. Chad heard the rasp of geese lifting from water and rising over the trees, and somewhere beyond the lavender field he could see a shift in the light, some slight movement on the path.

He touched the pod in his ear and spoke. "There's an approach. Can't make it out." He flipped open the scope on his rifle and trained it on the far bend through the silvery leaves of the olive trees.

Every man in the briefing room grabbed his own rifle and waited. Jacobits touched Ben's shoulder to wake him.

"It's a man," said Chad. "Coming around the back way." He lifted his rifle and trained it on the subject, a tall, thin man with glasses who walked quickly with long, bouncing strides toward the house. The man wore a dark green farmer's waxed jacket, and carried nothing in his hands, but Chad knew these situations, knew a weapon could be anything and could be concealed anywhere.

"He's going toward the kitchen." Chad's mind was very clear, and at the same time that he waited for the instant when he might need to shoot, he also thought of his beautiful Spanish wife and her huge pregnant belly, and these pictures were frozen for him in the silence.

"Give us a sit rep," Jacobits said calmly.

"He's alone. Wait, there's a dog with him. He's got a dog with him. What the fuck is he doing? He's at the door. Are we buttoned up?"

All of them heard the man's voice calling faintly up to the crack in the window.

"Kate! T'es là?"

Chad froze, and with the greatest care began pulling the barrel of his rifle back from the opening.

"Kate! Qu'est-ce qui ce passe? Tu vas bien?" He began knocking then, gently at first, and then louder and harder.

Ben nodded at Jacobits and pointed to his own chest. "I'll go," he mouthed.

"No, let it evolve a minute," whispered Jacobits. "Chad, what's he carrying?"

"Can't tell. My guess is nothing."

"Okay, then," Jacobits said, nodding at Ben. "Go."

Ben put his hand against the barrel of the Baby Glock lodged in the holster at his shoulder, and moved silently up the stairs to the kitchen. Suddenly, he began walking heavily across the floor. He ripped his tee shirt and holster off, and stood before the sink, leaning across it to peer out of the window. He began rubbing his eyes as though from sleep, and smiled at the man.

"Un moment!" he called out, and opened the door.

"Hello," said the man in English. "Where is Kate?"

"She's sleeping," Ben said. "Can I help you?"

"I am a friend. I have come to return her dog. She said she wouldn't be home until Wednesday, but I heard the car early this morning. Glockie was missing her."

Ben took the leash from his hand and tugged gently at it. "Come on, boy. Katie's waiting." He smiled and began to close the door. "Thanks. I'll tell her you came by."

He put his foot in the door before Ben could close it.

"Just a minute." He slipped his hand inside the heavy waxed coat, and Ben reached for his gun, swinging back around behind the door. "I brought her some *pain au chocolat* for *pétit déjeuner.* Kate always likes them in the morning and I stopped at the bakery in the village." He pulled out a white paper sack filled with pastries and handed them through the door.

"Thank you," Ben said, and carefully took the bag from him. He realized that he had no idea what Kate liked anymore, and he knew that pausing to wonder about it was a distraction that could get him and his team killed.

"Is everything fine with Kate?" the Frenchman asked suddenly.

The dog was straining at the leash toward the living room, and Ben dropped the leather strap and let him go.

"Yes," he said. "Sure."

The man smiled broadly and said, "Okay, then. I'll be off. Tell Kate to come by if she is able later today. I'm diving at Cosquer next week if she wants to accompany me."

Ben closed the door and watched through the window as Jacques Morel strode away down the path through the farmer's field. When he could no longer see him, Ben pulled the mike pod out of his pocket and lodged it in his ear.

"Okay," he said. "I'm buttoning up back here and coming down. He's gone."

"No," said Chad from the upstairs corner window. "Not yet. He's circling around to the front of the house. Stay there."

Ben moved quickly to the living room. He knelt beside the cool wall by the front door, and leaned hard against the doorjamb to anchor himself while he trained the Glock on a point, chest-high, along the seam of the door. He knew the pistol would be no defense if an all-out assault was on the other side of the door, and he was silently hammering himself for leaving his rifle in the basement.

"We're coming up," Jacobits said into the mike, and without even a vibration of the stairs, they came like in a hunt, confident and moving low, Marko, Serge, Alain, and Jacobits. Once on the ground floor they stood out of sight in the dining room, each with their rifles at hand, listening for a word from Chad. They waited there in the pocket, tension and silence bloating them.

"He's here," Chad whispered, and the Frenchman cracked his fist loudly against the front door. "No visible weapon."

"Kate!" shouted Jacques Morel. "Kate! I need to see you!"

Ben lowered his gun, and put his hand on the doorknob. He turned to look at Jacobits, lodging his chin for an instant on his tensed deltoid, and waiting for the sign to proceed.

When Jacobits gave the signal, such was the close understanding of these soldiers that he did not need to move his body, but barely lifted his eyebrows, and Ben knew it was time. The others reacted immediately, slipping quickly out of each other's line of fire and into position, gently hooking thumbs into the loops on their grenade pins, quietly situating themselves for fight or flight.

Ben opened the door and said, "What's the matter, friend?"

"Where is Kate Cardenas? Where is she?" the Frenchman shouted, and began to push the door open.

Instantly, Ben grabbed his arm and pulled him into the house. In one clean, swift motion, he twisted his arm behind his back and lay him face down on the floor. Without speaking, Jacobits handed him plastic flex cuffs, and Ben secured the man's wrists and ankles. Serge and Alain hovered silently beside him, their rifles aimed at the Frenchman's back and head, while Ben blindfolded him and then searched him for weapons and electronics.

"I think I've seen this guy at *l'École de l'Air*," said Alain. "Pull him up and let me have a better look."

Ben wrenched him up to a kneeling position and held his face into the light.

Alain nodded. "That's one of the teachers. I'm sure of it."

"Give me a sit rep," said Jacobits into the mike, and Chad immediately scanned the approach to the house several times.

"Nada. Not a fucking thing."

"Alain, you relieve Chad. Let's get this guy downstairs."

Marko lifted Jacques Morel onto his shoulders and carried him down the stairs to the basement stronghold.

Marko set the man's tall, bound body onto a dusty aluminum chair, while Ben knelt in front of him. He stared at the silver beard growth on the Frenchman's tanned jaw, and at the tiny, leathery creases on his face. Finally, he said to his colleagues, "This is no High Value Target. I'd bet my life that our friend here is maybe not even a target at all."

Chad came down the stairs and walked to his Toughbook, connecting to the Joint Worldwide Intelligence Communications System.

"You still having trouble with jaywicks?" asked Jacobits.

"No, we just slipped in. Intellipedia opened those sexy legs. Go on, give me something to validate."

Ben stood up and put his hand on the shoulder of Jacques Morel. He removed his blindfold, and spoke quietly to him.

"Buddy, I am going to ask you a few questions. I suggest you tell me the truth. Do you understand?"

Morel replied angrily, "Who are you? Where is Kate?"

"No, my friend. I am going to ask you questions. This is how it goes. What do you do at the college?"

Jacques shook his head suddenly from side to side in childlike refusal.

"I'm the nicest person in this room," Ben said. "It will be better if you help me out here with some answers. What is your name, my friend?" Without waiting for an answer, Ben roughly pulled open the man's jacket and took his wallet from the inner pocket.

"Jacques Morel. Professor at Aix. Chad, what do you get?"

"Nothing via SIPRNET. Scan his ID photo and let's run it." After a moment, Chad added, "Teacher, that's all that's here. Let me go to ALIEN, our new system. It connects all the databases and I can usually get anything there, classified or unclassified."

"Do it quick," said Jacobits. "We want to know if there's more of these guys in the forest."

"Come on," Ben said. "Tell me what you are doing here, Jacques." He did not answer, and Ben walked to the ordnance room at the end of the basement, staring over at the man. Suddenly, he snapped on the light so quickly the white glare surprised them all.

"You know, a long time ago I really hated being hated," Ben said. "Now I don't care so much." The old Frenchman's legs began to tremble together, and Ben leaned back on the bright wall and watched him.

"No, there's nothing," said Chad. "He's been a part-time teacher of ancient history at the École here for several years. That's it. He's part of the Ministry of Archeology. He conserves prehistoric rock art." Chad began to laugh when he translated this, and then all of them did.

"Rock art defender," said Jacobits slyly. "I like that job." He turned to Chad, "Tell Alain to come down here. We need him to have a look at this guy again."

Ben walked out of the stark light into the steel blue shadows of the main room.

"Who are you?" asked the Frenchman. "Where is Kate?"

"Why do you want to know?"

"She is my friend."

"Mine, too," Ben said.

Jacques Morel looked up at Ben through the murky basement light. His eyes were blinking rapidly and his fingertips were scratching hard and nervously at the metal seat of the chair, but he continued staring straight at Ben.

Serge approached Jacques Morel.

"Pourquoi vous êtes ici, Monsieur? C'est un rendez-vous?"

"Of course it is a *rendez-vous,* you imbecile!" Morel shouted. "*A rendez-vous pour pétit déjeuner.* I have brought *pain au chocolat et le chien!* This is her dog!"

"Put this man through the Paris database," said Serge. "I will get *Cristina* to check with the Ministry of Culture. Didn't he say he was diving at Cosquer? I have a friend in the DRASSM office in Marseille. They'll validate him or not and then we'll know."

"What is Cosquer?" asked Chad.

"Some underwater cave in the Med near Marseille."

The two men sat side by side among stacks of books that Kate had stored around the old drafting desk, and began to get messages out onto the JWICS system asking for immediate confirmation.

"Who are you to need proof of me?" Morel shouted suddenly. "You are in my friend's home with your guns and machines and she is gone. It is your identity that is in question!"

The day's new light began to travel into the basement, choked with dust the color of yellow ochre that glowed across the hidden corners of the room. Jacobits stepped forward to face Morel.

"Unfortunately, my friend, you are the one who is tied up so you are the one who is in doubt," he chuckled. "That's how it goes in bad guy work."

When Alain arrived he sat opposite Jacques Morel and began a series of non-coercive questions in French, quickly establishing what he knew of the *École de l'Air* at Salon. This time, Morel engaged, and after several minutes, Alain stood up abruptly.

"Colonel, I'm satisfied. Are you?"

Jacobits nodded. "What do you have, Chad?"

"Rock defender *extraordinaire*. Chief archeologist for the Culture Ministry. He's got basic security clearances from the Interior, and from the old DGSE."

"At last," said Morel. "Now take these ties off my hands and feet."

"No," said Jacobits. "Not now. Just because you're not on the bad guy database doesn't make you a good guy."

"What do you want to do with him?" asked Ben.

"Put a bag over his head and stash him in the storage room while we work. We'll figure out what to do with him later."

Ben nodded, and moved to hoist Morel onto his shoulders.

"Wait, I'm an old man! I'm 75 years old. I need some water and food. I haven't eaten all morning. I'm diabetic, you know."

"Didn't you say you had chocolate croissants for breakfast?" said Ben.

"I brought those for Kate. I am very thirsty and I need some food."

Jacobits nodded. "Go ahead, Cullen. But feed him quickly so we can get back to briefing."

Ben turned toward the staircase, but noticed a small movement in his peripheral vision. He looked once more at Jacques Morel, who had turned to stare at him through the thick, soiled lenses of his wire rim glasses.

"Cullen?" Morel asked. "I know a very wealthy man named Cullen, a longtime funder of our scientific studies. I have known him for many, many years. Tell me, what is your father's name?"

Ben hesitated only a moment and without answering he walked to the stairs.

"Is it James?" said Morel. "Is your father James Cullen?"

"No," he replied and disappeared up the stairs. At the top landing he paused, leaning against the wall. Slowly, he slid down and squatted on the dusty floor by himself. He scanned the room, noticing his heart rate rising sharply, and he knew that he was out of control.

His rifle lay across his knees, and he leaned over it. His face had broken into a cold sweat. He had never been outshot in combat; had never succumbed at the epicenter of a hidden market bomb. He had avoided many kinds of mortal threats, even the occasional spec ops care packages of heroin and violent sex. The only danger he had ever succumbed to was his own identity, and this had caused the murder of soldiers and friends. Now he could hear nothing, could only see the lost cuneiform writing on stone in the black drizzle of the polluted jungle again. He swept the perspiration from his cheeks and forehead, stood up, and walked to the window, peering out across a small garden of sunflowers at the side of the house, their flower-heads lifting up toward the thunderous dawn sky.

He heard footsteps behind him, and looked over his shoulder to see Jacobits on the staircase.

"Cullen, get back down here. Feed the old guy and let's get back to work."

"Colonel, sir, we need to talk. If he knows who I am, whether he's a bad guy or a not-so-good guy, I'm a liability to you now. My participation puts everyone in danger. I would like to be excused from the op, sir. *Haji* doesn't need to know that there's another Cullen out here just asking to be kidnapped. They might send more AQIM and we'd never get Hank and Kate back."

Jacobits stood evenly, balanced like an infantryman ready to spring. He held his rifle in his left hand, and the muscles in his forearm were tensed. He said slowly, "I've been trying to peg you, Cullen, but I can't."

Ben put his hands around the barrel of his own rifle, his fingers winding over the metal like broken roots. "Colonel, I'm afraid I will get us all killed."

"Holy crap, Cullen, did you really believe we would co-opt you into this just because you have a good reputation?"

"Sir?"

"I know a thing or two about constructing ops, Major. You are not here in spite of the fact you are a Cullen brother, you are here because of it."

And though there was no mirror in the room, Ben could see himself, every pore of his face, peering back into infinity. His muscles burned with adrenaline. He heard the static crackle of the radio in the room below, and where he stood by the window he smelled the spring morning air swell up for a hard, sharp rain. He, too, had been caught unaware by his own vanity.

"Why don't you tell me the truth then, Colonel."

"That is the truth. We all know they didn't lift your brother for the money. AQIM is onto something, but we can't get close enough to 'em to figure out what they're doing. Serge is here because *Cristina* thinks they will come for you. Our op is to take them, Leila Hosni and her team, and find out what the friggin' heck they are up to. You, son, are the bait."

"Where is my father?"

"Jim Cullen is on lock down in the U. S. of A. where he belongs."

"And my mother?"

"We took care of her. She's on vacation, Major. She's underneath the safest mountain in the world in the Colorado front range."

"So I'm your decoy?"

Jacobits nodded.

"What about Kate? What about rescuing my brother?"

The Colonel glanced away from him to the floor. He could feel the EPI quake hitting his muscles, the surge of epinephrine through his blood at the recognition of his own personal fear. He said to Ben, "You know as well as I do that the chance of them being alive at this point is minimal. Your father knows that, and so does the Ambassador. Now, even the President has been briefed on that."

"They might keep Kate alive for the intel she can give them."

Jacobits' face felt as cold as glass. He shrugged and said quietly, "Bury her deep, Cullen. And let's go find *haji*."

"What about Morel? Maybe he's one of them."

"No. He's nothing; just a neighbor."

"Are you sure of that?"

"Hell, Major, this isn't algebra. I'm not sure of anything. No one knows who the enemy is anymore. But I believe Jacques Morel is innocuous."

Ben did not answer. He had caught the word *believe* like in a trap, wondering about heaven and sundown and the rasping songs of the birds in the nearby forest. He believed that once the previous year he had seen a ghost in the Garden of Eden; he believed he had seen ten people blinded in the desert by a grenade launcher blowing bubbles. He did not know what else he believed anymore.

"They told me you were good, Cullen. So let's see if you really are. Suck it up and get the fuck downstairs and help us."

"I don't really have a choice, do I?"

"No," said Colonel Jacobits. "You don't."

Chapter 16

BEN CULLEN CUT THE FLEX CUFFS around Morel's wrists, and handed him a plate of cold beans and potatoes.

"Is this all? I want some protein."

"*Louis Quatorze a dit 'je veux' et on a coupé sa tête,*" said Serge, and the men in the room laughed.

"Manners matter," whispered Ben to Morel. "Be smart."

"I am not afraid of you. You are just some noisy Rambo destroying our peace. You and your president and your generals are the ones without manners."

All the men looked up then, including Morel. Against the barred and blackened basement window they heard sharp pelting as the warm rain began to smack the glass and the earth around them.

Jacques Morel stopped eating and laughed. "Don't be afraid of the rain, my friends. You are soldiers, after all."

In the far corner of the humid room, Chad looked up from the radio and the Toughbook. "We really are Kate's friends, old guy."

"Don't talk about her. She is a woman of sophisticated intelligence. You are just thugs of your country. That is why she ran away from you to France, because Kate knew your American intention is to destroy everything. Even her.

"I spent my life preserving the remains of human culture, and you Americans invade us and the rest of the world, and destroy it overnight," he said fiercely. "Look what you did in Ninevah and Ur and Babylon.

Searching for weapons that didn't exist you obliterated the records of the most advanced civilizations we have ever known. You trampled their relics and all of Litchfield's excavation work; decades of his work in Iraq were lost. You are like Attila and his Huns. Thank God that Lowell and I have our research here protected by the French government. No one, not even presidents, can get into our excavations."

Ben knelt beside a crate in the ordnance room, lifting a machine gun from its bed. His hands were slicked with packing grease and dirt, and around him were scattered small piles of termite dust. He paused silently, staring at these tiny mounds against the bright white ash of the soft basement floor, and then he looked straight at Morel.

No one else had listened to the old man's words. The others were gathered around the huge survey map, and even Jacobits had stopped paying attention. Ben heard the Colonel questioning the French team members about potential helicopter landing points between Marseille and the Spanish border. Suddenly, Jacobits turned to Ben. "Put a bag over his head, will you? His droning is driving me crazy."

Ben grabbed a sheet from the corner, but stood by Morel without moving. He knew one more thing about the old Frenchman than anyone else on the team, and he began to chase this one fact to ground like prey. Ben knew now that Morel worked with Dirk Lowell, and that Lowell had known his father for decades and had immediate access to him whenever he needed funds. He knew that Lowell had long seduced his father with scientific titillations, and that Jim Cullen had bought the respect of scientists and politicians and entrepreneurs with this connection.

Ben knew that the ability to identify the enemy was mostly an illusion. Once in Basra he had discovered a family who fed their children tiny explosives in sweets that looked like gold nuggets, and sent them into the streets to explode alongside the medics who were healing American soldiers. Once he had jumped from the roof of a hut in southern Afghanistan and had showered a hot valley path with enough brass to clear it of the Taliban militants, even as they held tight to the village women. But now, slowly and deliberately, he put the sheet down and stood back from Morel.

"What excavations are those, old guy?"

This time, Jacobits turned to face them; he stood and crossed his arms over his round barrel-shaped chest.

A light thumping sound reverberated through the basement, and the old furnace began to throb beside them, spreading the fire-glow like a blacksmith's light. The old Frenchman looked up at Ben, and wheezed a little as he inhaled.

"It's very damp down here," he said. "And the *mazout* burning so close is not good for me."

"It must be damp in excavations, too," said Ben. "You're with the French government, aren't you? How is that? You must be over seventy."

The question took Morel by surprise, and he paused. "In my country we do not discard our elderly," he said.

"Neither do we," said Ben.

Jacques laughed out loud. "You are such a disciple of your government, boy, you don't even admit to the obvious truth, do you? America has discarded many generations of its elders. A people loses wisdom when it does that. Your American compatriot, Dr. Lowell, came here to work, away from your universities, because he knew they would not respect his older ways in our profession."

"That's pretty ironic, Dr. Morel," Jacobits said from across the room. He strolled over to stand beside them, leaning on the steel lining of the ordnance room doorway. "In a search for history, American universities throw out the old people."

Morel squinted at him for a moment and then suddenly smiled. "You are not so stupid after all. It takes every technique imaginable to search for the philosopher's stone. Old men and young scientists, both." He put the plate on the floor next to his feet that were still bound together. "My ankles are hurting. Do you think I am a little less dangerous now and you could un-tether me?"

"Cut the flex cuffs," Jacobits said to Ben.

"Of course," said Morel, "Dirk Lowell is a pompous fool, but we wanted him to work here because of the affluence that follows him. Our preservation project will be funded forever due to his friends,

Mrs. McNally, the fat drunken lumber heiress from Alabama, and of course, James Cullen. They give us money so they can rub shoulders with scientists, so they can pretend to know something they don't. But we are not dependent on government money, which lends a certain freedom."

Morel leaned back in the small chair and put his hands behind his head, stretching his arms and long neck until the joints cracked. "I fought for years through the French courts to claim this exquisite cave for our foundation, and eventually I prevailed. It is because of me and Lowell's rich friends that we are able to own and protect this site."

"Where is it?" asked Ben.

"Oh, it isn't far from here, just up the Rhône Valley. Less than 150 kilometers."

"What's in it?"

"My boy, you have no idea. Absolutely no idea about what the people were capable of thirty thousand years ago. You Americans think you produce great artists, but those humans were the real heroes. It is a half-mile of wall paintings underground in these caves, the most ferocious animals you could ever imagine. Gigantic snarling cats and woolly mammoths, and enormous bison fighting. In the flickering candle light it is terrifying."

Morel put his huge hands flat on his thighs, leaning forward, eyes gleaming and his breath shortening with excitement. "Everything we know is really only knowing again. That is the most important platonic thought. The art these early humans made far surpasses our art. Of course, we cannot use candlelight anymore in the cave because of the wax residue it leaves on the wall pictographs. And everyone who enters must wear a special suit and boots to protect the rock and this ancient pigment from erosion by our modern germs." He paused and put his hands over his ribs. "My chest is hurting. I must be moved from this spot. I may contract bronchitis again. Last time I was in bed for three months!" Morel grunted and coughed loudly. "Actually, I misspoke. No one is allowed to enter the cave anymore except Lowell and his workers. It was during my hospital stay, that Professor Lowell noticed rapid erosion of the site and we closed it for a twelve month period of reparation."

"Interesting," Jacobits said. "How's that working?"

"I will see at the end of the summer. Even I have not been allowed in. Every new set of human bacteria destroys a piece of the art, so I agreed to stay out until the reparations are completed. My life is very chaste, you know. I work and write and wait for a glimpse of the alchemy of history. I am hopeful that they can save our cave paintings." He smiled gently and looked up at Jacobits. "I know I'm too old to be of much use. So I play chess with my dear friend, Kate, and sometimes I sit on my porch and have a Turkish cigarette while the sun is setting. And of course, I wait."

Jacobits shook his head. "When was your last inspection?"

"I am not an inspector! What do you think? We need artistic police? Lowell and I are partners in this. You know, my friend, scientists, whether or not we want to have dinner with each other, are dedicated, and very trustworthy."

"Except the ones who worked in the Nazi camps, of course. Or the Chinese scientists in Tibet," said Jacobits.

"You do not know the people of my profession, Colonel. They are honorable and ethical, if not always pleasant. What do you know, anyway? You come at people with guns and expect them to respond politely and meekly!"

"Come on, Major," said Jacobits suddenly. "Let's get back to work. Morel, we have to tie you up again."

The Frenchman's expression fell with sudden disappointment.

"Perhaps I could help you. I'm a very good chess player."

"You can help, professor, but you still have to be tied up."

Ben sat him in a chair near the huge floor map, and bound his wrists and ankles to the metal. He lingered next to Morel for a moment, with his hand on his shoulder, like a young man caring for his grandfather. He stared at Jacobits, who watched them in the stillness.

Finally, the Colonel nodded to Ben without speaking.

"I have met Dr. Lowell," Ben said to the Frenchman. "Several times."

"I am not stupid, boy. I realize that you are James Cullen's son. Some of your mannerisms are very much like his."

"Is Lowell that old guy who was at the embassy last night?" asked Jacobits.

"Yes," said Ben.

Morel pursed his lips at the two of them. "What is it you are looking for, *mes amis?*"

"Kate, of course," said Chad. "The bad guys took her." He said this with utter commitment and innocence, after many years and nightmare memories, absolutely unafraid of believing in good people and bad people and the simple difference between them.

"Pardon me," Morel replied, "but I thought you were the bad guys."

The men in the room did not rise to it, did not even move their heads. They each could tell him stories, of oil that had turned the color of blood, or friends beside them who had melted to sinews from flames; they could define those words 'bad guys' for him without hesitation, but they didn't.

Chad looked up from the computer, and called to Marko. "I just got the satellite infrared of local movement over the last six hours. Lay it out as I call it, will you?"

He began to read the coordinates aloud, and Marko placed colored weights across the floor canvas. They watched the picture appear, random coverage spinning out towards the *etang* marsh on the coast near Marseille, across the *autoroute* to the airport, a few spots through the forest surrounding Avignon directly north, but most were clustered up through the Gard province and once there, they stopped.

"They have not left via the sea," Marko said. "We know that for certain."

"And there are a shitload of *flics* overrunning the Marseille docks now. They just took possession of the remains of the *Mihrab*," said Jacobits. "AQIM disemboweled it. Empty. Completely sanitized."

"A helicopter could take them anywhere," said Morel. "From your coloring there, it looks to me like they moved up the river valley and then flew out. Maybe they had a helicopter waiting for them. Lots of

those big yachts have landing platforms on board. I think your father
has one, doesn't he Mister Cullen?"

Ben nodded, matter-of-factly. "His ship is not in Europe, Professor."

"It used to be. I have flown with him in his helicopter over the
Rhône Valley, years ago. We flew to Chauvet together before he gave
us a single dollar. He wanted to see it."

"Are you saying my father gave his helicopter to kidnap my
brother, old man?"

"Of course not. That would be irrational. But I am pointing out
that there are hundreds of places from which to land and disembark up
that valley. Anyway, this is where I think they went. Believe me or
not," he shrugged. "C'est la vie, c'est l'amour."

"If I was in a helicopter," said Chad, "I would get the hell out of
France."

"Of course," said Morel. "One would fly straight for the Spanish
border and the ferries at Barcelona."

Chad sighed. "That's exactly what I would have done, Morel.
Straight to Spain. You have no idea."

"That's how the gangsters get to North Africa now that we have
tightened up on their drug activity at the Marseille port. Through the
Costa Brava." He spoke with such certainty, Jacobits turned to look.
Morel smiled weakly. "I read that in a Reverte novel last year."

"What if they went up the valley by the Ardèche River and then
just stayed?" asked Ben. "Maybe they're staying for the ransom."

"Or maybe they're hanging around because they can't get out,"
said Chad.

"Why would they?" asked Marko. "Wherever they go in the area
we will be able to find them."

"You know," said Ben, "when we first moved into Baghdad years
ago I was in the forward squadron. I was the first guy through the
doors of the Baghdad Museum. By then the offices had been abandoned because of all the long nights of bombing, and when we went in
I found the strangest thing. All these photos of ancient Mesopotamian
art, all these Babylonian statues and Iraqi artists, and one single poster

above the desk of the Chief Curator, of a hillside castle overlooking the Ardèche River gorge. I always remembered that. Don't you think that's weird?"

"That would be Mansour," said Morel. "He studied under me for a few years. I took him to the caves at Alta Mira and Chauvet. I used to tell him what I thought we might find one day under the sea at Cosquer, and he always thought I was an old fool. Although now he is the fool, because we have found amazing art at Cosquer."

"A helicopter could not have gotten across the southern air space without us knowing," said Alain. "Any helicopter they have would not have made it into Spain."

Morel stared at the cluster of weights laying across the Gard province. He looked again and again at the path up the river valley, as though he were stroking an ancient bone in the sand.

"You can land on the meadow over there at Pont St. Esprit," he said. "I've done that before. You might land there and be lost in the Ardèche Gorges. This is a whitewater tributary. You can raft it or walk beside it."

"How deep is the canyon?" Chad asked.

"It varies. There are innumerable caves and crevices. At certain places it is seventy meters down."

Jacobits grunted loudly. "When's the last time you saw that cave you were talking about, Professor?"

"Seven months ago just before we closed it for the reparations. But they will not be near Chauvet. This is a scientific research site, with the most important artworks in Europe and we have spent millions of Euros saving them. They would not even know where it is, and even if they could find it, there is a steel door enforced with the highest electronic security. Lowell has seen to it that no one gets in."

"I still think we should take a look at it," said Jacobits.

"You will be wasting important time, Colonel. There are dozens of caves in the area. Why would you go to the one you can't get into? This is not logical. Can't you see that?"

Jacobits shrugged. "Gut feeling. Sometimes you can learn as much from instinct as you can from facts, Professor."

"Dirk Lowell would never allow the desecration of Chauvet."

"He may not have had a choice. Your precious cave may just be the roof of hell now, my friend."

Chapter 17

CHAD STARED AT Lieutenant Colonel Jacobits a moment and turned back to his computer. He was leaning over the screen, rocking back and forth on the old drafting stool, one hand tapping tremulously on the table beside him.

"There's something coming through from the embassy," he said. "It's a huge file." He pulled his knife from its Velcro flaps on his waist, and lifted the notched Recondo in the air. He took a soft flannel cloth and lay it across the short silver blade, wiping the shine back into the metal. "Taking a while," he said, still staring at the display.

"Let it run," said Jacobits. "We need to get our gear packed up and head out for the caves. Morel, we will accept your assistance as a navigator."

The Frenchman shrugged. "I suppose you'll kill me if I refuse to be a part of this."

Jacobits smiled at him. "That may be in the novels you read, but we don't do that kind of thing. If you refuse, which I hope you don't, we would just leave you here in the basement tied up."

"That would kill me all the same, Colonel."

"Sir, it's a film. The Ambassador's office says it's a new proof of life, with Kate."

Ben moved quickly to Chad's side, and was followed by the others.

"What is it?" called out Morel from his chair, but the team was already focused on the Toughbook, as darkened images began to appear.

The faces of Hank and Kate glowed out from the dim, uneven light on the display. White electric lights in wire cages were drilled into the walls beside them, illuminating the dirt and sweat on their skin.

Kate began to speak immediately, but suddenly Chad clicked the pause button and stared at her, frozen before them. One eye was swollen shut and blood had crusted around her mouth and nose. She and Hank knelt beneath a low overhang of an uneven wall, their hands tied behind them. Hank's face had not been harmed.

Chad inhaled sharply and said, "Okay. Seen enough of that?"

"Go on," said Jacobits. "Play it."

The camera zoomed to a newspaper propped against Kate. The *International New York Times,* dated that day, Saturday, April 20. She resumed speaking, reminding the American government of the deadline for the ransom delivery.

"Pause it again," Alain said abruptly. "What's on the wall there?"

Across the dark overhang above her head was a curved black line rounding over a hump in the wall that extended down to where the lights were attached.

"It's a drawing," said Marko.

"Yes, it is," replied Jacobits. He strode over to Morel and untied him. He took him by the shoulder and pulled him to the computer.

"There," he said. "Tell me where that is."

Morel stared at the screen without speaking. Finally, he said, "Play it from the beginning, please."

"You won't like it, old man," said Chad.

"Please play it."

Chad rewound the film and let it stream again, through the harm that had come to Kate, until Morel asked him to pause it.

"Right there," he said. "Stop on this frame, please." He looked closer at the small computer screen. "Can you make that bigger?" He put his finger on an indentation in the dirt next to the newspaper. As it swelled to fill the screen, Morel whispered, "*Ah, ce n'est pas possible...*"

"What?"

"This is Chauvet. The final chamber of the cave."

"How do you know?" asked Ben.

"This footprint. I have studied that footprint and measured it and thought about it for ten years. It is twenty-six thousand years old; because of its length and width, we have deduced that it is the footprint of an eight-year-old boy from twenty-six thousand years ago. He was in the cave and left his prints going only in one direction, actually going in the wrong direction, from the back of the cave to the front. For ten years I have thought about this, and wondered how he got to the back of the cave without leaving marks, and what happened to him after. There's nothing else like it in the world that we know of."

He stopped speaking, and put his huge hands in his pockets as though to hide them. "They drilled into those walls for the lights. They put holes in those paintings. It is like putting your elbow through a Picasso." Suddenly, Morel stopped speaking. "How did they do this? Why do they have Kate?" He leaned forward, his shoulders sinking to his chest. "Where is Professor Lowell?"

"Okay, Chad," Jacobits said, "map it now. Everyone else, pull your shit together pronto. We're outta here in fifteen."

"Traveling in daylight, Sir?" asked Ben.

"Yes, traveling in daylight. We have to get to the site and calculate our assault. We launch at dusk. Kate and your brother could be dead if we wait till dark."

"I will accompany you," Morel said. "I will do whatever I can."

Jacobits touched him lightly on the sleeve. "I know, Professor. We're all in it now for the same reason."

***

Hank lay on the floor of the cave, his head in the dirt, staring into the darkness at what seemed to be an animal footprint six inches from his face. He and Kate had been dragged from the forward portion of the cave through a low, narrow connecting channel, to the back. They had been dumped and chained in the very last chamber, and their captors had turned off the lights near them.

Hank's ankles and legs were bound together, and he was staked by this same chain to a steel pole in the ground. He could hear distant, rhythmic pounding, could feel it vibrating the thick walls like an old heart reaching for life.

Suddenly, a new harsher noise rang through the low cavern where they lay, hissing and turning to thunder like the sound of an invisible swarm of cicadas rising.

"Dear God," he whispered, "what are they doing now?"

"Drilling," said Kate. "It's nothing. It's just the reverberation because we're in a closed space. Don't worry about noise. Worry about the absence of noise."

"Do you have any broken bones?" he asked.

"I don't know. Maybe a cracked rib. It's a little hard to breathe now."

"Do you think you can still get us out of here?"

"If you help and if I don't miss anything."

"Look at this," said Hank. He put his finger into the soil in the center of the footprint. "It's an animal track of some kind."

"It's a wolf track," said Kate.

"How do you know?"

"Because I know where we are. It's a wolf print from thirty thousand years ago."

Hank looked at her like she was crazy. "Don't be ridiculous," he said. "It looks fresh."

"It looks that way, because no one has touched it for thousands of years, until now when you stuck your finger in it."

A faint amber light spread out from the forward cavern, scattering dimly through the narrow crawl tunnel between the two sections of the cave. Over their heads near the ceiling was the black outline of a bison, almost skeletal, so fragile and starving from a time when the ice expanding across the earth had destroyed all food sources.

"Do you think they'll torture me, too?"

Kate sat with her back against the warm slope of the wall. She did not answer him, and continued breathing, shallow and slow with evident difficulty.

"Do you think they'll torture me?" he asked again. He moved closer to her, sitting up gradually and leaning against her. "As long as we're stuck here together, you might as well talk to me."

"I'm trying to think."

"Maybe I can help you," he whispered and put his head close to hers.

"Cullen, just keep your mouth shut for a while."

He scowled at her, and then slowly, a look of utter amazement spread across his face.

"I know you, don't I?" he asked. "What's your name?" He could only see the outline of her hair and face as the dim light smeared across their small cell. "This feels like a dream," he whispered. "Who are you?" he whispered again, but Kate had leaned forward and was peering at the paintings she could make out on the ceiling, horses and bison in deep black outlines, animals that seemed to move with the shadows and the flicker of the light.

"Look up there," she said. "The lines on those paintings are broken."

"So?"

"Look, the back of that bull starts over there, and then there's a slight gap, and then it finishes on the round of the wall. Some of the animal bodies look as though they've been broken. They didn't used to be that way. I've seen the photographs from when they first discovered this place, and the lines were smooth. They were perfect."

"What the hell difference does that make?"

"Why would the walls of the cave shift?"

"Earthquake probably."

"In the last few years? Not likely." Kate's ankles and arms were chained to the same steel pole, and she twisted her body over the top to lever herself as high as possible. As she did, a wound was exposed, a gash stretching along her arm from her wrist to her elbow, and he noticed that the blood began to seep afresh from the crust.

"You better stop," he said. "You're bleeding again."

She was hunched against the low ceiling now, and she brushed her shoulder across the ridge where the cave paintings were broken. Warm dust fell from the rock, and Kate continued to stare at the ruined drawings. "Maybe they dislodged the rock walls with their drilling."

"So now we have to worry about a cave-in, too?"

"People believe there was another entrance back here that closed up during an avalanche in the Ice Age. That's the theory for why the footprints and tracks are all going toward the other entrance and none are pointed into the rear of the cave where we are. If Hosni and her team caused the walls of the cave to shift enough to make these changes in the paintings, maybe we can locate this other entrance shaft."

"How do you know so much about this place? Where the hell are we?"

"We're in Chauvet Cave."

"Chauvet? No, don't be ridiculous. We're not in Chauvet."

"You've heard of it?"

"Of course. Our family foundation has poured money into it for years. We are definitely not in Chauvet. They don't let anybody in there."

The humming from the front half of the cave stopped, and Hank closed his eyes for a moment. When he opened them again, Kate saw that he had begun to cry quietly. He put his chin onto his chest and whispered, "If that's the best you can do, we might as well give up. You're chained so tight you can't even stand up. How the hell do you think we can look for an opening like this?" He wiped his face against his shirt. "Stupid bitch."

Calmly, Kate said, "Do you still rock climb?"

"How do you know I rock climb?" Hank gaped at her, his eyes burning. "Who are you?" She didn't answer, and he began coughing from inhaling the dusty damp air around them.

Abruptly, he turned to look at her and began to shout. "Why don't you do something? Do you expect me to get us free? Here," he swung his body around and kicked hard at the steel stake between them, and the dust scattered even more.

"Keep your voice down. Don't bring them back here or they probably will take you for interrogation. We met each other a long time ago, and it doesn't matter now. I may need you to get up the shaft on your own. When I get us free from the chains, I'm not sure I can climb out. You may have to go and get help."

Suddenly a flash of light broke the darkness, and the rock walls began to crackle around them. Kate and Hank turned to look at the low passageway toward the sound.

Kate shouted, "Bury your head!" and they both huddled together with their faces in the dirt, their bodies lodged up against the cavern wall.

The ground began to shift, and sharp thunder resounded again and again off the granite walls around them. They heard the shatter of rocks crumbling and falling from the ceiling, and the dust rose up like fog.

•

Leila Hosni lifted her head and glanced around the Brunel Chamber. Slowly, she pulled her knees to her chest, black denim to black cotton, and pressed her arms to help her stand. Her black, curly hair was covered with dust from the cave-in, and her huge copper eyes were bloodshot and tired.

"Ali!" she called out, but a field of razor-wire lay between them. "Ali, come!"

The loping, steady figure approached her, then knelt beneath the dust from the debris.

"Yes," he scowled in raspy Arabic. "I am here. Where is Lowell?"

"Who cares where Lowell is?" she asked. "Where are the others? Where is Cullen?"

He watched her for an instant, so close to her beneath the burning air. "Magdy was in the small room. There are boulders all around him now and he does not answer me anymore. I think we may have lost him. Three others are caught in the room of hands, and one is outside. The man and woman, I don't know. Should I go for them?"

The shadows of the cave, of the world, swung to a stop, holding the ceiling down upon them.

"Get Cullen. Kill the girl."

"And your scientist?"

As the darkness began to clear, she whistled softly between her teeth. She cocked her head to one side, feeling the light shedding itself.

"Really, Ali? Kill him, too. We are finished here, and our job now is to return Cullen safely to his people. Then we can go home."

•

After a few moments, the noise abated, and Kate lifted her head. The cave was pitch black, but the dust had not settled and she could feel the particles in her mouth as she tried to inhale.

"It's okay," she said. "It's over."

Kate and Cullen lay inert for many minutes. She kept her head in the dirt, afraid to move. The entire left side of her face ached and stung, and she wondered now if their captors had cracked her jaw during the interrogation. The open wound on her arm throbbed, and she still had great difficulty breathing.

"Cullen?" she asked quietly, but he did not answer.

The stake between them had been dislodged by the rock-fall, but her hands were still chained to it. She rolled gently to one side to nudge him awake, and finally she heard him groan and saw that his body moved as he drew breath.

"Cullen," she said again. "Can you move?"

"Yeah." He began to shift himself to sit up, and she stopped him. "What the fuck happened?" he asked.

"No idea." She closed her eyes and thought of lying in a clean, cool hospital bed, her body washed of blood and dirt, with sunlight from some window skidding across her, pouring over her, swallowing her in easy warmth, until she heard him call her name like a child waiting for instruction.

She opened her eyes.

"Oh my God, were you fucking asleep?" he asked.

"No. I think I might have been trying to die."

"What?"

"Your mind reacts to overload that way. Sometimes it's just easier to let go." She sat up slowly. Her ribs felt like a brittle basket when she moved, but the sharp pain from before had softened to ache. "I'm going to stand up," she said. "We're still attached by this chain, but the pole broke out of the ground in the explosion. We can move now, but we have to do it together."

Hank nodded at her, and shifted his body forward. The chamber had been sealed into absolute blackness.

"Be careful when you stand. It's possible that things will not be in the same place as before."

"Are we going to run out of oxygen?" he asked.

"No, this space isn't closed that airtight. It was just a cave in. You can't do all the drilling they were doing and not dislodge some of the foundation seams. You know, I'm sure there is another opening somewhere back here. This whole cave is five hundred yards long, but it used to be two separate caves. That crawl space they pushed us through was the division. People believe that two different civilizations lived in here thousands of years apart, and that they came in through different entrances. The back wall here is calcite, like a crystallized door that came down suddenly in the Ice Age covering the older entrance, totally different from the granite at the front."

"This sounds like a damned fairy tale," he muttered, but followed her, moving slowly through the heavy, dust-filled darkness. They stood and stretched to test the limitations of the new ceiling, and lifted their arms together to locate any dislodged boulders that they could use to break free.

"It's just as dark with my eyes open as closed," said Hank. "This is impossible. We'll never get out of here."

The shackles at Kate's wrists still bound her to the dangling pole that chained her close to him. She stood quietly for a moment to focus. As though a current had worn away her will, she began to smell the musty San Diego bedroom again when he had entered uninvited and buried her naked, forced her face-down against the raw silk bedspread.

"I have to stop," he said. "I can't breathe!" His panic spilled out suddenly in a babble of high-pitched words. "I can't see anything, I can't see you or anything. How do I know if I'm even alive?"

"And how does that feel, Hank," she whispered abruptly, "wondering if you are dead from fear? Now do you remember who I am?" The timber of her voice sank deep like a growl, and he lurched back until the chains that bound them together stopped him. "We are not dead. We are only blind," she said. "If you want to get out of here, do what I tell you."

She heard the metal between them move, the chain links trembling against themselves as he shook.

"First, we have to work together to find a loose rock heavy enough to break the chains on our wrists. When we're free, we need to find the weakness in the walls that will lead us to the passage out. And we have to do this all fast, before they are able to open the passage again and come back here to get us."

"But we have no light."

"We don't need light. Light will suck the oxygen. Work with the tools available. We can hear and we can feel; it's easier without the light."

Together, they inched their way around the perimeter of the space, lifting their hands simultaneously to reach for the ceiling. A few times Hank grabbed at the air as though for an object.

"I keep seeing a rock in front of me."

"No, that's just hallucination. Your brain will show you light where there is none. Next you will see a shower of colors like fireworks, but that will be a hallucination, too."

"I thought your eyes were supposed to get accustomed to the dark so that you can at least see shapes."

"Not if there is no light to begin with," said Kate. "Come on, we have to keep going. We have to find a rock to hammer the chains."

"This place is made of calcite," he said. "You said that yourself. Calcite will crumble."

"There's also granite in these canyons. That's what we're looking for. A hunk of granite that was blown loose. With any luck, Leila Hosni and her bunch were only able to get Algerian chain. It's made from old steel that came from the Soviet Union and is a lot softer."

"I need to rest. I can't hold my arm up anymore."

They sat on the dirt and leaned back against the wall. The ground was suddenly cool and dry, and where they huddled it was easier to breathe, as though the air had cleared of the thick dust from the explosion.

"Are you cold?" Kate asked.

"Yeah."

"Me, too. That's odd. It's warm on the other side, but it's cold over here." She began to touch the uneven walls with her arms, leaning into the cool crevices. Gradually the darkness began to loosen, as though a sponge were soaking it up. A subtle smudge of grey spread above them, and Kate realized that somewhere light had penetrated.

"Look at this," she whispered. "This rock behind us is crystallized. That's why it's cold. Over here we are out of the main part of the cave. Stand up," she said. "Quick."

She looked above and could make out an open shaft in the ceiling, a slant of shuddering grey light that fell upon them.

"We need to get up there somehow. Can you climb?"

"I think so." He rolled to the side to reveal to her a small boulder he had been leaning against. "This could crack the chains, I think. Let me try." Hank put his hands on the rock and tried to lift it. "Put your wrists on the stone there as far apart as you can. I'll smash this down between your hands and hit the chain."

Kate stared at him. He had suggested such a simple action, an ancient action of hammering rocks on the ground, but she knew if he missed, if he broke her wrist bones, she would be unable to escape and would die in the cave.

She had no faith in him, or in anything. As a child in catechism, she had never really understood the point of faith. Courage, to her, was only a chemical, and her entire adult reality had been about survival. She could barely see his eyes now but remembered them from so many years ago to be pale and wary. She continued looking at the muted grey shadow that she identified as his body and face, and the light between them was so faint, a thin frost of dust covering them both like grace. She knew he was waiting for her.

It happened so quickly she could not account for it. Slowly she found herself nodding to him. She put her hands on a hunk of granite that lay on the cool ground, spread them wide and waited for him to pound the chain.

Hank knelt on the dirt and lifted the granite in the air. The chain connecting them to the pole was two feet long on each side. He knew he could only get the rock as high as his shoulders, and would not have the force of his body behind his movement.

"Are you ready?" he asked.

"Go ahead."

He brought the rock down on the chain, groaning as it hit the stone slab of the cave floor. He moved it aside to see barely an indentation on the metal.

"This is never going to work," he said. "I can't get high enough to slam it."

"Do it again. Keep going."

He lifted the rock, straining to take it higher. This time he felt his back and stomach contract, and he pounded the granite onto the metal. He repeated this many times, grunting and exhaling as he flung his body down with the rock, and each time the crash of the granite to metal created an echo of sound against the walls.

Harsh thunder reverberated around them, for five minutes, for ten, and finally Hank stopped and lay on the ground. "I have to rest. I'm exhausted. For fuck's sake, if we do break free we don't even know if we can get out of here. I could be using up all the oxygen we have."

"We do know, Cullen. Haven't you heard the sound coming back to us? This place is bigger and higher than we can see. If you can break this chain, I can get us out of here. Keep going. You're almost done."

Kate looked away from him and closed her eyes. He sat up and shifted to his knees, lifting the boulder as high as he could to pound it across the chain. He was sweating the last moisture from his body, wondering if he might ever again find water to drink. He struck the metal a few more times and saw the chain split. He struck it again and again and it cracked in half.

"There," he whispered. "We're free."

She leaned back, at last out of the radius that had held them together.

"Now what?" he asked. "Will they come looking for us?"

"Probably, when they finish digging out themselves."

He moved toward her until he stood not more than a foot away.

"I do know who you are," he whispered.

Quietly, she said, "We need to break the pole off your chain so that you can climb out first." She took the granite in her hands. "Spread your arms apart."

"How do I know you won't try to kill me?"

"My job is to get you to the embassy in Paris. If you want out of here, you better let me do this."

Reluctantly, he put his hands on the cave floor. As she lifted the rock high over her head, the entire left side of her body seared with pain. She took one deep breath and slammed down with all her force. She repeated this many more times until the metal cracked and separated. Kate fell back against the cavern floor panting, with her arms closing around her ribs to stop the sharp, hot throbbing.

"Climb up that shaft," she whispered. "See how high it is. If I can make it out after you, I will. But if it's too hard a climb, you'll have to go out on your own and get help."

Cullen nodded and edged his way along the small, cool bay of rock where Kate lay. The light was so faint, that he ran his hands up and down the walls, touching for crevices and ledges, for a space where he could fit his hands and feet to begin his climb. He moved to the back of the calcite chamber, and shimmied into a narrow space that had been protected in the explosion.

"I think I can get up here," he said, "and the cleft is so tight that the rock behind will stabilize my climb."

As he looked up the rock face, the shadow of a natural foothold about three feet off the floor appeared to him, and he climbed into it, using the wall as leverage. He lifted the rest of his body up, searching with his fingers for the next staging ledge.

He found indentations for both hands, and climbed again, still able to use the crevice wall behind him as support. He had moved about six feet up the shaft when he suddenly understood that he was using a ladder of crannies built by the people who had come before. He leaned back and rested, wondering whether he should bother to tell Kate. Instead, he continued quickly to the top of the cavern, where he scrambled at last onto a high deep ledge that stretched to a small plateau.

"Cullen, are you okay?" Kate called out, but he did not answer her. He had collapsed onto the ground, and was staring in amazement.

Before him lay another cave, bursting with splinters of purple light emanating from the far end. The chamber was at least two hundred feet tall, and parts of the floor had given way to deep canyons. Between his ledge and the daylight were immense crystal formations, white swords of translucent selenite shooting from the cavern walls, some as long as twenty feet and as thick as three feet in diameter. Among these prisms grew huge geodes of amethyst, bubbles undulating from the rock walls and floor like boiling water.

Hank lay on his stomach, gazing at the pale cathedral, warmed as though by an invisible mauve sun, unable to speak.

"Cullen?"

"I'm here," he called back. "I made it up."

The cave floor sloped upward toward a breach in the rock at the far end that was the source of the daylight. He stood and walked forward across the cave toward the opening. Deep fissures in the ground were everywhere. None was large enough to swallow a man, but as he moved through them, the heat intensified. The earth at his feet was newly split in places, and jagged cracks had appeared.

He had been climbing for many years, and knew enough about geological volatility, natural or manmade, to realize that the explosions deep in the ancient caverns had changed the pressure within the rock layers. Heat was radiating from this, and would intensify to the point that it would eventually escape, or it would bake alive whatever organisms were in the cavern.

When he reached the far end, he knelt in the soft soil in front of the narrow window of daylight. The granite of the ancient gorge-face had been split open at a weak point, a dark mouth that had been sealed millennia before by a rock fall. In the center, a three foot high slice of the outside world appeared to him, cut fresh through the thick layer of moraine that had tumbled shut when the glacial ice destroyed all life in its path.

Hank pushed himself headfirst through the jagged lips of granite. He slumped to the damp forest floor and looked up to the tree canopy to see the morning light glistening behind a soft, spring mist. He jumped to his feet and walked to the edge of the cliff to look down into the ravine. He sank deep to his ankles into the sponge of decomposed vegetation, and pulled his feet from the sucking, sticky earth to stand on a precipice of stone overlooking the river.

He knew he was dehydrated and needed water, and though he was unsure of his location, he believed the river was likely to take him out of the forest to a village or town. He stepped back from the cliff, and made his way through the dark, knotted oak branches, until he came to an animal trail that led down the hill. He paused at the trailhead, glanced back briefly at the breach in the rock where he had escaped, and turned to jog quickly down to the water.

Chapter 18

"CULLEN?" KATE CALLED OUT again. She rolled onto her hands and knees and pushed herself to a standing position. She pulled one arm tightly around her ribcage, forcing the pain to numbness with the pressure. After several minutes, she began to realize that he had left her behind. She stumbled to where he had begun his climb, and found the foothold he had used.

She concentrated on regulating her breathing, and began climbing with her eyes closed. She reached for the wall, and each time she found the footholds, she engaged every muscle in her body and with pure will, rose up to each new level. The sweat poured off her face, but she focused inward, executing the climb and attempting to separate her mind from the excruciating sensory data coming from her body. She made no sounds as she ascended the wall, and when at last she reached the summit, she collapsed hard onto the ledge, breathing heavily with her eyes still closed.

She lay there for several seconds until she began to hear a subtle hissing sound, like a small trapped animal. She opened her eyes and looked across the cavern to the magical purple light casting up through the frosted selenite prisms. She could feel the heat rising around her, and pushed herself to a standing position. Across the floor in front of her, steam was spitting up from the new cracks in the earth.

Kate took a few steps out onto the plateau, and felt the temperature increasing the farther she went. She understood that the heat intensifying and pushing up through the cracks signaled growing pressure. She began to run, hurling herself up the sloping cavern floor towards the slant of light at the far end. She heard the pounding of her own boots, but as she moved out across the cave, the noise began to muffle from the spongy ground as the floor liquefied around her.

Grabbing her side from the pain, she could not fill her lungs with air. When at last she reached the cave opening, she fell to the soft, warm clay, staring at the daylight. She leaned over quickly to climb through the slit, putting her hands on either side of the rock lips, and as she did she cried out loud from the jab of her broken ribs.

She tried to lever herself into the opening, but because of the pain she could not force her head and shoulders through the split. She lay back on the cave floor, resting for a few seconds, and then reached up to the sharp granite again. She pulled at the rock, using her arms to inch herself partway through the hole. At last her head pushed into the daylight and the damp forest air.

She squeezed her arms through the opening and grabbed the rock above her head with both hands. She pulled again in one intense muscle contraction, and swung her legs up to use the rocking action as leverage. She felt the heat like an open furnace billowing around her legs inside the cave, and she rocked herself up again and pulled as hard as she could. Slowly, she brought her chest out into the daylight, and lodged her boots on the inner lip, pushing with her quadriceps to move her torso through the cave opening. At last, she inched free, and dropped to the rusty iron-rich soil of the forest.

For many moments she could not move. She could still hear the steam hissing through the rock opening, but now she also heard the frantic sound of a songbird in a nearby tree. She lay with her eyes closed, her sweat forming a sudden layer of cold around her. She began to tremble, and tried to open her eyes.

"I need to get away from here," she heard herself say aloud, but even her own sound was muffled and hollow. She had no energy to move and stared up into the tree canopy, confused.

She tried to remember where she was, and why, and thought about lifting her head for a better look, but decided it would require too much effort. Then, she understood that she was drifting into shock, and she bit down on her lip, hard enough to draw blood, in order to pull her focus back again.

She stood up slowly. She was in the middle of an oak wood, and through the trees she could see the white limestone face of the gorge across the Ardèche River, glowing smooth as oil. The cool, damp air began to awaken her from the shock, and she knew she desperately needed water to drink. Her first thought was to attempt the trek to the river, but the pain was so strong she did not believe she would be able to make the climb down the gorge.

She walked through the stubby oak trees to look out at the water, down to the canyon floor three hundred feet below. The opposite wall fell away in a sharp, sheer drop to the river, and on her own side, a single dirt goat trail led through the scrub and oaks descending in a series of uneven switchbacks. Above her, the cliff rose another two hundred feet with no discernible path.

She began to waver unsteadily. She fell to her hands and knees and crawled back into the trees, far into the deep shadows. She collapsed against the trunk of an ancient oak, cloistered from the wind and the sunlight by the heavy, low branches. She noticed a bee-eater on the bark above her head, its slender scarlet throat suspended taut as it perched in wait. She put her fingertips out to touch it as it turned to face her, but she could not reach it, and the bird glanced away from her. She closed her eyes.

Chapter 19

"THERE'S AN OLD ROMAN ROAD raised above the middle of the marsh beside the train track leading north from here," said Jacobits. "It's five clicks to the outskirts of St. Just, and from there Chad can drive us up onto the plateau just above Chauvet. We can't get any farther in with the Iris, so we'll pull it down the ravine. Our primary goal is the rescue, but our Commander-in-Chief also requests that we keep Miss Hosni and her friends alive and get them back for interrogating. Any questions?"

Marko stepped aside from the others and climbed quietly into the back of the Desert Iris strike vehicle.

"Okay, time hack," Jacobits called out to the men. "Chad, count it down."

Marko remained in the Iris, watching himself in a small mirror that he had affixed to the back of the driver's head rest. He had dampened his face and skull with water from his thermos, and now took a silver-blue blade to his jawbone. He began to peel the stubble away from his face, scraping it clean.

"Marko," Jacobits called out. "Get with us. Check your watch."

Marko ignored him, and reached his arm back over his head with the razor. He drew it forward across his scalp again and again as the light blonde tufts of his hair fell to the floor of the truck, and then he pulled it across his heavy brow-bones, until his entire skull was as smooth as satin. He packed his razor and the mirror in his kit, and squatted in the sunlight at the edge of the truck bed. Finally, he nodded at the others, pulled his sleeve back and looked at the second hand on his watch as Chad counted back to zero.

"Let's get a move on," said Jacobits.

Chad jumped behind the steering wheel of the Iris, and waited. Ben, Morel and Alain climbed in the back and dug into their gear, but Jacobits remained outside staring at Marko.

"I get the feeling you slipped off the bus," he said slowly. "What's going on?"

"Don't worry about me, Colonel," Marko replied. "I am *aitz-kor* of your team. Do you know what that means?"

"No, I don't," said Jacobits.

"It means I am your weapon. We have lost a few people together, Colonel, but this woman saved my life. I am beholden to her."

"I understand. We all owe her one thing or another."

"In my country we call this *mendekio*."

"Vendetta?"

"Correct."

Jacobits nodded, and then suddenly asked, "Do you even have a country anymore?"

"No, Colonel. I do not. That is why *mendekio* is important."

The sound of the engine began to grind around them, and they both moved to their places.

Before them the marsh extended to the edge of the forest, with the Ardèche Gorge rising to the left, and above these sheer cliffs, pristine white clouds were suspended against a soft, robin's egg blue sky. Once they reached the causeway, the vehicle continued to roll forward but began to churn heavily from side to side.

"What's going on up there?" Jacobits shouted.

"Can't help it, Colonel. The road is covered with craters and hunks of twisted metal."

"What the fuck? Have they mined it?"

"No," answered Marko. "Only the good roads are mined, and they would have disguised their holes. This simply means they have used this road well."

Jacobits leaned over the back, and saw a stream of oil seeping into the patchy weeds and dirt across the path.

"There's oil back here. Check the gauge," he shouted to Chad and Marko.

"We're intact. That oil stretches for half a mile. It looks like this has been used pretty recently."

"Is it passable?"

"Anything's passable in a Desert Iris," said Chad. "Just hang on." They rocked hard over the terrain, descending into the center of each deep hole and climbing out again, easily and powerfully as Chad applied slight pressure to the accelerator. Before the new suburbs of St. Just, their path petered out into a farmer's field of grapevine rows surrounded by a perimeter of fruit trees. Here, they broke off to the west down a muddy farm track until they reached the sloping mountain road up the back of the canyon.

They began the ascent on a pebbled trail leading into the forest. Around them was the smell of lavender and peaches, deep fertile farmland capable of bringing abundant crops century after century. Ben was watching the crisp spring sky, thinking how different the clouds were here, sugar-white and spun of pure mountain moisture instead of the grey mix of gunpowder gases and grimy rain that covered the desert where he spent most of his days. He couldn't really remember spring in his own country, and tried to recall the last April he had spent at home. Sometimes in the silent transport to a battle, he would get a quick sensory flicker in his mind, the magnolia-lined street where he grew up on the island of Coronado, or the smell of exhaust and flowers in D.C. But mostly, the America he remembered was an old photograph of his parents at a summer barbecue, or a sentence from the Gettysburg Address that he had reluctantly memorized as a child.

They were nearing the trees now, and Chad slowed the Iris to take a hairpin turn when Jacobits suddenly lifted his rifle at the faraway sound of a human voice. He moved to the front of the vehicle, and leaned between Marko and Chad.

"Keep on," he said. "Keep going to the forest edge."

Instinctively and silently, the other men touched their weapons, checking readiness of guns and grenades without moving their eyes from the horizon. Within seconds they reached the cover of the oaks.

"Now, slow," said Jacobits, and the engine silenced to a low whine. The voice came clearer to them for a moment, a male voice calling from the forest, and then at once it stopped.

Ben jumped down from the vehicle, followed by Alain and Jacobits. They scrambled through the mud and shadows, stopping just before a clearing of sunlight. At the far edge beside a narrow animal track, lay Hank Cullen.

He lay face down, and he was pulling hard at the old trunk of a fallen oak tree, attempting to move himself across the dark soil. His legs dragged behind him over the decomposing vegetation, as he tried desperately to inch forward into the sunlight.

Ben ran to his brother and knelt beside him.

"Hank!" He put his hand firmly on his brother's arm, and looked up to scan the forest clearing.

Alain cracked open the medic pack he carried on his belt.

Hank stared at them confused, and jerked his head down to bury his face in the dirt for protection.

"Hank, it's me. It's your brother."

He raised his head gingerly to look, slowly understanding the presence of rescuers around him. "My legs! I fell into the ravine. My legs are broken."

Alain squatted beside him, and tore his blood-smeared pants open to expose his bruised legs. He began to feel his calves and thighs for fractures, and Cullen did not move or speak.

"Where is Captain Cardenas?" Jacobits asked.

"Who?"

"The agent who was captured with you. The woman."

"I'm sorry," Hank replied. "She didn't make it out. They held us in a cave and there was a cave-in. She's dead."

"No!" said Morel, and moved forward to squat beside them.

Ben put his arm out to block Morel. "What happened to your captors?"

Hank did not answer him, but spoke instead to Alain. "Can you splint my legs so I can walk?"

"I don't see any breaks." He dug his fingernails into the fleshy part of Hank Cullen's left calf, so deeply that a crease remained after he removed his hand, but Cullen did not respond. "See if you can roll over and sit up."

"I can't. I can't move."

"Try," whispered Alain. "Let me see."

"Do you think I haven't already been trying? You sadistic frog. I fell over that fucking cliff and landed in this ravine. I can't fucking move."

Ben moved his hands down the curved shaft of his brother's spine, feeling for breaks.

"We'll have to carry him out of here," he said.

"What?" shouted Cullen.

Jacobits said, "Ben and Serge, you two take Cullen and the Professor back to the Iris, plow it behind the old chapel, button it up, and wait. Alain and Chad, you come with me and Marko. And Alain, radio in to make sure that helo is ready for us down here when we need it. We'll try to wait for the dark to exfiltrate, but we may need to get outta here quicker."

"No, I'm coming with you to rescue Captain Cardenas," Ben said.

Jacobits narrowed his dark eyes, and pulled the knit cap from his head. He wiped it across his face and continued staring at Ben. "Major, you heard him. This is not a rescue. It's a recovery. You know what that means. And I need you out here, standing guard over your brother and not getting yourself shot. Rescuing one Cullen brother and losing the other would not go over well with the Ambassador or with the Pentagon."

"Colonel, to be honest, I think you need me in the cave with you. The only reason you wouldn't, is if you had started believing the Cullen family is more important than this team and our real mission."

Jacobits did not answer immediately. He put his fingers unconsciously on the stiff rose scar near his eye, stroking it hard. The others were silent, looking on at them.

Finally, the older man said quietly, "Okay, Major."

Marko stepped forward suddenly. "We're ready to go, Colonel. We need to move."

Chapter 20

KATE AWOKE IN THE EARLY EVENING with the delicate insects of
the warm forest hovering over her face. Their sound was like a human
hand tapping on a door, and she listened for a few moments, staring at
the silvery pink spring-growth leaves on the white oaks around her.
The deep forest where she lay glowed with moonlight, and she sat up.
Her dizziness had disappeared, so she stood and walked carefully to
the path. The pain in her side and face had numbed, and though she
moved slowly, it no longer hurt her to walk.

When she reached the trail, she stood quietly to adjust to the night
light before she began the descent. Two huge crows, black as ink,
squawked above her, and the new slice of moon rising in the sky shone
sugar-white through the oaks. She had no protection, neither weapons
nor armor nor goggles, but she knew her subconscious brain had
numbed the pain so she could move to save herself. This had happened
to her once before in the Caucasus, where she had been near an indus-
trial explosion that harmed her so badly she was able to walk free to
the docks at Sokhumi, but then lay paralyzed in a hospital for six
weeks after. She respected that an opportunity had been given to her
now, and she understood that she needed to find help quickly.

She walked carefully down the dirt trail, pushing the low
branches aside and keeping watch on the ground to make sure she did
not trip or fall. As the moon rose higher, it turned to yellow, and

flickered through the thick trees like candlelight. About halfway down the mountain, she thought she heard a voice in the forest, but she was in the center of the deep oaks, and she made herself ignore the sound.

As she descended her speed increased, and she became impatient and breathless. Finally, she came upon a clearing, and rested at last on a decayed tree trunk that was half eaten by age and covered with woodpecker holes. She put her head in her hands, panting heavily.

Suddenly, she heard footsteps nearby, and she dropped immediately alongside the trunk, clinging closely to it in the dim moonlight.

She did not believe the voice she heard, a male speaking in French, a voice so familiar that she knew it was a dream.

She heard the man say her name softly, and she looked up over the ravaged bark to see her old friend, Jacques Morel, coming toward her. He sat in the dirt beside her and put his arms around her shoulders. Above them hung a map of veiled stars and the moon frozen against the mountain.

"I had to sneak away from them to come find you. I knew you were not dead." Kate sank into his chest, not speaking or moving.

"Sneak from who, Jacques?"

"Your American friends, Kate. I knew you would be alive."

"I don't understand," she said, and held her hand out to him. He took it in his and stared at her, unable to control his own tears.

"We can't stay here, Jacques," she said at last. "We have to get to cover."

"Look," he whispered to her. He pulled a small, worn knapsack from his shoulders and unhooked the rusted metal clasp at the top. "I brought provisions for us. Food and water. And medicines for you." He stared at her face and said tenuously, "What did they do to you, Kate?"

Behind him she could see the shadows folding across the buttes in the moonlight; she could make out the sparkle of anger in his eyes and she nodded at him.

"Nothing that a medpac antibiotic won't fix," she said. "Let's move back into cover and see what you have."

She rolled slowly to kneel beside him, and gingerly pushed herself to a standing position. He hooked his arm under hers, and together they walked to the trees.

"Here is water," he said. "Sit and drink. I have food, too. In these little packets."

At last, Kate smiled. "I never thought I'd be grateful for an MRE," she said.

"What?"

"A military meal ready to eat."

Morel ripped open the packets and handed them to her. "Eat slowly," he said. "You are very hungry. Don't get sick."

They sat on a soft pile of mildewed leaves and undergrowth, and Kate put her head back against a tree trunk.

"I don't have a weapon. I can't protect us out here."

"But I have weapons! Look." Morel pulled a semi-automatic Heckler & Koch out of the pack and handed it to her. "And a knife just in case," he added.

"How did you get these?"

"Because I am part of the American team and they understand that I need to protect myself."

"What American team? Do you know how to use that gun?"

"No," he shrugged. "Really, I stole it from your people. They have taken over your house, a Colonel and a Basque man and others. They said you had been kidnapped, but they were not moving quickly enough." He held the Recondo knife in his brown, bony hand. "I want to get you to safety. To a hospital. And then I will go back to Chauvet. I need to find out what has happened to the research."

She took another drink from the flask he had offered her. "We are so far past that now, Jacques."

"What do you mean?"

"Do you know who these people are?" Kate put the container on the ground, wedging it slowly into the vegetation with painful force, and Morel noticed that her wrists were crusted with blood where she had been chained. "They are not common criminals. There are more cultures at stake than the ancient one in that cave. Anyway, I think they probably have destroyed Chauvet altogether by now."

"My dear Kate, please do not say that to me!"

Kate winced at the sharp sound of his voice. "Jacques, there were several explosions in the cave. There may be nothing left of it. And there's something else. There was a Western man with them. An older man who was not a soldier."

"Was he American?"

"Possibly. But he could have been English."

"Ah, that was Dirk Lowell. He's been in charge of my research project for years. They must be holding him, too."

"He wasn't a prisoner, Jacques."

"What do you mean?"

She closed her eyes for a moment. With her eyes still shut, she spoke again, hoarsely as though the very last drop of energy in her body had now been spent.

"I have a broken rib and I can hardly move. I need to hydrate before it gets any colder or I'll go into shock again. My ribs need to be taped, and I have to disinfect these wounds and get some antibiotics into my bloodstream. Can you help me? I'll tell you what to do."

"Of course. And then I will kill the people who did this to you." He reached over and ran his aged fingers gently through her hair.

"What you want to do and what we need to do are entirely different. It takes years to learn that, and more years to believe it. We can hide here while I hydrate, and then we need to get back to the team to help them find Cullen. That's the mission objective."

"We have Cullen already. But he told us you were dead."

Kate leaned her head against his shoulder. She closed her eyes again, and said, "We are way past the golden hour, Jacques, and I could pass out before you finish. If that happens, don't stop. You may save my life."

Morel had taken the med pack from his old, canvas knapsack, and he held it now between his hands, his thumb trembling over the Velcro closure.

"First, you need to do some checks. My airways are clear, but take my pulse to make sure my heart can pump the oxygenated blood around. Do you know how to check that? If I'm below one hundred I'm probably okay."

Morel nodded, and took her wrist between his fingers, counting silently by his watch.

"Now look at my circulation. Make sure my skin is not cold or cyanotic. I'm sure I've lost some blood, so there's less of it circulating. If my skin is going purple or blue you will need to act very quickly."

Morel put his hands across her face and neck, chest, and ankles.

"No, you are safe," he whispered.

"You don't have to do a neurology exam. I can focus and I definitely can feel pain, Jacques. Look in the supplies you have. There should be a dose of injectible antibiotic in there, primed already. Can you find that?"

He examined the syringes and held one up to her, reading the label out loud.

"That's it," she said. "You need to stick this in my quadricep, right into the muscle, and then discharge it slowly. The slower you do it, the less pain I'll feel."

She closed her eyes and waited for him to execute, and as the needle plunged into her flesh and the serum began to shriek through her body, she suddenly saw darkness surrounded by a baffled ghost and a silenced God and a white crane in the distant horizon.

"There," said Morel. "Are you all right, Kate?"

She did not answer his question. "Get my pulse, and then see if you can find tape in the pack." She began to slip her arms from her shirt, but jerked back sharply from the raw throbbing of her ribs. "I'm still stiff. Can you find morphine patches in the box?"

Morel opened the packet.

"Check your watch now. Wait twenty minutes and then apply that. Can I have more water?"

He put the bottle into her outstretched hand.

"Tape my ribs."

He tugged gently at her shirtsleeves, until she sat upright against the tree trunk in only a blood-spattered white bra.

His jaw slackened and he stared at her wounds without speaking.

"My bleeding has stopped. Take the tape and start just below my bra. I think the seventh rib is the one that's broken. You have to tape me as tightly as you can so I can move again without so much pain or I'll never get out of this forest."

He wound the medical tape around her body many times, still without speaking. He held her narrow shoulders and smooth belly so firmly and so gently that Kate closed her eyes.

When he had finished, the perspiration dripped from his face and he crouched alongside her, exhausted.

"Do you need more water?"

"I need an IV," she whispered. "I'm fading out. First put the morphine patch on my back, and then find the bag and line. There should be one in the med pack. You'll have to find a vein and hold the bag for a while. Can you do that?"

Without answering, he tore the patch from its paper packet and lay it across her shoulder blade. He pulled a syringe from the box, and tied a rubber tourniquet above her elbow. Morel watched for a few moments as she pumped her fist to raise a vein on her forearm. He began to stroke her arm.

"I know it's hard," she said. "I'm dehydrated now so it's even harder. Just go for the top of my hand." She turned her arm over and rested the palm of her hand on his knee. "Here, use the one below my index finger. That's the easiest."

"It will hurt you if I stick it in your hand. There is no flesh there to absorb the pain."

Kate smiled gently at her friend and said, "I'll be okay with it, Jacques. You need to get the needle in, tape it down, and snap the IV line into it. Run it wide open, that should get me about 20 cc's a minute. Can you see the gauge?"

He nodded and rubbed his index finger over the target on the top of her hand. He brought the needle to her skin and pierced quickly into it. When he was sure he had caught the vein, he taped the needle flat from her wrist to her knuckles, and attached the coiled IV line to the syringe. After, he sat next to her and held the bag high overhead.

"You'll get tired of that," she said. "Shoulder height is fine."

Morel lowered his arm. "Will you be all right now?"

"Sure," she said, and paused. "You are saving my life, you know. I wouldn't have made it much longer."

"Hank Cullen said you were already dead. He told us that you died in Chauvet in an explosion. Why would he say that?"

Kate lay her head back against the tree and for a moment it felt comfortable to her, like the familiar curve of the oak headboard of her own bed. The night had become silent in the deepening darkness, and as she closed her eyes again she imagined the stars spitting silver across the sky, bursting through the leaves over her head.

Morel watched her sleep for a few minutes, but did not close his own eyes. He forced himself to fight off his exhaustion, and he stared deep into the trees around them, scanning back and forth, again and again, to defend their position. His hand was on the gun, his bruised fingers spreading across the barrel.

He was not afraid of this forest. As a boy, he had hunted wild boar here with his father, and over the past fifty years he had hiked every trail of it searching for evidence of lost peoples, for bones or art or detritus. He knew where the Romans had fought the Vocontii Celts for this land, and where the ancient Greeks had sailed up the Rhône to the Ardèche River gorge in their search for tin. As a young researcher, he had dived naked into the river from the hot, broad beach at the Pont d'Arc, and that same summer he had made love for the first time on that beach to the young girl who later became his wife. This forest was a map to the history of his life, and although he had come infrequently to the gorge since Dirk Lowell had taken over the Chauvet research, Morel still remembered its geography like a diagram of his own ancestry.

Morel's arm had started to ache as he continued to hold the IV sack, and he shifted slightly to relax his shoulder. He could hear the toads singing in the distance by the cliff, and he felt the vibration of the crickets rising through the heavy night air from the thick patch of new-growth oak tendrils at his feet. He thought he recognized these sounds, but the toads' voices rose too sharply, and travelled toward him. The sounds rose higher above his head, spreading in a symphony of flying creatures, bats pursuing him in the damp night. Then he knew that these creatures had become human, the timber of men's voices whispering to each other in the trees far across the other side of the clearing.

Every muscle in his body tightened, and he heard his own temples pulse with pumping blood. He opened his mouth slightly, uncontrollably, and wondered why he had begun to smile. At once, he realized he was not smiling at all, but had unconsciously bared his teeth. He listened for a few more moments, and then slipped his fingers through the smooth metal groove of the butt-joint of the 45.

Suddenly, Kate opened her eyes and reached for the pistol.

"Don't," she whispered. "Wait and listen."

Five men walked into the clearing and paused in the cracked moonlight. She smelled burning tires around them, like the earth had been sown with exploded grenades, the smell of soldiers.

They were not fifteen feet from her hiding place. She knew they would see her the minute they scanned in her direction. She stared at their faces, but did not know them. She looked hard again at them, and saw only boys surveying the clearing.

A nightjar began singing above her head, loudly through the cool night as though it had escaped from its torpor suddenly and Kate swung her head around to find it.

This movement brought the men rushing for cover away from the moonlight, crouching on their knees with rifles poised.

Kate lifted the gun slowly, resting it across her arm for stability. She leveled the weapon at the head of one man. He wore a dark green battle dress uniform and a thick black balaclava mask. His face was covered with camo paint, and he was scanning the woods but did not yet see her.

He dropped his rifle slightly, and the moment she saw his eyes and his short, stocky frame, she realized it was Jacobits. She stared at each of the men until she was certain that the other four were not his captors but were her team.

She needed to move or speak to self-identify immediately, but she knew that moving or speaking might also draw fatal fire.

As the fear opened in her stomach, a charge of adrenalin surged through her bloodstream and she escaped sharply from the fog of ache and dehydration.

She took a slow, painful breath, pushing all her strength into her voice, and shouted to them the answer to one of her identifier questions. "1-9-5-2!"

The men immediately lowered their rifles.

Jacobits rushed to where she lay, and squatted beside her, smiling.

"Captain Cardenas, as I live and breathe." He smiled and put his hand on her shoulder. "We don't really need to run your ISOPREP, kiddo. I think I can still recognize you. What's the sitrep?"

"She is doing well now," replied Morel. "I brought her provisions and *medicaments*. She has broken ribs and lacerations, but her dehydration has abated."

"Thank you, Professor, but I was actually referring to the mission. Captain?"

"We were incarcerated in a cave, Sir. There was an explosion that blasted our section shut, and we found a secondary entrance."

"You did?" asked Morel. "You found the other entrance?"

Kate nodded. "Yes, Jacques. It was there all along. You were right."

He dug his brown fingers into the lichen-covered soil, his eyes opened wide in amazement.

"Cullen escaped," Kate said, "and then me. I collapsed in the trees outside of the entrance, and have no verifiable intel about Cullen or the enemy at this point."

"Alain, come check her out," said Jacobits, and the young French pilot swung his backpack over his shoulder. He opened it, and lay his medical supplies on the ground.

"We have Hank," Ben said. "He's safe." He stood behind the others, hesitant to move closer to her. He watched as Alain touched her wrists with antiseptic, and smoothed the blood crust from the long, jagged wound on her forearm. Ben's stomach was tight and knotted, like dried out cat's gut splitting from wear. He clutched the shank of his M4, and smelled the dank fruity odor of decomposing leaves and carcasses around them. It could have been a moment for him to drop a coin in the mouth of another dead colleague, but this night he knew that she had been brought back to him. In this torrent he stood without moving, solid and scared at once, staring at Kate's face and afraid to speak again that a stutter might give him away.

"If what *Cristina* believes is true, *haji* won't leave here without the Cullen boys," said Jacobits. "They are tracking through this forest somewhere coming after them and all of us, and we need to identify their coordinates before they identify ours. Our job is to take Leila Hosni alive now before she takes us. She has the best tech available, except for ours. Chad, wake 'em up at Bolling."

Chapter 21

CHAD SQUATTED BEFORE THE SCREEN, watching the drifting countries come into focus.

"They're awake, Colonel," he replied. "Look, here's Beaver Dam, Oregon."

Jacobits chuckled, "Somebody get those guys a compass."

Marko stood behind Chad. "There may only be seconds," he said. "We do not have time for humor." He pressed a wad of crumbling chewing tobacco between his thumb and forefinger, and let the flakes fall to the earth.

"You oughtta stop with the Hansel and Gretel," said Chad. "The bad guys will know we've been here. Pick that crap up, please."

Marko nodded and leaned over to grab the tobacco from the soil.

"And chill out, buddy. Are you nervous?"

"Always," Marko replied.

Chad turned back to the Toughbook. "Here it is," he whispered, and the milky satellite pictures of their forest sharpened on the screen, followed by the imagery analysis from the DIA specialists at Bolling Air Force Base and the Huntsville space operations center. "*Haji* is circling down the mountain on the goat track to where we dumped the Iris."

Jacobits smiled. "God bless the guys flying those damned UAV's."

"Alain, what's the verdict on Captain Cardenas? Can she travel?"

"The morphine is low dose by patch now, at an even pace. She is hydrated, and I will replace the tape with a rib belt to give her core stability. She will be able to walk in a few minutes."

"Of course she cannot walk," Morel said immediately. "I will stay here with her until you return. If the other group is heading down the mountain, we will be perfectly safe here."

Jacobits looked at Alain again. "Can she engage?"

"No."

"That's not the answer I wanted."

"I'm viable, Sir," said Kate.

"She has two wounds that I will need to staple, and she needs hospitalization." Alain lifted her shirt from her body and began to cut the tape away. When he had finished, her torso lay entirely exposed, wounds smeared with blood and dirt and small, circular burns, pock marking deep into the flesh on her stomach and breasts.

Jacobits took a long, deep breath. He leaned over and waved away a fly that hovered on her face.

Ben's face was hidden in the dark, but she watched for him, suddenly wishing for mercy for all of them as her trigger finger began stirring against the earth.

"So, Professor," Jacobits said, "I need you to show us the absolute quickest way down this mountain to our vehicle. We need to get to the Iris before Leila does."

"That would be jumping off the cliff," Morel replied. "I have done it several times. Do you have rope with you?"

Jacobits nodded. "Of course. We're in the mountains, aren't we?"

"Well then, the best place to launch would be about five minutes from here."

"Take us there," Chad said, packing up the mobile comms. "Let's go."

Marko bent forward to Kate, offering his arms to lift her.

"I think I'm okay," she said.

"No, you're not," said Ben suddenly. "You are not okay." He stepped forward and between the two men, they helped her stand.

Once at the cliff, Morel squatted low near the edge, feeling through the damp vegetation with his fingers.

"We have always used the spruces here to anchor. The mountain rescue team checks them regularly." He pulled a large white blossom from the soil at the broad base of one of the trees and held it up. The flower glowed like dogwood, translucent and dripping with moonlight. "Just here," he said to Chad, "If you anchor at this tree we will land very close to where we left the vehicle."

Chad squatted in the tangled hillside brush, and pulled equipment from his backpack. He tied nylon webbing to the tree as an anchor for the rope, and slipped a harness over his pants. He clipped a cara-biner to the webbing, and pushed the rope through the belay tube. The friction from this device would allow him to control the speed of his descent. He put on heavy leather gloves, and backed up to the cliffside.

"We're doing multiple lines," said Jacobits. "First Chad, then the rest of us together. And Ben, you take Kate tandem. Professor, you help them launch. Kate, you'll be in a helo soon on your way to the American hospital in Marseille. Tomorrow you'll be sippin' mango juice in Germany with those nasty ass American army nurses taking care of you."

As the soldiers pulled their gear and readied for the drop, Chad checked and rechecked his harness, carabiner, and figure-eight rappel device. With one hand holding the rope in front, and one threading it behind, he began the descent into the deep slot down the mountain. He shifted his body forward and began rock-walking backwards into the darkness. He was unable to see clearly, and could not guide his body around the gnarled trunks growing sideways off the volcanic cliff rocks. Foot by foot, he slipped himself down, slapping into huge branches that were growing from giant trees on the canyon floor, ducking and bending as the thick growth scratched at his helmet and legs.

After five minutes of rappelling and bushwhacking, he whispered into the mike, "I think I'm almost there. Can't see a fucking thing, though, even with NVG's. Don't hear anything, either. What IA do you get from the guys at Bolling?"

"They're sending data," said Jacobits. He was mid-cliff, and gripping the rope fiercely with his right hand, his brake hand, to slow his descent while he watched for the shadows of the tandem rappel above him. "They can see movement on the goat trail. They're telling us that Leila is still winding down the path with her boys. With any luck, we'll be there to meet her."

Ben stood behind Kate, their backs facing the canyon abyss. Morel slipped the harness up between her legs, and gently added webbing patches around her chest. Ben girth-hitched a runner through her belay loop, creating a cow's tail with the rope. He took a Prusik and girth-hitched it through his own loop, extending it slightly so he would hang just below her body on the descent. He loaded the rappel device with the rope, and clipped his and Kate's carabiners through the rope and the rappel device. Morel tested the lines from the tree with his own body weight, and nodded at them.

"Okay, Katie, here we go," Ben said gently into her ear. He put one arm around her body and gripped the front rope, and with the other he held the brake line behind them. "Just lean back on me; put all your weight on my chest." She nodded to let him know she could do this, but as he stepped back over the cliff, he felt her entire body tighten against the pain of the jerking motion. "I'm sorry," he said. "We'll be down soon. I'll do my best."

They descended about one hundred feet without speaking, and each time Ben eased down the rope he heard Kate whimper. She was sweating profusely from the pain, and he stopped their movement to allow her to rest. They dangled in mid-air silently, and when he released the brake to continue, they began to swing suddenly toward the cliff. The closer they swung at the deeply angled wall, the more speed they picked up, and suddenly he saw the glowing blue basalt rushing toward them.

Ben instantly lifted his legs up perpendicular to his frame, boots first, to keep their bodies from slamming into sheer rock.

"Hang on to me," he whispered, "this is gonna be bad." Kate opened her eyes wide and stared as they rushed toward the jagged volcanic rock. Just before they hit, Ben put his free arm out toward the cliff to shield her from the crash. He took the force on his elbow and wrist, and on his knees, using his joints as shock absorbers for her against the jolting pain.

Somewhere in her mind, Kate heard the throbbing of thousands of tiny wings, vibrating behind her ears, and felt a burning powder slipping down from rib to rib, burning and chewing inside her gut. She closed her eyes and listened, and then she blacked out, all the world was sleeping, and her body became a sack of skin in Ben's arms.

"Kate?" he called out. "Katie, talk to me." They hung in the cool night, NVG green bursting all around them. When the pain in his own knees subsided, he released the rope slowly, trying to keep the descent smooth. He knew that she would not answer him, and he touched her neck with his fingertips, tapping gently in a prayer of Braille.

Chapter 22

JACQUES MOREL WATCHED their shadows sink down into the deep indigo night of the forest. He did not step into his rig, but let it drop to the damp dirt at his feet. Turning from the gorge, he strode quickly into the thicket beside the path, pushing aside heavy branches and climbing over familiar boulders in the silence. He felt the half-life of the dark Ardèche under his fingers, and he began to chop through the countryside quicker and quicker until at last he leapt toward the sprung steel door of Chauvet Cave.

Breathless now, Morel lurched his lanky frame under the low, jagged doorway, panting as he crossed the narrow threshold. He had not entered this cave for months, but he would never forget the ritual of entry. He knelt immediately on all fours in order to crawl through the long tunnel leading to the chain of caverns. At the end he stood, bruised from the rocky passage and hobbling from the arthritis in his knee joints. He wiped the back of his hand across his sweating face, clearing his eyes, and peered into the sacred abyss before him.

The stainless steel ladder and bridges lay crumpled like tinfoil across the broad Brunel Chamber. Thick mist of dust and sour smoke billowed at him from the next Chamber of the Bear Hollow, obscuring the far depth of the caverns. On the wall beside him, AQIM had installed a steel-caged light by drilling into the calcite. The fixture had jarred loose in the explosions, leaving the painted rock cracked and broken. The perfect representation of a panther in gallop, blown in tiny dots of red pigment onto the wall twenty thousand years before, now lay in chunks on the floor, fissured by the American Black and Decker drill that Leila Hosni's team had used. And beneath the light, sat a stainless steel gurney surrounded by other metal tables. Morel pressed his lips together, breathing deeply through his nose. He felt his eyes stinging and watering in the smoke, and he stepped forward to the ledge.

He eased himself down the fragile walls, using the twisted steel carcasses as a ladder, until at last he let himself fall to the soft floor. Ancient bones of cave bears lay around him and he stepped gingerly among them like old friends, toward the Gallery of Hands. There he stopped, staring at the overhang of scarred, scarlet rhinoceroses that had been painted by the shaman hunters.

He ran his long fingers across the wall. All of the paintings had been exploded to pieces, and one of the modern generators used by Leila's soldiers still throbbed and sputtered underneath the ancient animals.

Morel turned to the low chamber that led to the caves of the earlier era. He looked about him for material that might burn, and found in a corner the greasy remains of a recent meal, a lamb chunk drowning in fat. He lifted this in its ceramic bowl from the clay floor and held the flame of his lighter close until the grease ignited. Holding it as a lantern, he stooped low, moving slowly along the cavern until he came to the wide mouth of the Hillaire Chamber.

The oppressive smell of burning fat mingled with the dust, and he wheezed heavily as his lungs began to give way. Around him lay more piles of cave bear bones, preserved alongside the bones of numinous humans who occupied Chauvet. Skulls of recent men and ancient ursines lay strewn together, dry and polished, gleaming in the shadows. Slowly, the walls began to vibrate with an unnatural rhythm, and Morel heard the sputtering of a human machine somewhere beyond the chamber.

He walked forward, the burning sheep fat bouncing light across the caverns as he moved. At the back of the cavity lay the great Panel of the Horse. Thirty feet long, the mural had been etched by hand in the soft putty surface of the clay wall: a beautiful, wild animal striding, immense and strong, to the left across the folds of the stone. The belly of this massive animal was lacerated vertically with parallel lines, representations of the cave bears on their hind legs tearing down at the walls as they awoke from hibernation.

Beneath this miraculous art, slumped against the floor, sat Dirk Lowell, scientific hero, with his eyes closed, and murmuring heavily into the grease-flame.

"Lowell!" exclaimed Morel. "Are you all right? What happened here?"

The old charlatan looked up at him, quietly cleaning his clay-covered hands by smearing them across his flannel shirt. He lifted his shoulders in a silent shrug, and smiled.

"I'm fine, Jacques. All things considered. Nothing that a stay in the Ritz can't fix once we get back to Paris."

"Dirk, how did they ever get into Chauvet?"

He shrugged again. "You have always been so naïve, my friend."

"But it's ruined. These paintings," Morel whispered, "all of these paintings. What happened?"

"What happened?" he repeated, his voice drained of any energy. "Well, many things happened. I have had a life you would not believe. But, it is true... I imagined things a little differently, that is for certain." He smiled, and the cancer-collapsed flesh at his throat began to quiver. He leaned back against the dusty remains of the horse panel, and with a sweep of his liver-spotted hand, his soft fingers fluttering in the damp air, he whispered, "An error of judgment on my part."

Morel pulled the Heckler & Koch from his jacket pocket and pointed the barrel at Lowell's body.

The man's eyes widened, and he whispered, "Don't be absurd, Jacques. We will find other Chauvets."

Morel squeezed his tanned, wrinkled fingers slowly against the trigger, and watched as Lowell jack-knifed back against the horses in the flickering light. The man's body squirmed and snapped against the cavern, shuddering and slumping at last to the dirt.

Jacques Morel reached over and grabbed the blueprint of veins at Lowell's wrist to search for a pulse. Finding none, he slipped to his knees against the wall of cave bears, the tears streaming down his face.

Chapter 23

BEN LAID KATE'S LIMP BODY on the ground and bent to release the tungsten clips that held her to his lines.

"Hey, buddy, what's up with Katie?" Chad squatted by an oak tree, camouflaging radio-controlled SLAMS he had spiked into the earth.

Ben carried her out of the open clearing back to where the Iris was parked. Beside the well, a rectangular, weathered stone stood over the bubbling water, chiseled two thousand years before with the image of the Celtic river goddess, Sirona. Over the face of this pagan woman someone had gouged a cross deep into the granite. An oak tree grew behind the old marker, and from its branches modern farmers had hung ribbons and small crosses, hedging their religious bets by dressing the well as their ancient Celtic families had done.

Ben placed Kate on the ground, and leaned over to check her breathing. He put his hand in the cold water, and sprinkled a few drops on her lips and forehead.

Jacobits crawled to the back of the Iris and peered out at the sound. He jumped down and walked over to them.

"What happened?"

"We hit the cliff and she passed out."

"Alain, bring the med station over here," Jacobits said into his mike. "Kate is unconscious." He knelt beside Ben and pulled a lighter from his pocket. He rolled her sleeve up to her elbow and held the flame to the skin on the inside of her forearm, slowly counting to three, but she did not stir.

"That's enough," Ben said.

Jacobits stared at him. "I'll tell you when it's enough, Cullen." Beneath the balaclava, his wrinkled eyelids were pale pink, his eyes black and fierce.

The two of them knelt in furious silence, as Alain rushed over with his backpack. He pulled a syringe from the bag, held it up and tapped at the clear plastic to settle it. Then he slipped the needle into a vein on top of her hand, shooting life back into her.

Within seconds Kate began to stir. Ben took her hand and held it, and Jacobits whispered, "Dear God," while he watched her eyes open.

Alain grinned at her. "I am delighted to welcome you back."

Jacobits took a deep breath and stood up. "Cullen, you and Alain get her into the Iris with your brother, hook her up to an IV, and get back out here. We're just about ready to receive our friends."

Ben lifted Kate from the ground on his own, carrying her away from the well to the vehicle. He laid her on a thin mat on the cool, steel floor next to Hank, and stood over her for a few moments.

Kate looked up at Ben and said simply, "Thank you."

"My God, she's alive," said Hank.

"Yeah," replied Ben. "But you knew that all along, didn't you?"

"What do you mean?" Hank asked.

Alain knelt beside Kate and snapped a new IV into the line taped to her knuckles. He glanced up in the silence at the brothers.

"*Et voilà,*" he said quickly. "This last *sac* and you'll be good, I think." He wrapped a flak jacket around her body, but the hollow dip of her collarbone still lay exposed to the cold. He reached out to cover this, and she looked up quickly. Neither of them spoke. A large forest moth landed on the floor between them, its violet paper wings ceasing to tremble as it settled.

Alain heard the sound first, a strange tinny noise coming across the floor of the vehicle, discordant, somewhere in the dark.

"*Qu'est-ce que c'est?*" he asked Kate.

She shook her head.

Now, they all strained to quiet, and it continued, metal across metal, sounding farther off than it was.

Alain turned toward the sound and walked to the far corner of the cabin, squatting on the floor. Before him lay a raccoon, with its paws smashed. Unable to escape, it continued to push the claws of its back legs against the floor, scraping across the ridges furiously. It began to screech at Alain, hissing and baring its teeth while it scrambled hopelessly in place.

He pulled the SOCOM pistol from his belt and applied the suppressor. Quickly, he lifted the gun, shot the animal through the head, and the bullet snapped through its brittle skull. For an eerie moment, no one moved; they were so close to the Ardeche River that they could hear the churning of its rapids across the dips and boulders of the riverbed.

"Okay, that's it," Alain said. "Back to work."

"I gotta go, Katie," Ben said. "You'll be fine now."

"I know," she replied. Ben grabbed a rifle from the storage box and loaded it. He put it in her hands. She nodded at him without speaking again, and he jumped down from the back hatch of the truck to join the others.

•

Jacobits' team had lived through IED and mortar attacks, random roadside bombings in no-name villages, yet the absence of an enemy at night still caused their instincts to grind like overheated engines. Chad had bermed himself into a ridge suspended over the mountain path, burrowed into the safest scuttle hole he could find. He would be the first to respond when the enemy engaged. He checked his gear and imagined AQIM tripwire circling the trunk of every tree, waiting to blow his face off.

Alain and Serge sat in the cab of the Iris in silence. Somewhere in the forest around them was a mother lode of anti-tank mines, explosives, raw IED materials, and perhaps surface-to-air missiles. They knew that Leila had been here, but were unsure where exactly, and all they could count on lay visible before them: their own plastic explosives, rifles, beds, sleeping bags, and a few bloody bandages.

"*T'es branché?*" Serge whispered to Kate through his mike.

"Yes," she said, and he heard her voice in echo, both through his live ear mike and across the hollow truck.

Near the riverbank, Marko set himself on a rise of earth above the chapel, and lay on his stomach in the wash. He sank his face into a pool of sweet-smelling mud and waited, his entire life, he thought, swinging on the simple hinge of the next fifteen minutes.

"They're on their way now," Jacobits said calmly. "As long as we have bullets we'll be okay. We have orders to wait until their first fire, but then we can take them out as they cross to the river road. *Cristina* has promised us some spectacular analysis, so open up your left mike now and pay attention." Not one person responded. "Can I get a friggin' grunt from you guys?"

There was no laughter or crackle of radio voices, no fly of brass bullets lifting birds up off the trees, nothing to indicate they were still out there, but Jacobits knew that his team was grinning at him.

Ben knelt below the ridge of the berm, in a cavity on the muddy embankment swollen with freezing water. He heard a voice whispering through the mulberry branches that overhung the path, coming to him like the rasp of a ghost.

Jacobits slipped down the muddy berm beside him.

"Any minute," he said. "NVG time now. Leila's gonna try to sneak by us and we gotta see her in those slimy shadows."

Ben nodded, pulling his goggles down over his eyes. He tried to speak, but his throat was dry. He thought he could hear .50-caliber machine gun fire up the hill, yet Jacobits did not move.

"They are not engaging," whispered Jacobits calmly. "Why aren't they firing?"

"I thought I heard something," Ben said.

"That's just your anticipation, Cullen. They're coming, but they haven't thrown a fuckin' thing at us yet."

"Holy shit," said Chad. They're nearly in our kill zone. What the fuck is going on?"

"No idea," Jacobits replied. "Just hold off until I say."

"This part always makes me crazy," said Ben.

"The waiting?"

"Yeah." He held his fingers over the muzzle of moonlight reflected in the mud before him. "Just waiting."

"Cullen, I got no idea why they aren't firing, but we're in a good position whatever they do. Don't worry."

"Oh, I'm not worried, Colonel. Either we win or we friggin' die. I just pray to God that I don't kill the wrong people. Who's with Kate and my brother?"

"Alain and Serge," replied the Colonel. "Okay, Chad. They're here, count off their approach."

"We're in their kill zone in five. Four. Three. Two. One." No sound came from the forest, no reverberation and no lights from fire.

"Still nothing. Really, Leila? What the hell are you doin'?" Jacobits clamped a small diameter pipe to the rifle barrel. He leaned forward into the mud and whispered, "We're not waiting anymore. Could be suicide."

Slowly and firmly, he put pressure on the trigger of his gun, and several hundred yards out, between the heavy trunks of the forest oaks, he saw a blinking light. His goggles magnified this into a bright smear of emerald glow across the clearing. "All right, friends, we're in this now."

It took nine seconds for the impact. A single shot smacked through the branches, digging into the bark with a small burst. Suddenly the banks around them began to throb, and a large tremor followed, engulfing Jacobits' body.

"I'm an old guy," Jacobits said, "I don't like surprises."

Chad blasted an RPG across the forest, slamming through the branches to the clearing where it exploded. Immediately the AQIM soldiers hammered themselves into cover and began firing their machine guns. Explosions and flashing lights pumped relentlessly through the dark, the bullets ripping through branches and bouncing off the granite boulders around them.

Chad reached for the radio switch, and with a single index finger he flicked open a thunder of large artillery shell explosions rigged at the entrance to the clearing.

Within seconds, Marko began launching mortars across the broken hillside, and soon they could see a body twisted at the base of an oak.

"We got the forward there at the tree," whispered Chad, and the explosion of bullets and tracers and mortars going in both directions was deafening.

"The Iris is not retaining fire!" shouted Alain quickly. "Why are they avoiding our vehicle? That's the obvious place for the asset. We're ready for them, but there is nothing."

"Maybe Leila wants him back alive," snorted Jacobits.

Ben watched the surges of fire bursting through the forest, and struggled to ID the sources. He counted down between the flash and snap of the closer bullets, and knew the berm where he and Jacobits lay had now been targeted. Bullets fell around them from several vantage points, and he understood that they had to relocate or within minutes they would both be dead. Quickly, he scanned the landscape, searching for a defensible location. He identified a sniper perch overhead, set beyond into the forest by about fifteen yards.

"Up there," he said to Jacobits. "I'll take it and establish." The Colonel nodded to him, and suddenly Ben lurched forward into the chaos and bone-splitting thunder. He did not know where the fire was coming from, where his own people were, or whom he had to kill in order to reach the sniper. He was sweating and scanning for his buddies, and then suddenly his thoughts were silenced, he was lost in the fight, and the only parts of his soul still intact were his fear and his desire to kill.

He flung himself onto the ground, and lifted his weapon. He looked up only once to measure through the scope, and then he began to fire. He shot until the barrel of his gun glowed red. The toxic smoke of the battle surrounded him, and the shattering noise across the bottle green forest closed out all hope of communicating with his team.

He crawled forward with his rifle, firing through the trees at the
sniper in the perch, until gradually the sound of shots over his body
abated, and he realized that he had killed the man in the nest above
him. He dug his fingers into the mud and grass and pulled himself up
the forest bank.

The man lay with his legs outstretched and his arms by his sides.
A pool of blood soaked through his clothing, and Ben saw that bullets
had penetrated his back and neck. Blood coursed into the wet earth
around his boots, and Ben leaned over and quickly pushed the body
down the back of the hill so he could take its place. The deep vibration of mortars rocked the battle space around him, but he spoke
calmly into his radio mike.

"We're secure up here, Sir. I've got your back."

Firing from the west rose like a shrine above the treetops as Jacobits, stretched flat, began to climb from the sludge of the riverbank.
He plunged through the long, wet grass toward the hill.

Ben turned to this western flashing and began targeting the seat of
the shelling, but the French voice in his left radio feed was directing
him east. The *Cristina* team was calmly analyzing the satellite images
from a thousand miles away in Levallois, and now directed him toward
a fire pocket that fell on the ridge below the mountain path.

He knew he had to believe them: they could see the entire region
by the satellite, while he only had a view of the window in front of
him. He turned east and began to fire.

"Chad, are you secure?" He spoke furiously into the mike to his
buddy at the eastern edge of the battle. "*Cristina* is calling us to cover
you!"

"No immediate threat here. Anyway, how the hell can they see
anything from the satellite with all these trees and cliffs?"

Ben's eyes widened, and he could feel the pummel of his pulse. As
he hesitated, his guts rose up into in his throat, filling his mouth with
a sour taste. He had been to this space a hundred times, where not
even a knife could separate caution from cowardice.

He paused, drifting for a fraction of a moment out of the battle,
weighing the intel, weighing the threat to Jacobits, watching the

curve in the road out of the trees. His fingers lay inert on the warm barrel of his rifle, but he began to stir like an animal anxious to take down its prey. He knew that there were two kinds of dead, those you killed and those you could not protect, and suddenly he saw the ceiling of red tracers and bullets above Jacobits, clear like in a candle flame.

He shouted, "Launch to the west! The Colonel is caught by the river and Leila's boys are keeping him from getting up here to safety in my berm."

"Copy." Chad clicked the warhead into place and lifted the long barrel to his shoulder. He knelt in the soft pine needles and held his body like a tripod. Through his NVG's he identified the source of nearby shooting. Holding steady, he released the mortar with a deep reverberation, and watched it spinning through the night, green smoke trailing behind it. The RPG sank in the distance, and then lit the horizon with a wild starburst at the base of the trees. Chad ripped the NVG's from his eyes to keep the flash from blinding him.

"Was that a hit?" he called out. "Alain! What can you see?" but no one answered him.

Jacobits crawled forward under a new, unstoppable rain of explosions, puffs of smoke skidding off the trees as hundreds of rounds roared across the forest. He hugged the earth with his arms and his belly, clenching his thighs to the muddy grass as he squeezed himself forward by sheer will.

Ben spun around back to the west to counter the heavy gunfire slamming into the ground around Jacobits.

"*Vingt mètres a l'est,*" the *Cristina* voice said calmly.

"*BOGINT!* Ignore that! Leila's target is the Colonel!" he shouted to his team. "Keep firing on the west to cover him!"

Jacobits pulled himself through the mud, rising at last onto the ridge and collapsing. His huge barrel chest heaved, and he fell heavily to the ground.

"Are you hit, Sir?" Ben asked.

"No," he said, and grinned. "Just old." He rolled over slowly onto his stomach. He leaned on a mud-mound in the perch, and carefully pulled his rifle into place, measuring the geometry of the forest and the strength of the wind. His eyes were bloodshot from the damp, smoke-polluted air, and he closed them to rinse the sting away.

For an instant the night went silent, and then the explosions began again, louder and denser than before.

In the next instant, a deep reverberation ripped through the sky. A thick umbrella of rusted light glowed above them, and Ben smelled garlic soaking the air.

"Holy shit," he said to Jacobits, "they're firing WP."

Suddenly, streams of white phosphorus emanating from the east fell like spider webs around them, their smoke bursting into flame at the first contact of oxygen. Even the forest ground, once damp with the spring rains, now ignited instantly with flecks of WP burning into the earth, embedding and flaming farther and farther up the hill toward them with each explosion.

"Just when I thought I could relax and have a cigarette," said Jacobits, but his voice was airless and hollow.

"They're firing WP out of the east," Ben whispered.

"Shit, the French were right again. Those guys in *Cristina's* analysis lab told us to heave our crap onto the east and they were right. I don't know how they friggin' do it."

"I shouldn't have called us off the east," said Ben.

"That's true, Major, but if you hadn't, I wouldn't be alive."

"Tirez sur l'est! Y'en à cinq seulement qui restent là bas!"

Suddenly, the radio mike opened with Chad's voice. "I can see three of the five guys from here! Colonel, they're launching WP straight at you. Everything they have. Get the fuck out of there!"

The sky was brutal, lit with the ghost-glow of phosphorus, severing the moonlight from the earth. Ben's muscles ached and his skin stung with tiny quills of pain. He snapped his head around, scanning for an escape route. Each second they waited lowered their percentage for survival, yet he could no longer see the terrain around them. The explosions had trapped them in a burning cone of stinking gas.

"Alain!" called out Jacobits. "Give me a sit rep now!"

"Asset is secure, Colonel. They have not engaged with us still."

Jacobits paused to catch his breath, and then began a long, low growl. "Whatever the hell Leila's plan is, Ben and I need a retreat path now!" Then, shouting at his mike through the burning forest, "Mark a retreat for us A-SAP. This is *SPRINT!*"

He repeated the SOS in French, and said to Ben, "Help me think, dammit!"

"Can you get to the river?" called out Marko. "It's behind you about ten meters. If you move to the north down the berm you will fall farther into the white phosphorus. If you move forward you will be in their kill zone."

"If we move at all we'll be in the WP," said Ben frantically. "We're surrounded by it now."

"You can get to the river." Kate's voice came suddenly, even and strong. Ben heard her resolve as though she were sitting next to him, rerouted through the radio waves. "I can see trees sheltering a path for you. Exfiltrate to the river." Her words shot into the filthy night, eclipsing everything else.

Ben looked quickly at Jacobits, and started to speak.

"I'm here behind Marko," she said. "We'll give you cover. They can't target you on the down slope, and even if you catch the WP, the cold river water is your remedy. Go," she said, "go now!"

They lurched over the lip of the berm, throwing themselves onto the cool bank, rolling and covering their bodies with a mud shield against the inferno.

At the bottom of the hill, they were still surrounded with white smoke and fire. Between them and the river lay five yards of flat, burning earth. Jacobits dived forward into the fire, and Ben followed. They felt the flecks of burning compound attach to their clothes and their exposed skin, as they charged into the chemical firestorm toward the safety of the river.

Jacobits pushed through the heat and pain, and at last fell forward into a shallow lagoon lined by the huge roots of a bank side oak. He lay panting in the water, frantically rolling his burning body over and over to extinguish the lace of fire on his clothing.

"Take them out!" shouted Kate. "Get AQIM now! Can anyone see the eastern seat of the firing?"

"Smokescreens are all over," said Chad. "I can't see a damn thing now!"

Ben lay on the riverbank in a cloud of white smoke, about two yards north of Jacobits. He felt the WP embers burning into his back, and he could no longer see or hear. He knew he lay in the center of a volcano, and that his body was engulfed in a searing purple heat that brought him to the edge of an odd, deep calm. He stopped struggling against it, and began to drift out of consciousness. And then somehow, he found the smell of dampness, the sweet rich odor of fertile, black soil, seductive like soft rain over the ocean. He began pulling himself closer to this sweet, wet odor, at first slowly for comfort, and then with rising strength he clawed at the mud, wrenching his body toward the smell of water. He contracted every muscle to pull forward, and finally threw himself over the riverbank, where he pitched at last into the deep cool water.

"The Colonel is safe," said Marko. I can see him in the *gave*. But *haji* is advancing. I think they're moving toward Cullen in the Iris."

"Where is Ben?" Kate asked. "Do you see him?"

The radios were silent until Chad replied, "Katie, either he's in the water or he's fried. But right now we gotta stop the fuckers firing the WP or we'll all be barbecue."

"What about the Iris?" called Marko.

"Can't see a damn thing through this WP," Chad said. "*Cristina's* stumped, too. No images from them. Nothing. *Haji's* drawn a circle of WP around us, so they can take the Iris!"

"If they come here, we are ready," whispered Serge. "Whether you can get to us or not, we can contain them." He crawled to the back of the van where Cullen lay, and squatted beside him, rifle poised.

"At least give me something to defend myself," said Hank Cullen.

Serge shook his head. "I can take care of you, *Monsieur*," and he rested the side of his face against the rifle butt.

"It's me they want!" rasped Cullen furiously. "They want me! You know who I am, right? At least let me protect myself."

But Serge merely looked at him through the dirty half-light of the cabin, nodding absently while he listened for footsteps outside.

Then through the hot mike, they all heard Alain speak, his accent gentle and precise. "Leila is visible. She and another are in a nest up the hill. It is the last hill before the clearing, and it is from there that they are shooting the *phosphore blanc.*"

"Hang on, guys," said Chad suddenly. He lifted the automatic grenade launcher from the ground, and began to run with it, a hundred meters up the path with bullets smacking the mud all around him. When he reached the trees, he turned around and knelt to the ground for an anchor. He wheeled the barrel into place and began launching grenades back toward the seat of the WP attack.

Chapter 24

KATE KNEW IN THAT MOMENT, he had created the cover she needed. She tore off her night vision goggles and raced up the hill toward Leila's position. Gunfire light burst all around her as the forest roared with weapons. She squatted beneath the smoldering oaks, where ashes were pressed into warm chalk at her feet. She lifted her rifle, and pitched her spine against the oak trunk. Edging methodically around the tree, she scanned for AQIM on the hill close to her. She held her finger gently across the safety of the rifle, leveling her gun sight beneath the hard deck of flashing shots and explosions, focused on the cool death-embroidered breath of the forest. She monitored the shadowy spaces between the thick branches, her breathing short and shallow.

Then she saw Leila in the throat of the battle, crouched in the indigo crevice of a basalt boulder, while a soldier beside her attempted to load WP grenades into his FAMAS amid the furious blasts from Chad's attack.

Leila shouted, and suddenly the man stood straight up into the night with his hand on the butt of his rifle for balance. He discharged a missile toward the bottom of the hill, but it fell short of the kill zone. The grenade sank instead into a tree trunk, exploding bark and soil into the flashing night.

Kate caught the man in her sight, held her breath, and pulled back steadily on the trigger.

She took him in the head, and his skull shattered like an eggshell. His body snapped back against the volcanic rock, kicking sharply to the right, and he slumped beside the boulder.

Kate wheeled her sight to Leila Hosni, but she was too late. The AQIM woman had jumped from the bank and started toward her. Dark screaming tumbled from Hosni when she lunged forward, spreading her arms and legs out wide along the ground as she slithered between the fiery white oaks.

Within seconds she was upon Kate, covering her with the smell of burning tar. Furiously, she put her teeth to Kate's shoulder and tore the outer cloth apart. She planted her body atop Kate's and quickly grabbed her collar, with her fingers inside and her thumbs outside, readying for a nutcracker choke. She turned her hands sharply inward and began leaning forward, applying the pressure of her entire body to Kate's throat to snap it.

Gasping, Kate grabbed Leila's right elbow in her hand, and began to slide her other fist in front of Leila's leg. Leila pulled up to avoid the arm-bar, and punched Kate in the face several times, quick and hard. On the last punch, she leaned back for leverage, and at that instant of shifting balance, Kate opened her legs and twisted her shoulders.

She pushed off her feet, torquing quickly, driving her hips against Leila's until she forced her to fall back. Immediately, Kate flipped on top of her, and drew her clinch pick from its sheath. She sank the short, rounded blade into Leila's side, and the woman released a guttural cry. Kate jammed the blade at her body again, this time aiming for her stomach, reaching across her own body. In an instant, Leila brought her legs up high over Kate's back, slamming them down on her neck.

Leila pitched back with the force of her entire body, hurling the weight of both their bodies against the ground so hard that the knife fell from Kate's fist. The AQIM woman saw the blade on the forest floor, and grabbed it. She rolled forward and anchored across her body so hard that Kate could not breathe.

The noise of shots around them had slipped away, as both teams held their fire from the hill. The air reeked garlic from the white phosphorus, and the still-burning embers smoked through the oak leaves and branches. Like a glowing, marbled cloth, it covered their snaking bodies. Kate brought her left leg in and began to push up with all her force to free herself. She felt Leila's arm pull back slightly, and she knew her adversary was gaining leverage to sink the knife. Unable to block it, Kate tightened her muscles to receive the stab.

She heard the sound of a branch snapping above her, somehow cracking the air all around them. She waited for the blade to pierce, but instead the woman heaved forward upon her chest with the whole force of her body. Leila's knife arm lay beside Kate, as though severed, and she realized a dead body slumped over her now.

She pushed herself free, and knelt on the ground. Leila's pulse had ceased entirely, and blood drained from a bullet wound at the base of the woman's head.

A figure came out of the forest and squatted beside her. He held his rifle in one hand and put the other on her shoulder.

"Ça va?" asked Marko.

Kate tried to speak but could not. The adrenaline was slipping away, folding her into silence. Suddenly, her throat muscles clenched in a sharp spasm, and she put her fingers on her neck to massage the flesh just below her jawbone.

"Kate?" he asked softly, but she did not answer. The blood, dark as raw oil, from the wound in Leila's skull had spread to a splinter of bone lodged in the soil, and had formed a pool around it. Marko put his index finger into this, and drew a line down his throat, stroking it until it dried upon his skin. He whispered to himself quietly, turning the pages of some lost scripture.

The soft rain began again, shuddering across them. Kate stood up and leaned against the tree behind her.

"Thank you," she said to Marko.

He nodded. "They still need us at the Iris. There are three AQIM soldiers left at the bottom and they are well stockpiled."

They turned together and ran down the damp path. The moon was rinsed by the cool rain, and the forest was queerly silent of shooting and of birdsong. A third of the way down the hill, Kate and Marko slowed simultaneously, staring at the open ground that lay before them.

"Go wide," Kate whispered to Marko. "Into the trees." He nodded and they veered off the path, pounding into the soft mulch of leaves and dung. They stopped at a huge ancient pine, scanning the dark forest for evidence of artillery. Both buttressed against the rough bark, rifles raised.

"The path is mined," Marko whispered.

Kate did not need to answer. She knew that this goat path had been engineered, and knew it so certainly she could feel the truth trembling on her lips. She did not know if AQIM would blow the path from a cell phone, from radar, from trigger wire, or at all. They might have even laid traditional mines that would explode on the gentlest of pressure. She believed three men remained on the AQIM team, but she did not know which battle stations had been obliterated by Chad's RPG fire, or what lethal detritus had been left under the forest floor.

"I lost my radio connection in the fight," she said. "Can you get intel from *Cristina?*"

Marko pressed his finger on the pod and waited for the feed to begin. It came with difficulty, rough sounds that scraped against a wall of air slowly turning to words, and then faded out entirely.

"The white phosphorus has blinded the receptors at Levallois," he said. "*Cristina's* satellite cannot penetrate, and I've lost the connection with the Iris, as well. We must find our own way down, Kate, and do what we can."

Before them lay a solar system of trigger wire, and in the distance she could see thin, blue flames rising up from the black river. No radar could guide them through this lacework of hell to reach it.

"We'll head back up and over the other side," she said.

"Our colleagues will not have that margin of time, if they are still alive."

Kate squatted on the ground, balancing her rifle across her thighs. Smoldering lichen clung to the soil around her, and the air passages in her throat began to constrict. She knew from the childhood stories of her friend, Jacques, that many paths down the mountain existed. She thought about what he had told her, of his youth and his research, but each time she tried to remember his words, her mind was pulled back to a deep, black weary slumber.

Near her lay the barely-breathing body of a charred Bonelli eagle. Unconsciously, she scooped the soil and pine needles to form a protective berm for it, and watched the even pulsing of its breast.

"This bird will not live, Kate."

She looked up at Marko suddenly, and shrugged. "If we clear this forest fast enough, it may have a chance."

Marko shook his head and stared at her. His eyes were the color of pure blue glacial ice, glistening in the exploded night against the black camo paint on his sunken cheeks. He knelt alongside her. "I love Americans. You are all so desperately hopeful."

"I know there are other ways down this hill," she said. "Jacques described this forest to me a dozen times." She continued pushing the pine needles and mud up to the bird's body. "I can't," she whispered, not looking at him. "I can't remember anything now."

Marko could smell the heavy sweet odor of sticky foogas in the air around them. Somewhere nearby, napalm and petroleum lay waiting to blow the earth out from under them, but he remained still, knowing it was only a simple chemical reaction that had moved her from action to inertia, had moved her into darkness.

"It's all right, Kate. You are exhausted, quite literally. Let me guide us," he said. "I do not believe the wire will be dense. Leila's men did not have enough time to lay it well. I can get us through the clearing."

He knelt so close to her that she could smell his sweat washed through by the swollen mist of the forest.

"A lot of people have saved my life," she mumbled "Some even without meaning to. A lot of people have tried to kill me, too. I know it's crazy to think this, but right now I can't tell the difference."

He stared at her as though into a vast horizon, and said quietly, "We need to get to the base, Kate. That's all we need to do. I have had years of experience with improvised explosive devices. You know that. I have laid these traps on a hundred occasions. I know what I'm looking for."

She stood up, still bewildered and staring into the high pine and oak branches overhead, those draped with fire and those that were safe.

"I think I see some artificial impressions in the soil there," he said. "If you follow me, we will get through the mines."

Kate took both their rifles and walked to the edge of the open area. She held them like votives, standing at the wet purple earth that marked the beginning of the mined path. She balanced tentatively on this imaginary filament, waiting for him to come to her.

"Here," said Marko. "Allow me to move your bird out of the way just in case you are right. Sometimes," he grinned, "you Americans are right."

She smiled at him as he lifted the eagle in both his hands holding it to his chest. Instantly, a deep roar thundered from where he stood, shaking the tree trunk and searing it with flames. Smoke billowed across his body, and he pitched from side to side.

Kate was knocked to the ground by the explosion. Quickly, she scrambled forward through the cloud of pale dust to the fire where Marko lay. She grabbed his boots and wrenched them hard, again and again, dragging his body into safety.

The smoke and burning extinguished quickly into the heavy air, but Marko's lower chest and stomach had been torn open by the blast. Bright red blood frothed upon the ground, and Kate lifted his shoulders and head into her arms.

"Fucking bird," she whispered. "They didn't mine the road, Marko; they filled the poor bird."

He looked at her like a dazed animal who could scarcely hear, and she put her mouth close to him. "Marko, I can smell thermite. I'm sorry. I'm so sorry."

She pulled the black knit cap from his skull, and used it to wipe the paint and traces of gunpowder from his face. As she loosened the clothing around his neck, his body began to shudder. She slipped her jacket from her arms, and hooped it over his open wound. She could feel his muscles sag, and stared as his veins drained blood around her into the dirt.

"You will be okay now," he said.

"It was my fault," she whispered. "I should have remembered what Jacques told me. I'm so sorry, Marko."

He could no longer move his hands or legs, but Kate saw that his pale eyes were clear and focused again.

"*C'était inévitable, Catalina,*" he whispered. "In the end, I don't think God really meant for us to be human."

The sweet taste of almonds rose from her gut, twisting like venom.

"Oh yes," she began but by then his pulse and his breathing had stopped.

She laid his head carefully against the soft earth, and gently stroked her fingertips down over his eyelids. She pulled his body far back into the trees and removed any indication of identity.

She stood up slowly and slung the French rifle over her back. She took her own M4 and moved back to the animal track, invaded by the smells of artillery, and by the sounds of newly rising shots snapping through the sweet forest pines.

Chapter 25

KATE ARRIVED AT THE RIVER as the darkness began to thin into Sunday's dawn. The sounds of battle had disappeared from the forest, and small birds now clustered on the branches of the chestnut and oak trees like a string of dark pearls against the pink light. In the quiet of the swampy riverbank, they had begun singing again, sharply as if glass were shattering over the water.

She squatted alongside her friends and laid Marko's rifle in the mud beside her. Alain and Serge were hunched over the inert body of Colonel Jacobits, and Ben lay a few yards off nearer the river.

"Give me a sit rep, Alain."

"We have identified the bodies of two more AQIM. So that leaves one, unless our estimate was wrong. Personally, I believe we got them all," he said. "As for the wounded, no inhalation injuries for either the Colonel or Ben. We removed all the WP embers we could find from their skin and applied the compresses to stop the heat and residual burning. The Colonel has about fifteen per cent burn coverage. Ben got off lighter. Most are superficial or partial thickness. He was lucky. I can't find any evidence of deep or full thickness wounds. We started rehydration for both of them, but I don't have enough sacks here. It will take eight hours of IV fluids to get them going again. We must get to a hospital."

"What about the asset?"

"Did you hear me? They may not live unless we move them now."

"I understand that," she said. "What about the asset?"

Alain paused tenuously. Huge crows lifted up along the face of the fiery red wall on the opposite side of the river, and both soldiers turned to the noise.

"They did not touch him. Nothing hit the Iris, or even close. But he fell off a cliff, Kate. His back isn't broken, his legs are not broken, but he can't move. We have no clue why. He needs a real doctor. All three of them do. Chad thinks he will be able to get the Mobile Communications Unit working again. He thinks it will be about fifteen minutes. If so, we can get a helo here to lift us to Marseille."

He glanced at Kate and saw that she carried a second rifle with its familiar French-angled stock.

"Where is Marko?"

She shook her head slowly with her eyes wide open. "We took out Leila Hosni and her assistant, and then I lost Marko to an IED."

She looked toward the shore, where Ben lay in the lapping water. Patches of the dawn light cast across the bank and spread up the towering granite walls of the gorge. She saw the dark outline of an otter slip silently into the river.

"Where is Chad?" she asked.

"He's on his way with the meds from the Iris."

She leaned over Jacobits' heavy body, and felt the heat still rising from his clothing. The forest had fallen silent, and around them all lay the sweet odor of scorched chestnut leaves that had been dampened by the crystal water of the Ardèche River.

She took Jacobits' hand and held it, stumbling into a prayer that she could not quite remember.

When Chad arrived, he pulled saline solution from his backpack and saturated several clean compresses to lay across the Colonel's chest.

"What can I do?" Kate asked him.

"Get Cullen's legs elevated, pronto before he goes into shock."

Kate let go of the Colonel's hand, and walked to the river's edge. She built a mound of leaves and branches, adding wet stones from the shallow bank to raise the level. She lifted Ben's legs atop this, until they were higher than his heart. Then she sat beside him, and watched over him as the rising light threw gold across his face. She waited for what seemed a very long time, until the dawn had transformed the immense granite walls of the gorge into glowing orange ramparts. Ben's eyes were open and focused on her, but he did not have the bandwidth to speak through the pain.

Finally, Chad approached them.

"Okay, Katie. We're good to go. Colonel's ready to be loaded into the Iris. What's your pleasure now?"

"Do we have radio?"

"If I can work on it for a while."

"There's one more combatant in the forest. And we have to recover the ordnance from the cave. We can't leave WP laying around a French province."

Chad said quickly, "How do you infiltrate a NATO border with these old M79's and a thousand gallons of shake and bake anyway?" He glanced at Serge, and then away to the chestnut trees behind them, their tops shorn from the shelling, their branches dangling like carcasses.

"I think we are all aware that the production of *le phosphore blanc* happens principally in Arkansas, my friend," Serge said. "So we also might ask the question as to how the shipments get from Pine Bluff into the hands of the AQIM in order to be brought later into my country."

Without responding, Chad moved a few yards toward the medpac debris. "Just tell me what you want me to do, Kate."

The soldiers waited before her in the harsh sunlight, silent and shadowed against the risen sun. The landscape of mud was pockmarked black and white, like an old war photograph, granulated and crisp with smoke. When she spoke, her voice cracked.

"I'm not intending to leave without recovering Marko's body and finding out what happened to Morel."

Blunted brushwood, charred and softened, slapped at the shore alongside them.

"Of course," whispered Serge.

"Haven't seen Morel for hours," said Chad.

"Let's get the injured in the Iris, get the communications back, and Alain and I will go for Marko."

The four of them moved out slowly toward the vehicle, at first plodding parallel to the river through thick, unmanaged territory. After a hundred yards, they neared a rent in the bank, and there the great bluffs shot up suddenly two hundred feet toward deep blue canyon sky. An animal track turned inland toward the old chapel ruins, and they followed it through the mud and fallen chestnut husks until they reached their vehicle.

As they approached, they saw Cullen lying near a tree a few yards from the Desert Iris. His eyes were closed, and he had managed to roll onto his side to put his face in the shade.

Chad stopped briefly to stare at him, and muttered, "Looks like *el rico* is feeling better. Or maybe he's just dead." He walked past him toward the vehicle, and put his finger to the soft film of white dust that shimmered across the hood. "Not sugar, baby, that's for sure."

He swung open the door and slid the steel ramp to the ground.

Kate and Alain lay Colonel Jacobits in the dark cabin and covered him with a blanket. Water pooled between the ridges of the corrugated floor, festering the smell of soot and garlic in stagnant streams.

Alain took his jacket off and laid it across the Colonel.

"Once we get rolling you'll be okay, Sir," said Chad.

Kate was standing where she had previously lain, staring at the violet glow of blood she had left behind, now mixed with water.

"Why would water be in the vehicle?" she asked.

"I don't know, Katie. Maybe the rain leaked through."

"An Iris? Not possible."

Alain and Serge lay Ben alongside Jacobits.

"How long were you gone from here?"

"We've been in and out of here all night," said Alain. "Water is not a lethal trap, Kate. Besides, if the AQIM had been here, they would have retaken the asset."

"Katie, what the hell?" Chad said as he bent for the ordnance. He pulled rifles and grenades and the MCU into his arms and packed them inside the door. "It's over now. Breathe a little."

She nodded and sat beside the vehicle, leaning back into the wild foxglove that burst with purple across the forest floor. A hundred birds lifted into the sky from the trees like a flight of silver. In seconds it was over, and Kate felt electricity burn slowly back into her limbs.

Chad lay on his belly in the mud, checking the MCU against the motherboard, whispering to the console and to the analysts back in the dreary Parisian suburbs.

A blue heron stood at the shore, as still as ice, gazing down across the seething white water tumbling over jagged boulders in the riverbed.

"Got it," Chad said suddenly. "Give me a test."

Kate put slight pressure on the pod in her ear, "Request the helo now," she said.

Each of the others put index fingers to the tiny mushroom-shaped cushions in their ears, instantly clicking into communication with the MCU, with *Cristina,* and with Nellis far out in the Nevada desert.

"You're a genius, Chad," she said. "Now find us a rendezvous out of this forest. You got GPS yet?"

"I have everything, baby."

"We'll go for Marko and Morel, but tell *Cristina* to haul ass with that helo!"

Chapter 26

KATE AND ALAIN CLIMBED up through the dense, muggy forest to the plateau above the gorge cliffs. The sun drew out the sweet, sharp smell of the pines between the sycamores, and she sank slowly to her knees in the dark soil. She stared down the cliff at the slip of glistening water, now like crinkled tinfoil in the distance, and heard the pounding moan of a woman crying in her ear.

"I'm sorry, Alain. I may pass out. I have to rest. Do you have anything left in the med pack that will help?"

He took a syringe from his supplies and held it eye level, tapping the vial clear of bubbles.

"This will mitigate the pain and give you some energy for a short time. And then that's it for the miracle of medicine, Kate."

A blue dragonfly shuddered to calm on the spring tendrils beside her, surveying for predators and food. Kate waited quietly while the ice-cold burn shot to her heart. Her muscles twitched and jerked, and she closed her eyes again, this time seeing a dream of herself standing before a circle of soldiers, bound and kneeling on stiff straw, and pleading to her for mercy.

She heard Alain breathing, and she said, "Marko's body is about half a mile from here. We can stow it and go on for Jacques."

They crossed through the woods that covered the hot, open plateau. They stopped against the rock face, in a dank corner of light articulated by the shadows of the burned pine branches overhead.

Beneath them lay Marko's body covered with needles, his chest blown to pieces like the heart of a fallen god. Without speaking, they dragged him far into silhouette, onto the wet grass, and they left him there, covered with the hot umber clay of the forest.

When they arrived at Chauvet, the sky was blue and empty, and the sun shone so hard on the busted steel door that neither of them could touch the metal. Orange nasturtiums hung from the hillside, broken free from the crumbling soil. Kate kicked through them to the steel, swinging the door inward, and she moved forward into the cave.

They found Morel inside the mouth of the cave, rocking on his haunches in the bursting light that shone like a halo around the granite. He was surrounded by empty cartridges, and did not stand when they approached.

"There must be something here that will drop this stone again," he said. "I shot everything I had at it, but now I have no more bullets left." A handgun lay in his grasp across his thighs. "I suppose I used too many bullets on the devil who came back here for the equipment."

"What do you mean?" asked Alain.

The blood had drained from Morel's face. "The old scoundrel and the gibbering man. I killed them both." He nodded to a body deep at the bottom of the cavern, a thin, dark-haired man lost again to antiquity.

"You're not bad with a gun after all, *mon cher ami,*" said Kate.

"It is no accident." He put his hands out to touch one of the orange flowers that had broken from its smooth stem astride the dark doorway. "When I was born my father fired a shotgun blast behind my mother's head to make me come out. I always suspected there would be ramifications for that," he said, but he did not smile and his voice was as powerless as the slip of sand in an hourglass.

"Jacques?" asked Kate softly, "can you walk with us? This is the last call. A helicopter is coming to take us to Marseille. You need to come now."

He looked up at her, drumming a rhythm in the soil with fingers grimy from machine oil.

"Do you have explosives left in your sacks? I must shut off Chauvet before it disappears altogether."

"Close off the boy's footprints?" she asked. "You spent your whole life studying this place."

"*Comme la lune de sang,* like a blood moon waiting for light," he whispered. "Now that we have opened it, the politicians and their armies will destroy it forever like everything else."

Kate reached to take his arm.

Once on his feet, Morel jerked free of her. "Please help me," he pleaded. "This is part of the mission. None of us had any right to this place."

"You know, he's right, Kate. We do need to seal it off from the local police. *Cristina* can reopen it when they need to."

The three of them lay SLAMS around the inner lining of the stone entrance. They stood far back into the warm sycamore and pine shade while the small blasts spun thin cords of light around the rock archway, soaking the air with ammonia.

When it was done, Morel turned from the cave and moved first down the ancient animal track, his head sunken against his chest, guiding the others in silence. After a few kilometers, they heard the sound of the helicopter blades, scraping the sky like swans coming to light on water, and they quickened their pace through the afternoon forest to follow the sweet, sick trail of exhaust.

Chapter 27

THE MORNING LIGHT began to slip through the vertical slats over the windows, casting Ben's shape into black. He was covered in cool Egyptian cotton, sheets so fine they might have been drawn from silk.

Kate stood beside his bed, and watched him open his eyes. He put his hand flat on the curves of his chest, and smiled at her, nodding at a vase of red tulips sitting on his bedside table.

"Who gave me those?" he asked.

She was out of uniform, wearing a soft, sleeveless ivory dress trimmed with bone-colored lace and ribbon, foaming like cream over her skin, and leaving him dreaming even as he awoke.

Kate walked to the table and opened the card. "Ambassador and Mrs. Henderson. It says, '*You're a heck of an airman. Feel better fast.*'"

He shifted to take the pressure off his back. "How long have you been watching me?"

She smiled, suddenly embarrassed.

"I came to take you to the press conference. Remember?"

He nodded. "I know. Come closer. When do we have to leave?"

She approached the colonial four-poster, an antique among many that had been carefully placed in this Washington home of James Cullen.

Ben reached to touch the lace at her neckline. She sat next to him, and he stared at the tawny plump curve of her breast against the cotton. "Is this okay?" he whispered and placed his lips on her glowing skin.

A sacred heart carved from raw, unpolished cherry wood hung above the bed, and as he put his arms around her, the old walls creaked against the huge sculpture.

She closed her eyes for a moment, and he pressed against her. Then she felt him slip his fingers beneath the lace. She could hear her blood humming, and all the voices within her calling out over bone.

"What time's your plane to California?" he asked.

"Late tonight," she said.

She lifted his hand, taking his fingers in her mouth, one by one. He pulled her body down across his, and brought her face close so he could kiss her mouth. They lay quietly for a few moments, but her chest was pulsing tightly.

"Easy, Katie," he whispered. "It's up to you."

"Does this hurt your back?"

"A little. But it would hurt more not to."

"Why is the air so dry here?" she asked, and buried her face in the old tee shirt he wore. "Do we have enough time?"

He smiled lopsidedly, and kissed her again, and this time her lips tasted like cool blackberries. He put his fingers in her long, soft hair and pulled it back from her face.

"I wonder if all these years have made me a better lover," he whispered.

She began undressing, lifting the ivory lace over her shoulders, removing her bra and pants until she stood naked. Her smooth olive skin, marred by darkened combat scars, gleamed in the splintered light across the room. She lay beside him on the cool sheets, and he rolled slowly over her, propping himself on his elbows above her body so he could see her.

"Go ahead," she whispered, and put her soft hands on the tensed muscles across his shoulder blades. "I wanted you to. For so long," and they filled the narrow room with that simple notion until both of them could fall asleep, without flex cuffs or radio static or prisoners' heads slumped before them.

•

Kate lay quietly with her hand on Ben's warm shoulder. She stared at the healing sores gleaming on his back like a field of cheap ruby chips, and she could hear a television from another room, the voices melting into a muffled stampede. She dressed quickly while he dozed, and slipped down the thick hallway carpet in the direction of this noise.

She found a second bedroom, empty, with the door swung wide. A large flat panel television was mounted on the far wall, tuned to the C-SPAN channel. The window was cracked open slightly and a mild breeze ebbed at the bubbled, Colonial glass. She sank into a wing back chair facing the screen. The camera lingered on an older, dark-haired woman, lovely and fit, who stood in the center of gleaming, wooden stairs, and this woman seemed to be waiting, biding quietly with a slightly saddened face.

Kate realized this was Ben's mother, and almost immediately she heard someone moving behind her.

"What are you doing in here?" Ben asked brusquely from where he stood in the doorway. "This is the room Hank uses when he's in DC."

She said, "I heard the television noise and came to see. Look, it's your mom arriving at the White House." She glanced at her watch. "We only have an hour. We should get dressed and get on the road soon. The traffic will be bad and the lines at the White House will be long."

He was wearing jeans and no shirt, and she stood up and put her fingers on his chest.

"Are you okay?" she asked. "Are you annoyed?"

He looked at her through years of short-fused trust.

"No," he said, pulling her close to him. "I'm just wound up. I need to get through today, and then I was thinking we could go away together somewhere for some R and R."

"Okay," she said. "I would like to do that."

"You understand, Katie. We're a little different from most people. Trusting people is not really that easy. Once I dug a grave with my fingers. Have you ever done that? Near Bagram. My hands were stained for days. It was a woman, a tribal princess, and she double-crossed us. I shot her. She was bent in front of me with her head on the ground and I shot her through the neck. Her dress was gold, really soft, and she had this gold hood, too. I put a hole in it and killed her because she killed our fox and our medic. I had to do it, you know. We couldn't trust her and we couldn't keep her with us on the op. People like you and me, when we've seen stuff like that, done that stuff, it's hard to be normal again."

Kate listened to him intently, and moved her body alongside his.

"I want you to meet my mother....again, I mean," he said. "There's a private reception at the White House today, after all this is over. Will you come?"

"Yes," she said.

"Hank will be there, Katie. I can't do anything about it. He's part of my family, part of our family. I'm sorry. I know he's the last person on earth that you'd want to see now."

Kate nodded. "It's time to go to the reception. Do you want me to help you get into your uniform?"

He kissed her forehead, and turned to the television.

"They're televising it?" he asked.

"It's just C-SPAN."

He sat on the chair, with Kate in his lap, and they continued to watch as Hank Cullen was brought through the Rose Garden in a wheelchair.

Kate looked away from the screen and said, "Jacobits called me this morning. He spent the last three days directing staff from his hospital bed in Germany. The doctors try, but they can't keep him quiet." She laughed out loud and added, "He finally convinced them to give him his laptop in the hospital room. Big mistake. And the nurse told me that they keep taking away his cell phone, but somehow he always has another one hidden under the sheets."

Ben smiled. "He's okay, though?"

"Sure. He's the bullet. He never breaks. But they're hassling him for the final report, and he refuses to seal it until he can get all the pieces together. It's driving him crazy and he's driving Ramstein and the Pentagon crazy."

"I don't understand his problem. We got Hank back alive. That was our job. What else is there to say?"

"He says the intel doesn't make sense. I've seen Jacobits take his time with these reports. I don't even think he's filed the wrap-up on the explosion at Lajes last month because he still can't figure out how they were able to blow up the airfield."

"Life's too short to focus on things you can't control," Ben said quietly. "People like us just need the facts in the final report, Kate, not the philosophy. Leave that to the analysts and to the big bosses."

She flicked the television to mute, and leaned forward to put her mouth against his.

"Hank was an asset before, but now it's different," she said. "You know I will try today; no one can say I didn't try. But after this, I'm done. I don't want to make you choose me or your family, but I think you may have to." Her hair was lit by the spring sunlight, and she stared at him as her chest tightened.

"I know," he said. "When we both get to San Diego we can go away and work this all out. He's not really even my brother, Katie."

She turned back to the screen. Hank was in his wheelchair at the precipice of a low, carpeted ramp, on his own now in the shadows of a White House hallway. Ben's mother moved beside him, still waiting for her husband who was making his way up the ramp among the crowd of White House well wishers.

Kate saw Hank with an I-phone in his lap, holding it with both hands, and then she saw him lean forward across his knees, and the phone fell to the ground.

"Look at this," she said. Hank began to cough, retching as though lifting thick phlegm from his lungs. He sat up and began rubbing his ear, patting the side of his head, his eyes wide open with bewilderment.

"What's wrong with him?" she asked.

Ben's mother moved quickly behind Hank, and wheeled him out of camera range.

"Who cares?" Ben lifted her off his lap. "We should get a move on. I'll go get ready."

When she turned back to the screen, she saw that Hank Cullen was with his father and step-mother in the Oval Office, and he sat in his wheelchair beside the President of the United States.

Cameras began to flash across the room, and she heard the muffled voices of the White House press corps in the background while they waited for the photo opp participants to be arranged. She saw the President put his hand on Hank's shoulder and she remembered the defeated look in Hank's eyes as she lay alongside him beneath the Ardèche forest ceiling, when the birds lifted from the trees before the battle. His face was clean now, and he wore a powder blue shirt beneath his suit jacket. She thought that the color of it brought the pallor of ice from his skin.

Chapter 28

BEN AND KATE REMAINED side by side at the North Portico of the White House compound, while journalists and guests stretched behind them in a single-file line out to Pennsylvania Avenue. A Marine facing them blocked their passage into the magnetometer metal scanner. He paused and scrutinized Ben's uniform.

"Sir, I need some information first. Your ID, please."

Ben gave these to the Marine, and waited. He knew how late he was, but he did not try to hurry his entrance. He watched his own reflection in a mirror under the cameras that were affixed to the roof-line, and he saw his own blue uniform alongside bloated crows waiting in formation for food scraps from the crowd.

"Sir," said the boy in a nervous voice barely scraping the end of adolescence, "we need to move you in quick. They were expecting you earlier."

Ben nodded and called over his shoulder to Kate. "I'll see you after the press conference. I'll come find you before the reception."

Kate's stomach knotted with his comment about the party. She had no body armor, no boots, and no grenades. She had no intel that day to survive meeting Ben's brother again, nothing on her side but her own nerves. Suddenly she yawned and licked her lips, frightened at a language without strategy or weapons.

After Ben had disappeared down the corridor, the same young Marine led Kate into a bullet-proof cubicle.

"Here's my phone," Kate said, barely audibly. She took it from her purse and pushed it across the table to a uniformed woman.

"You're okay with your cell phone, Ma'am. No pictures, though; not without professional accreditation."

At the back of the kiosk stood another Marine, younger still and half shadowed by smoke-tinted walls that appeared to be glass. He held his M4 across his chest, and stared at it grimly as though on terrified radio silence. Kate could dismantle his weapon and reassemble it in a matter of minutes, but she moved around him gently, as she would near any man in battle. He rubbed his fingers along the shining black body of his rifle, and as she passed, he looked up furtively, at her breasts and her legs under the soft creamy fabric. Tears of sweat slid down his smooth face, and he stared back at his gun silently.

The first Marine pointed to a sunlit corridor.

"Down the hall, please, Ma'am."

Kate reached the thick, oak doors of the East Room, swung wide open with the stuffy warmth spreading out to her. An aide checked her name off an electronic list, and allowed her inside.

Sound technicians had installed cameras and microphones along the perimeter, with tangles of cords snaking between the metal feet of the tungsten stands. An arrowhead of two hundred gilt chairs angled around the podium far down in front, and all of it was draped in the sallow light from crystal chandeliers hanging over them as big as lions. Secret Service agents lined the Cross Hall behind the curtain opening, and Kate knew that a handful was also around her, disguised as reporters.

She stopped near the doors, letting journalists and photographers brush past her. A group of men in ill-fitting suits stood along the side-wall talking and waiting. One of them, with skin the color of poached salmon, looked over at her several times. He was tall and bone-thin, with dark grey hair and large black eyes. Kate stared back, wondering if she knew him, and he smiled at her, nodding. His cheeks were pockmarked with old acne scars, embedded deep and the color of pomegranate seeds.

Some of the regular press corps sat by themselves near the front, tweeting to their fans on smartphones. A Fox reporter was already on air with his awkward, wiggling back to the podium, giving biographical points about the soon-to-be sworn Secretary of Commerce, James Cullen.

Kate noticed the tall man leaving his colleagues to approach her, and she saw that he carried a thick, black rubber tube in his hands.

"Hello," he said. "I'm Buddy Wyatt. I'm with 'Mother Jones'. Are you a guest or a journalist?"

His suit jacket was soiled with a smear of gravy across the breast pocket, and he raised his voice when he spoke the name of his employer. Kate leaned away from him, wondering if he were Secret Service, but the grey skin encircling his deep-set eyes glowed a faint, sick lavender, and she decided he must be telling the truth about his work.

She pondered a moment, and then replied, "Reporter."

"You must be new in town, then," he grinned broadly. "Who are you with?"

She mumbled, and looked away to the front of the room for Ben. "I'm waiting for a colleague," she said.

He smiled and put his slender fingers on her shoulder.

"No, dear. I meant, who is paying you to be here? Who do you work for? Would you and your colleague like to sit with me? I just have to give this cord to the Fox people. I can get us the best seats. I'm in the corps. Be right back," he said, grinning again nervously and not waiting for her answer.

When he had walked away, Kate moved to an empty golden chair in the back row, and from there she saw Ben's mother take a seat at the front, followed by the two Cullen brothers. Ben pushed the wheelchair, and swung it alongside his mother at the center of the front row. A barrier of low, limp potted plants stood between the family and the presidential seal.

Hank put his arm over the back of his stepmother's chair, settling in easily next to her, and he leaned close to whisper something in her ear. Kate stiffened when she saw this, at the thought of Hank being so near to any trusting woman, but abruptly she saw him change, and he began shaking his head sharply. He put his palm to his ear, rubbing it hard and pulling at the lobe as though trying to scratch something deep inside.

Kate felt a shadow rising behind her, and she heard Wyatt's nervous voice.

"This is not a good spot," he said. "I can get us much closer to the front. If you're not in the corps, you'll never get a question sitting back here."

Kate looked up at him. "No, this is fine."

He moved around the row and sat next to her. "Okay," he hesitated, "whatever you say." He smiled, and touched her knee with his cold, spindly fingers. "I don't have anything to ask old man Cullen, anyway. We already know his commerce plans. He's gonna help the prez drain natural resources from the developing world and pocket the profits."

Kate stared straight ahead, watching the podium without speaking again. Hank was rubbing his ear hard now, and he began to clear his throat. His coughing grew louder, and he leaned forward over his knees.

"What's with our friend, the CEO?" Wyatt asked loudly. "Did you hear he broke both his legs rock-climbing on vacation in France? Pretty unlucky, huh? Not that his kind of war criminal doesn't deserve it."

Ben stood abruptly from his chair in the front row, and turned to face his brother. He bent close beside him, and put his hands on Hank's shoulders to stay the heaving of his body. He slapped him hard on his back to dislodge the object, and the Fox reporter stopped speaking at the camera and turned to look. A different kind of murmur, a soft thrumming of anticipation, spread across the large room as all present, the media and the guests, stared at the Cullen brothers.

"Well, shit!" said Wyatt hoarsely across the crowd, his mouth cracked open in a broad grin. "Good television if he chokes to death!"

People around them began to use their cell phones, and Kate saw Ben hold his arm out to shepherd his mother through the side door and out of the room. After, he took hold of his brother's wheelchair and followed her to stand among the Secret Service agents.

Kate turned back to the *Mother Jones* journalist, and whispered to Wyatt, her eyes widening. "Why would you say that?"

"Say what?"

"That he would choke to death."

"It was just a joke, my dear. You'll never make it inside the Beltway with such a literal, naïve mind," Wyatt said. He halted mid-sentence and added, "For God's sake, who do you write for, anyway? *American Girl?*"

She turned away from him. She could still make out Ben and his mother, through the open side door, holding his brother's wheelchair near a narrow stairwell. Three Secret Service agents clustered around them, nothing distinguishing them but their heft and the bristle-cut above their collars. The jacket of Ben's uniform was stretched tight across his muscled shoulders, and he stepped forward to allow one of the agents access to guard his brother. The agent swiveled Hank's chair around to face the doorway, and Kate could see he held a glass of water in his hands, and that he was smiling again.

A small cold pressure rose behind her breastbone. She closed her eyes, but the pictures of him remained, sitting unharmed beside her in the dark of Chauvet. He had been overcome with panic, even though AQIM had fed him, and had neither attacked nor tortured him. They had so carefully avoided harming him, even in the blur of battle.

Suddenly, Hank Cullen leaned over his knees again, and began to cough.

"You'd think he was a smoker," Wyatt muttered, "that sounds like my morning wake up cough, although they say he's a health nut." He chuckled to himself without looking at Kate.

The thought sank through her gut like a fistful of needles, and she stood up abruptly.

"Oh my God," she whispered.

"I wouldn't leave just yet," Wyatt said. "The show is about to roll."

Without responding, she moved quickly down the row and out the back door of the East Room, careful not to run, but pushing steadily through the incoming news people until she reached the hallway. She scanned frantically for an area that would afford her privacy, and finally slipped into a shadowy corner formed by two powder white marble columns.

With trembling hands, she grabbed the secure phone from her purse and pressed the single button that connected her to the Colonel.

"Hello, Captain," growled Jacobits. "You done with your fancy White House reception yet?"

"No, Sir," she said. "But I need to ask you something."

"Sure, Captain. At your service."

"Are the details at Lajes still classified?"

"You're on leave, Captain. Forget about it."

"Did you file the report yet?" she asked, with more urgency than he expected.

Jacobits paused. "Don't be a gravedigger, Kate. This is the point where you need to let it all go, enjoy yourself, and come back ready to move on to the next assignment."

Her voice was shaking, but she repeated the question, "Did you file the report, Sir?"

"Yes, I did. The Pentagon is examining it, Bolling is analyzing it, and that's all I can tell you. Strictly need to know at the moment. Nothing has been released."

Her hands were clammy, and she felt the perspiration drops on her temples as they rolled down the sides of her face. "Is it conclusive?"

"Didn't I just tell you it was need to know?"

Kate replied, "Was the explosion caused by an internal body bomb in the prisoner? Please just tell me if that part has been determined."

He breathed deeply in response, rasping and annoyed.

"Captain, I'm not releasing classified information because you say please. You know better than that."

"Colonel, we picked that prisoner up in North Africa, in AQIM territory."

"I know that."

"Hank Cullen was kidnapped and held by the AQIM forces."

"Correct."

"Now Cullen is here at the White House and he's doing exactly what the prisoner at Lajes did in the plane. Coughing. Convulsing."

For several seconds she could only hear him breathing, sucking hard at this information and holding it like a bellows.

A bowl of bright yellow lemons lay on a table beside her, waxy and perfect. She picked one up and began clawing her fingernails across it, lacing its thick skin with gashes while she waited.

Finally she could not wait any longer.

"If it was an internal IED that blew up the airfield in April, what if they did the same thing to Hank Cullen? What if Hank is a suicide bomber? Sir, he's with the President. He's in the White House."

"You're way out in left field, Captain. Cullen is not a suicide bomber." He grunted quickly. "You're making me think you've lost it, Kate."

"You said yourself we got lucky to find him alive. Maybe we didn't get lucky. Maybe they gave him back to us. I think they had a reason. Sir, when Marko was killed, the explosives were planted in the body of an eagle. It might not have signaled anything or meant anything, but what if it did? Maybe it wasn't just an accident."

"Oh, for God's sake, Captain. You're looking for ghosts and clues like a crazy person now. So Cullen's coughing. So what? He was MRI'd by the best hospitals in the world. There's nothing in him that they didn't find."

"But they were focused on his spine, Colonel. And his legs. A body IED could be anywhere, and it could be tiny. Remember the IED that blew up the UK defense minister last year? It was the size of a dime and it was slipped in the padding of a bandage on his shin by a doctor in the National Health Service. It took a month to figure that one out after he died, didn't it?"

She was speaking so quickly that she had lost her breath and paused. She stared down at her arms, so fragile to her in the hard daylight of the corridor; she knew she sounded irrational, and she also knew that every mistake she had ever made had been because she had ignored a hunch settling in her gut.

"Calm down, Kate, and think about it. Who's going to detonate it? And how the hell would they get in range? Are you crazy? These people can't get into the White House! We found the detonation device at

Lajes in the prisoner's molar. He was his own trigger, a real suicide bomber. He swallowed the bomb, got himself in range, and then detonated it on purpose. Hank Cullen is not a suicide bomber. And nothing and no one gets into the White House that isn't meant to be there. Even if you're right about them planting an IED, there isn't any way in hell they could get in range to set it off in that compound."

"I don't know how they will detonate it, Colonel. But I believe they will." They both stopped, then, and the empty hallway fell to silence.

"Cell phone." The voice came nervously from the other side of the marble columns where Buddy Wyatt stood in his wrinkled suit, sweat dripping from his face. The light from the hall surrounded him like sulfur-glow, and he walked forward. "That's how they do it these days, isn't it? In war zones, in Belfast, wherever you are if you get in range you can detonate a bomb with a pre-wired phone. And everyone takes their cell phones into the East Room. Hell, right now most of the press corps is in there tweeting on them. The White House issues a hundred new credentials for events like this. I'm part of the corps, and even I don't know half the people."

"Colonel, did you hear that? Cell phone!"

"Who the friggin' hell are you talking to, Kate?"

"Who are you?" Wyatt asked her suddenly. "What are you doing here?"

"There's no time, Colonel," she said, ignoring Wyatt, "I have to do this."

"Kate," he whispered, and then paused for a few seconds. "Okay. Go, then. I'll call our guy in the White House and see if I can slow things down. But I can't cover your back on this, so you better be right, Captain, or we'll both be flippin' chipotle for the rest of our lives."

Kate hung up without responding. She turned to Buddy Wyatt, who was jotting notes on an index card as he waited before her. She took his pencil and card from his hands.

"Give that back to me!" he said, and touched the scars on his cheek unconsciously with lead-soiled fingers.

"Mr. Wyatt, you will have to come with me."

"Why? Where?"

She touched her phone again, and as she did, Buddy Wyatt began to shuffle away. Kate reached up and grabbed his forearm, twisting it to spin him around like a man made of rubber. He began to shake his head violently, through the last vestiges of numbness, and she held him calmly until his body went limp and his spaniel eyes filled with tears.

Kate whispered to him, "You understand what's happening?"

He shook his head slowly from side to side.

"No," he said.

Kate pressed the keypad of her phone, and instantly Ben's voice responded.

"What's up, baby?"

"Keep Hank away from the President. Don't let him out of the hallway."

"Katie?"

"I believe he has a body bomb planted in him. Someone in the press conference is going to detonate it, maybe with a cell phone. Get him out of the White House while I go for the trigger-man."

"What's happened? What's going on?

"Just take care of this. Trust me."

"They're about to start, Kate. The President is in the Cross Hall, and we're waiting with him."

"Then get him out now! But if I'm not quick enough, just make sure the President is safe."

She pulled Wyatt from between the columns.

"I need you to help me, Mr. Wyatt. We are going back into the East Room."

She brought him to stand in front of her, so close that she smelled the odor of cigarettes laying across his clothes. She prodded him forward onto the polished marble floor back toward the open doors.

"Look at these people now. Look at this audience. Who is press corps and who are guests? Who are the ones you've never seen before?"

"There are dozens of new people. I don't know where to start!"

"I don't care how many there are. Identify them for me. Quickly, Mr. Wyatt!"

"I can't do it from back here," he sighed. "We'll have to get up front so I can see faces."

"Hurry then," Kate whispered, "they're about to start."

He gazed around the room. Traces of pink were dragging down the gold-swaddled white walls as the chandeliers were relit. "No. There's been a delay. None of the cameramen are in place. And there's no music. The President always comes with music."

Buddy Wyatt began pulling her down the side corridor toward the front row, weaving a path between the frustrated, mumbling media crowd. People stood from their seats and stretched, moving into the aisles, blocking his view. Wyatt stopped alongside the front row and stared back at the sea of faces and bodies without speaking.

"Listen to me." She wrenched his hand up toward her face, grabbing it tightly, and she could smell the tobacco squeeze off his fingers like traces of tar. "If we don't figure out who it is before the President brings the Cullen family in, he and half this room will go up in a blast. Do you understand? Start talking to me. I need to stop the trigger. Who in this audience have you never seen before?"

He shook his head furiously, his eyes and mouth wide open, and Kate could see that panic had begun to suffocate him. "This is impossible. There are too many of them," he hissed.

"What about the woman on the far side? In the pink silk jacket? She doesn't look like a journalist."

"Don't be ridiculous. That's the Japanese Ambassador's wife. She's getting a degree from Georgetown in economics. That's the only reason she's here." He took a deep breath and indicated a ginger haired man in a navy suit. "He's new," he whispered.

"He's Secret Service."

"Look up this aisle," Wyatt said. "Near the back, the former Chief of Staff is sitting there with a woman who's not his wife. And he's taken off his shoes. Why did he do that?"

"Wyatt, don't tell me the gossip, find me somebody who would blow up the White House!"

"For God's sake, I don't even know what I'm looking for! I don't know how to help you with this. Honestly, I don't even know who you are. For all I know, I could be looking for you!"

He began to step back from her toward the side door, when his large feet tangled in a camera cord. He lurched forward, his body slamming onto his hands and knees. Bedraggled and shaking, he stayed on the floor, clinging to it with his eyes focused on the carpet. "The truth is, lady, I don't want to die, so I think I'm going to get out of here now."

Kate leaned over and grabbed his arm hard, feeling his bones through cloth and flesh. She stared at him and said under her breath, "No, you're not, Mr. Wyatt. You're going to stand up and be a hero."

She turned back to the room, the audience washed now in the golden pink chandelier light. Thin strains of piped music slipped quietly from speakers high on the walls, and the reporters quickly returned to their seats. The chandeliers dimmed, and cameramen moved to their equipment. Cautiously, Buddy Wyatt stood up.

Chapter 29

HE SCANNED THE PACKED ROOM slowly. "A woman or a man?" he asked.

"I don't know."

"Old or young?"

"No idea. I just know that something about this person will be irregular, and I don't know what that will be."

The music grew louder around them, rich violins building to brass, and finally the melody line of 'Hail to the Chief' filled the room, as the President began his carefully paced walk down the Cross Hall to the open doors and the podium.

"Hurry," whispered Kate. "Keep looking. Hurry!"

She grabbed her phone and pressed the keypad. "Where are you?"

"With my family following the President down the hall."

"It's too late, Ben," she said. "I can't identify the trigger. This room is going to blow and our only chance is you. Get Hank away from the President! Don't let him get into the press conference. Don't let him go through the curtains!"

Buddy Wyatt scanned the room frantically, staring straight into the slipping light.

Suddenly he stopped moving. "Why does it have to be someone I don't know?" he asked.

"What?"

"Look there. The man at the middle of the third row. He's holding a cell phone shoulder level. But they're starting now and even the corps has stopped tweeting. This guy is a foreign correspondent from *Publico*, the Portuguese paper. Look at him!"

The man held a phone in his left fist, white-knuckled and tight. His forehead was waxy with sweat, and his round, brown eyes narrowed toward the podium. As he lifted his arm, his chest and shoulders were possessed with an uncontrollable tremor.

Kate raced quickly up the aisle and lurched into the row, maneuvering past the feet and knees of shocked journalists as she neared the center. She saw that the triggerman held her in his peripheral vision, watching her whale-eyed as he stared all the while at the podium. Quickly, he lifted his cell phone a little higher for a clearer path to the front.

The curtains behind the Presidential seal began to part, and the President stepped through to the microphone, while inches behind him, in the shadows of the Cross Hall, waited the entire Cullen family. Suddenly, Kate heard Ben's voice, low and rough from the front of the room as the curtains opened to reveal James Cullen and his family, with all but Ben smiling and still.

The Portuguese man turned his head toward Kate, for an instant watching her advance, and then he jerked back to face the stage and repositioned his phone.

Kate was too far away to touch it, but she dived toward him, extending her arm as far as she could toward his hand, hurling herself across the people between them.

She landed on top of him, knocking him sideways over the next reporter. Kate grabbed for his phone, but he pulled away from her and stood up. Before she could move again, a deep, hot pain seared her leg. The burning was so intense, she could no longer control her body and her arms fell to her sides. Her leg throbbed with the bullet as it melted into her thigh, and she fell to the floor, rolling off of the chair.

Two Secret Service agents rushed toward her, grabbing her by the shoulders from between the chairs, while a third man held his pistol high and firm over the crowd. Kate opened her mouth to call out her name and rank, but she could not squeeze any sound from her gut, and she fell back, inert, while they carried her toward the side door.

In seconds, Kate was at the edge of the room, slammed onto the old granite face down. One of the agents knelt on her back, and yanked her arms around to handcuff her. The other agent held a pistol to her temple with rock-steady hands.

Three more agents who had been hovering behind the curtains, immediately surrounded the President at the podium. One man threw him to the carpet and covered him with his body, as the other two knelt quickly alongside, guns aloft, scanning the East Room crowd.

The chandeliers hanging out over the audience began to tremble, their crystal teardrops cracking together, and a thunderous explosion deep in the bones of the building heaved at the room with such force it seemed as though the skull of God had blown apart. The electric lights shuddered to dark, and the crowd's sudden hush rose to a terrified shatter, as people began to scream and run for the doors.

The Secret Service agents dragged Kate into the corridor, and held her there, while around them thick, dark smoke swirled above the stairwell growing blacker and bigger as it rose, and the red light of its fire slithered up the walls to the landing. The old staircase crumbled, and smoke at last reached the open doors of the East Room, pouring across the golden chairs.

A Secret Service agent lifted Kate over his shoulder and ran from the building into the garden. He lay her on a soft narrow lawn surrounded by pink tulips, and all around them ambulances were arriving. A dark-haired doctor ran toward them down the red brick path, and began directing the set-up of the emergency triage station. Medics unfolded gurneys and pulled equipment from the shelves and bags of their vehicles, while people raced past them toward the iron railings to save themselves from the suffocating smoke pouring out of the White House.

The Secret Service agent dragged Kate close to the ambulance and cuffed her wrists to the wheel frame.

"Bullet wound to the thigh. She's involved," he shouted to the doctor. "I searched her and contained her, but be careful. I'll send someone to stand guard if I can," and he ran back into the fray of smoke and shrieking voices.

Somewhere in the distance she could hear the familiar sound of wing-beating rotors slashing at the air, the sound of salvation or a sandstorm over graves. She saw Buddy Wyatt's face looming above her with his huge sunken black eyes, and the doctor kneeling beside her. He put his face next to hers and asked her name, but she could not muster her voice. She heard the sound of thunder around them, and saw the doctor smile at her through the howling like a priest filled with grace, and then she closed her eyes again.

Chapter 30

KATE AWOKE TO THE CHILL of the dying day, and to the low yelp of a dog from somewhere across the gardens. The spring-lit sky over the Potomac swelled black with rain, and the crowds in Lafayette Park at last began to filter away, as the violence ebbed. She saw the sky and the magnolias above her, all of it dripping with the smell of carbon, and she turned her head to release a wave of tension.

She lay flat on a stiff gurney beside an emerald lawn, her back aching and the gunshot wound in her leg swollen to a smooth, tight melon that had begun to burn again. She lifted her arm to touch the pain, and she realized that she was no longer cuffed.

"What time is it?" she said aloud, asking no one in particular.

"You were pretty damn lucky," came a man's voice.

Her face was suddenly covered in shadow, and she looked up to see the gaunt body of Buddy Wyatt standing beside her.

"Did you realize that you took a bullet?"

She nodded. "How many?"

"Just the one," he replied. "The agent was aiming at your head, but you flew out so quick he only hit your leg. And it was just a surface wound at that. Didn't touch your bones. I understand a shattered femur could have put an end to your career." He stopped speaking and put his cool, spindly fingers on her arm. "You know, you really should have told me who you are. Just because I work for *Mother Jones* doesn't mean I can't be a patriot."

She smiled at him. "I know that. Thank you, Mr. Wyatt. You really are a hero after all."

"I guess you can call me Buddy, Captain Cardenas."

She nodded and put her hand to touch his. "What time is it?"

He looked at his watch, the old leather band held together by a bent paperclip. "I don't know. Stopped again. I imagine about three o'clock."

She lifted her head and saw that a slow sense of balance lay across the gardens. The area had been cleared of all but Secret Service agents and a few medical personnel, and they moved calmly.

"It's over then? Was it a single assailant?"

"Looks that way," said Wyatt. "At any rate, the Marines and Secret Service are walking, not running anymore."

She grinned at him, and asked, "Is the President safe, Buddy? How many casualties were there?"

"Four dead that I've heard of. They haven't made an announcement yet, but the Fox guys, of course, have some unattributed info. I'll go and get it all in a minute. About a dozen injured so far, mostly East Room staff. The Secret Service got the President out first, took him up and away on a joyride with some F-16s flying shotgun for him. Funny how we can get the Air Force and the Secret Service to work like clockwork, but not the economy."

Thin, grey light lay across his face as the clouds shifted overhead.

"Who died?" she asked quickly through unmeasured breathing, feeling her voice tightening to a choke. She knew his answer might further change this mercurial day, but Kate could not contain her need to know, regardless of the fear in her stomach.

"I don't know any names," he said casually. "They haven't released them."

"Were there any military among them?"

"I'm sorry, Kate, I don't know. Who are you looking for? I can go make inquiries."

"Major Ben Cullen," she said. "Air Force."

He opened his eyes wide, and the irises were the pale color of moth wings.

"The Cullens? You kidding? I haven't seen any of them come out of the White House, but I haven't heard anything, either. They may have lifted them all out with the President for all anyone knows."

"No," she said, "you don't understand. Please..." She closed her eyes and whispered, "I'm so tired."

Buddy Wyatt touched her again, tentatively, and said, "I guess you are. They've been pumping you full of morphine for the last hour."

"My leg is killing me..." she began, and then she heard an unfamiliar voice.

"I'll fix that."

She felt a hand's light pressure on the bandage over her thigh, and she snapped her eyes open. She sat up suddenly, dizzily grabbing at the air and pulling the IV lines with her.

"Easy, Captain," she heard someone say, but she fell back to the gurney again. A doctor stepped forward into her view, bending slightly over her legs. "I'm Doctor Browning." He stood beside Buddy Wyatt, a man of similar age and height, but his eyes were filled with kindness and confidence. She relaxed against the thin pad on which she lay. "We have a bed for you at the hospital now. We're about to get going. I'm very sorry that we ran out of ambulances. You're going to have to share this one and it will be a little cramped." He went quickly to the door of the vehicle and opened it.

"What about the Cullens?" she asked, her voice rising quickly. "Did they make it?"

Buddy Wyatt pointed to the contrails of jet exhaust across the sky. "I'll go see what I can find out. I think the President's transport just landed again. They must have decided it's all clear."

A nurse appeared at her feet, and Kate felt herself being moved, gurney and all, backwards into the ambulance.

The nurse placed a transparent plastic bag on Kate's stomach, and a medic behind her lifted the back of her bed to make room for both patients.

"Hang on to these, dear," she said. "These are your possessions."

"Before we go, there is someone out there who wants to speak to you, Captain," the doctor said.

Kate smiled with relief. His voice was knowing and so smooth, and she immediately realized that Ben must be alive and waiting for her outside. She had always known that she could not lose him again so soon, and that somehow in this high angle of hell, he would find her.

She looked out the open back door of the vehicle, but only Buddy Wyatt remained outside, waving furiously at her.

"I'll see you at the hospital!" he called out. "That is, if you don't mind a visit from a *Mother Jones* reporter," and he laughed nervously.

The nurse closed the back door, swinging the latch tight, and Kate felt her throat contracting. The ambulance pulled away, swaying and lurching over curbs and out onto the parkway while a stream of tears covered her face.

"You're a very special passenger," said the nurse, her own blue eyes twinkling. "You saved the President's life, I hear."

Unable to speak, Kate simply stared at her. Her back ached and her thigh felt as though a knife turned in the wound.

"It's okay, dear. Don't try to talk anymore. In a minute I'll press your little button here and the pain will go away for a little while."

Kate took a deep breath and asked, "Do you know if the Cullen family made it?"

"Some of them did, honey. You are sharing this ride with one of them, behind you in the wheelchair," said the nurse. "We have him on morphine, as well, only he's sound asleep and we're hoping he'll stay that way until we get him to the hospital."

Kate closed her eyes again, collapsing back into the steel that cushioned her from the patient in back of her, from Cullen. Her ears and forehead were drumming with harm, and for the first time in years, she stole a psalm from her childhood and began asking for mercy.

The drumming grew louder, pounding against her skull, and the nurse said to her, "Dear, your bag is ringing. I believe someone is calling you. Would you like me to answer it, or should I just turn it off?"

Kate put her hand in the plastic bag and took her phone.

"Captain?" growled Jacobits. "You okay now? How's your leg?"

"I'm fine, Colonel. You know about my leg?"

"Hell, Kate, I know everything. You know that. I'm even patrolling the corridors here now. These damn nurses tell me everything."

"Do you know what happened, Sir? Who survived?"

"I'm glad you're okay, Kate. I'm fine, too, thank you for asking." Jacobits' laughter could be heard across the cab of the ambulance, but Kate did not respond. "The doc says you'll be up and around in time for your leave with the Major. Kiddo, you were one lucky warrior today. Smart, too. No chipotle for us," he said and guffawed.

"What did you say?" she asked, but he was laughing so hard he did not hear her.

"I talked to your dad, and your uncle is flying out to Washington to take you home. How's that for wheeling and dealing for my team?"

"Colonel," she interrupted. "What did you say about leave with the Major? What do you mean?"

"You and Cullen taking some time off together. What's the big deal? You need a little romance, don't ya think?"

"Ben made it?" she asked suddenly.

"What drugs have they been pumping you with? Of course he made it. You and Cullen saved the President's life. Saved the day. Hank Cullen was the bomb, and because you went for the detonator, Ben had a couple extra seconds. Shoved his brother straight down the staircase to the basement and blew him to hell and back. There's medals in this for you and Ben. Choice of assignments. Whatever you want, Captain."

Down her neck she could feel the sinews slacken.

"Ben is fine, Kate," Jacobits said. "He was thrown against a marble column. Broke his collar bone, is all. Where's your situational awareness?" he asked. "According to the doc, Major Cullen is sitting behind you."

She jerked forward and tried to turn around, but only caught a glimpse of the receding edge of his shadow before she fell back onto the rigid bed. She closed her eyes and saw a hurricane of pumice and amethyst battering against warped glass. She gripped the memories so tightly she thought she felt spots of blood on her fingers, and then she let it all go into an ache, steep and sweet, that collided gently with her heart.

The End